Steve Juke is a 64-year-old retired policeman. He is married and has three children, six grandchildren and three step-grandchildren. Over the years, he has told many bedtime stories in which he has used his overactive imagination and created many fantastic animal characters such as Taff the Giraffe, Bryon the Lion and Tornrny Turtle. When he became a fulltime child-minder, he decided to write and created *The Awesome Lives of Tommy Twicer*, which hopefully will be the start of many more.

To my wife, Gail, without whom I would not have been able to write as she took the lion's share of child-minding.

To my granddaughter, Teigan, who I made up the characters for so that she could write the book. She didn't, so I did.

Steve Juke

THE AWESOME LIVES OF TOMMY TWICER: PART ONE

The Origin of Taff the Giraffe

AUSTIN MACAULEY PUBLISHERS™

LONDON · CAMBRIDGE · NEW YORK · SHARJAH

A CIP catalogue record for this title is available from the British Library.

ISBN 9781528909563 (Paperback)
ISBN 9781528959315 (ePub e-book)

www.austinmacauley.com

First Published (2019)
Austin Macauley Publishers Ltd
25 Canada Square
Canary Wharf
London
E14 5LQ

Thanks to Austin Macauley Publishers for having faith and publishing this book. Being Welsh, I had wanted a Welsh publisher, but I am not a Welsh speaker, so they weren't interested; and to Tim Williams, who recovered my story when my Word crashed.

Foreword

Do you know a twicer? Some of you will without even realising it. Some of you may be a twicer without realising it, for most people haven't a clue what a twicer is. That is because a twicer is a nickname given to certain people named Thomas but not just any old Thomas. No, these Thomases are named Thomas Thomas, and Thomas Thomas can be shortened to Tom Thomas or Tommy Thomas; they can be called Tom Tom but in Wales, where Welsh miners used to make up nicknames for each other, Thomas Thomas became Tommy Twicer.

Tommy Twicer: it has a certain ring to it, doesn't it?

Twicer doesn't ring with other names, like you wouldn't call David David, David Twicer, would you? It just doesn't sound right, does it? He would probably be called Dual Dave or in Wales, Double Dai. What about Robert Roberts? I'll leave that one to you.

No, a Twicer can only be a Tommy. Unless of course, some clever clog comes up with another suitable name.

This story is about one such Twicer who was a Thomas Thomas, who lived and worked in Oakdale Colliery in South Wales for most of his life, but it was not just his name that was double, it was his life or lives that were double; for although to the miners, he worked with, he was just plain old Tommy Twicer from Ashville Oakdale, he had led the most extraordinary life anyone could ever live. Not just one life but two, which made our Tommy Twicer a true Twicer in more than just nick name.

Our Tommy Twicer's lives were truly awesome.

The Origin of Taff the Giraffe

Chapter 1
Saving Abercwmzoo

I'm going to tell you a story. It's a story that I thought would never be told but now it has to be told. It's a very long story and probably the most unbelievable story you have ever heard, I know because when my bamp (my bamp was my grandfather) told me but I didn't believe him, but it is all backed up by historical facts as you will find out. You will soon see that it's more than a story; it's a history lesson as well. A virtual history of the twentieth century and the part played in it by one extraordinary man with a double name and a double life.

My bamp was a storyteller and he used to make up stories about animals which he would tell his children and grandchildren at bed time.

When I was a little girl, he told me the story of Taff the Giraffe and his best friend Brion the Lion with a tie on and glasses who live in Abercwmzooa, a magical place hidden in the Sirhowy Valley in Wales. Whenever I stayed at Nanny and Bamp's house, he used to tell me stories at bedtime. I loved the adventures Taff had and what made them even more exciting was that they all happened close to where Bamp lived and so they happened in places I knew. They were also magical because Bamp said he knew Taff.

As I grew up I began to ask questions, questions like: How did Taff get to be a Welsh giraffe? And how did he come to live in Abercwmzoo? And how do I find Abercwmzoo?

Bamp told me that it was a secret and that he had sworn that he would never tell anyone as it was important to keep Abercwmzooa secret from the rest of the world.

When my bamp was getting on though, he called me and said, "Teigan, the time is now right for you to know the full story of Taff the Giraffe and Abercwmzoo as if they ever need help from outside, I fear I may not be able to help them. So if you are willing and able I want you to be their liaison with the real world.

He then came up with this awesome story about how Tommy Twicer, an old friend of his father, had brought Taff and a whole circus of animals to Wales and how they had to hide themselves away due to such a controversy that they all had to run and hide.

So one day Bamp sat me down in the living room of his house to tell me the story of Tommy Twicer, Taff the Giraffe and Abercwmzoo.

"Teigan, are you sitting comfortably, you want to be comfortable as this is going to be one hell of a long story. One you will think unbelievable but it's true. I know because I was told it by the most unbelievable source when I stumbled into Abercwmzoo myself," he told me.

"Every part of it is backed up by fact so you will see for yourself that I have not made it up," he added.

"You want to know the origin of Taff the Giraffe and if I made up the stories about him. Well yes and no is the answer."

"Yes, he is a real giraffe. He was born in Swansea, Mumbles Bay actually, and I've met him."

"You've met him?" I said.

"Yes and I know his story, I was told it that day in Abercwmzoo, my bamp told me and now I am telling you. The adventure stories I told you I made up as children's stories for you and Taliya. (Taliya's my sister.)

"I'm telling you now because I have been Taff's liaison with the outside world ever since I met him but I am getting old and it's time to pass the mantel to someone else. Someone who can be trusted to keep the secret and keep Abercwmzoo safe. At present Caerphilly County Borough Council are committed to keeping the Sirhowy Valley beautiful and unspoilt but there is a new regime in all councils nowadays, one focused only on profit and they may not safeguard the green belt and that could endanger Abercwmzoo and I want you to keep Abercwmzoo safe," he told me.

I was flabbergasted.

I gawped and said, "Will I get to see Abercwmzoo and will I meet Taff?"

"I suppose you will have to," he replied, "but first let me tell you the full story for you will see for yourself why this has to remain a secret and just how awesome it is."

My Bamp was an ace storyteller and when I was young he used to tell me and my sister Taliya brilliant stories about different animals like Taff the Giraffe and his friends from Abercwmzoo. He also told us stories about Tommy Turtle, Sammy Shark, Dolly Dolphin and Sally Seahorse and many more, and what was great about them was he said all of them were true stories. That's what my Bamp told us and he was a policeman so he wouldn't tell lies, would he?

If Taliya or I doubted him he'd say that's the truth, just like Billy Liar said in court to the Judge when he said my Bamp's dog, Willow, snuck up on his dog in the snow and bit his tail so badly that it needed to be amputated, then snuck off again without any sound being made by either dog, and even more amazingly no dog footprints were left in the snow. "And that's the truth Your Honour," Billy Liar told the Judge. Judges are people who are supposed to know when people are telling the truth or lying because how is justice to be served if a judge cannot tell truth from lies. Well that judge believed him and Willow, who was the gentlest dog you ever did see, was branded a dangerous dog from that day forth.

I mention Willow because he was the one who found Abercwmzoo.

Bamp always recorded Once Upon a Time for us to watch on TV as well because he said all fairy tales are true, they had to be, how could someone have made up such fantastic stories from so long ago. They had to be true, or at least be based on fact, for in those days there was magic all around and people saw and believed in it. *How else could you explain it? Do you think someone imagined it?*

Anyway I digress, back to the story or to be exact, the history lesson.

Bamp didn't start at the beginning of the story he began with how he came to learn of this fantastic tale and how it was all down to his beloved dog, Willow.

He began by explaining about Taff and Abercwmzoo.

Taff was born in Swansea back in 1917, just before Christmas but he did not stay there, even though it is on a beautiful part of the Welsh Coast.

Taff is a giraffe who lives in the hidden magical village of Abercwmzoo which is hidden deep in the heart of the Sirhowy Valley in South Wales. He told me it is within walking distance of Oakdale somewhere between Hollybush and Pen-y-fan Pond. It is west of the Cock of the North or was it east, I can't remember but it was down that way, somewhere past the Cwrt-y-Bella Church.

My Bamp never got round to showing me where Abercwmzoo is, as he said it was a secret and best left that way. When we were young my sister Taliya and I tried to find it, we even took Willow for a walk down that way along the Sirhowy Walk past Manmoel Crossing and went as far as Bedwellty Pits, but we never did find it. We didn't even get lost because Willow knew exactly where he was and led us home without any trouble. He didn't lead us to Abercwmzoo though.

Even my aunty Hannah couldn't find it and she used to ride her horse Copper on treks through the Sirhowy Valley from Smugglers run, her riding centre in Manmoel all around Tredegar, Croespenmaen, Pantymilah and even to Ebbw Vale looking for it, but she never found it either.

Bamp said he met Taff one chilly Sunday morning when he took Willow on a long walk. Well, it was more like Willow took Bamp on a long walk. They went down the hundred steps towards Blackwood then turned up the Sirhowy Walk towards Argoed along the river and up to Cwrt-y-Bella church where Willow caught a pigeon in his mouth and wouldn't let it go. Bamp said he chased Willow for over a mile through the woods shouting at him to drop it but Willow wouldn't. It was not until he and Willow were deep into the woods that Willow was spooked by something very, very tall, did he stop and Willow let the pigeon go. Willow hadn't hurt the pigeon, he just liked carrying it. That's because Willow was a Springer Spaniel and Springer Spaniels are gun dogs with soft mouths, good at carrying things without damaging them.

They were now in a bit of a clearing in the woods and although he couldn't see the sky above him, Bamp said there was a strange little village in front of him different to anything he had ever seen before. Bamp said he had lost his bearings and had never seen this village before and that was strange because he had lived in Oakdale all his life and had been a policeman in Blackwood for many years and had never seen anything like it in his life. For a moment he said he was a little afraid but then he remembered the saying he always told us, 'There's nothing to fear but fear itself' and he composed himself.

It was then that the very, very tall thing spoke to Bamp in a kind of Valleys accent with a hint of West Walian saying, "Hello, bore da my name is Taff. Who are you and how did you find Abercwmzoo?"

"Well," my bamp said, "he almost fainted." Willow barked and ran off and the pigeon ruffled its feathers and flew up into a tree.

After closing his eyes, taking three deep breaths and counting to ten, Bamp opened his eyes again. Taff was still there, standing tall but bent down with its head next to Bamp. His eyes looking straight into my bamp's eyes. He was the most unusual and unique young giraffe Bamp had ever seen and was wearing a long blue and yellow woolly scarf and bobble hat.

In fact Taff, who was a very intelligent looking giraffe, was also puzzled.

"Am I dreaming?" said Bamp.

"I don't think so," said Taff, "because I'm here and you're here and I'm not dreaming. The thing is how by the beard of Myrddin did you get here, this is an animal sanctuary, a village for animals only, and hidden from the world by Myrddins magic." (Myrddin is the Welsh name for Merlin the Great wizard who looked after King Arthur, and we all know he was Welsh and from Carmarthenshire.)

Taff said, "I'd better take you to see Mrs Trumperov, our teacher; she will know what to do and she can tell you all about Abercwmzoo and how we got here. She knows lots of stuff, but I don't know if she'll know how you got here."

So Taff led Bampy and Willow through Abercwmzoo to the school house where Mrs Trumperov lived. On the way he saw lots of different animals; there were lions, bears, monkeys, horses and even a hippopotamus.

At the school house Taff knocked on the door and they heard a voice from inside say, "Come in and wipe your feet first, we don't want dirt in the schoolhouse."

Taff, Bampy and Willow went inside and were confronted by a rather portly and motherly elephant in a pinafore and dust cap who was busy dusting the school desks.

"Um I thought this might happen one day," said Mrs Trumperov with a look of resignation on her face. "We'd best sit down and have a cup of tea, as I have a lot to tell you which will explain our presence here. It covers a dark period of history before even my Bamp was born. You may know parts of the history but you must swear that you will never show another person here or our very existence will be jeopardised and we will have to find somewhere else to live. When I've told you our story, you will realise how hard that would be," she said.

So she stopped dusting and made a pot of tea.

I don't believe this, how can this be happening? thought Bamp and I bet you're wondering that too, aren't you?

Mrs Trumperov sat him down at a school desk and poured him a cup of tea and said, "This is a very long and amazing story which I think will help you see why it should remain secret."

Well it was an amazing, very long and important tale with a lot of twists and turns. A story about war and peace, of royalty, politics, intrigue and revolution. A tale full of fantasy where fact merged with fiction, making the impossible seem possible.

But really it was a tale about a boy who had a dream. A boy who, with his girlfriend and animal friends, struggled through many hardships which finally ended with them coming to live in Wales and ending up in Abercwmzoo after World War One. And what's more, it is backed up by historical fact.

My Bamp told me he listened to the whole story captivated as although he knew parts of the history he just couldn't have imagined that such an epic story could have culminated so close to home and even involved past family and friends.

He reminded me that he was only telling me the full story because he wanted the story told if further development was to be made to the Sirhowy Valley as it would endanger the existence of Abercwmzoo.

Well it is. Trees have been copped down all around Smugglers Run and Croespenmaen and wind turbines and solar panels erected in the green fields. A huge new school has been built where Oakdale Colliery used to be and because of the projected house building programme the Council are planning it is already said to be too small to cater for the rising population of Oakdale which will require a further school expansion inevitably followed by more housing and the loss of more green land and woods.

Abercwmzoo is now in great danger and its story must be told to prevent its extinction.

Chapter 2
Tomas Tomaschevski and His Dream

Mrs Trumperov began to tell Bamp the story which began at the start of the last century about a hundred years ago, which was a long time before my Bamp was born. As she was a teacher and had lived during that time she told Bamp the full story which was full of history, politics, culture, war and adventure with a little bit of fantasy as well.

The story began at the turn of the last century 1900, which was the beginning of the 20th century, when Tomas Tomaschevski, the son of a Polish farmer who had married a Russian dancer when he was a rebellious young man and dreamt of being a musician, was born in a town named Tuchola. It was a time when there were no televisions or mobile phones or Game Boys for kids to play with and there were not many cars or buses about either. Things were a lot simpler then but because there was such a lot of poverty, most people were poor and uneducated. Children had to grow up quickly and were put to work at a young age as there were no child protection laws in those days. It was the time when our great grandparents were children.

The world was the same and although there were different attitudes there was still a great divide between the rich and the poor. It was a time when the Class system was in place, there were the great Royal families, great landowners and industrialists, working classes who were poor and then the poor who either begged or were put in work houses. Just like today, really, but we have the Welfare State.

Europe, that's the continent we live in, was different too. Countries were different but the race and religions of their populations were the same and there were always wars starting between one country or state to gain independence or national sovereignty. Again like today, really. Despite all these nationalistic struggles, the thought of a First World War was about as plausible as men walking on the moon. Many things are not much different today as they were in our great grandparents' day.

Wars are terrible things where people fight other people over some big issues which usually consist of national sovereignty. Europe at that time was a volatile continent which was mainly ruled by a number of empires. There was France, The Austrian/Hungarian Empire, also known as the Hapsburg Empire, Russia, Prussia – which was Germany and the Ottoman Empire which was the Turkish Empire. Prior to the 20th century the Ottoman Empire spread over much of Europe but its power was on the decline and it was becoming known as the Sick man of Europe. The Austrian/Hungarian Empire also spread over Eastern Europe and between them and the Ottoman Empire they ruled over the Slavic States around the Balkans and bordering them was Russia.

The Balkans were especially volatile because not only were the influences of the different empires, they were populated by people of different nationalities and religions such as Orthodox Christians, such as in Eastern Europe, and Muslims of the Ottoman Empire.

At the start of the century, there was a strong nationalistic movement amongst the people of the Balkans and Serbia, which was partly populated by Slavs, had fought and freed itself from Turkish rule. It had grown into the Kingdom of Serbia including Serbs, Croats and Slavs. Serbia was also looking to expand its kingdom at the expense of the Austro-Hungarian Empire. Then you had Bulgaria, Bosnia and Herzegovina, Montenegro, Macedonia, Rumania, Albania and even Greece.

All these countries were looking for their own national identities and fought to remove the Turks from Eastern Europe and establish their own territories. Each had their own agendas and there was also hostility against each other which meant that alliances between them were also very fragile.

The Balkan States had formed an alliance to fight for independence against the Turks and later with Russian help against the rule of the Austrian Hungarian Empire which had also become fragile.

The Balkan League consisted of Serbia, Bulgaria, Greece and Montenegro.

With all this conflict in Europe, Britain did its best to stay neutral and adopted a policy called Splendid Isolation, which meant it would stay out of European squabbles thus saving money and resources which could be used on the British overseas empire. Britain at this time had the largest empire in the world, with countries in Asia, Africa, North America, South America and Australasia.

With all these mounting squabbles, a major war in Europe seemed likely, though a World War unlikely because three of the leaders of the major empires were related. They were in fact cousins and grandchildren of Queen Victoria who was queen of Britain. There was George 5th, King of England, Wilhelm 2nd Kaiser of Germany, and Tsar Nicholas 2nd of Russia so you would have thought that the outbreak of a major war in Europe was highly unlikely.

However, events leading up to 1914 proved otherwise and led to the outbreak of World War One. This war was the most horrific war there had ever been and was thought, at the time, to be the war that ended all wars, as so many people died during it.

Unfortunately however, it was not. Just about twenty years later a Second World War started.

Now it wasn't by accident that Taff came to live in Abercwmzoo in Wales, it was all down to the dream of that young Polish farmer's son named Tomas Tomaschevski from Tuchola.

In 1914 Poland did not exist as a country. Instead, it was divided into three states each being part of other countries' empires, which had conquered it through wars. There were a lot of wars in those days. Tuchola was in the German Prussian state of Pomerania; then there was Galicia which was part of the Austrian/Hungarian Empire and the Congress Kingdom of Poland, which was part of the Russian Empire.

Tomas was 14 years old and the youngest of three brothers and two sisters. His father wanted Tomas and his brothers to be a farmer like him. As well as root crops he kept livestock such as horses, cows, goats, ducks and chickens and when Tomas was old enough his father put him to work. His job was to look after his flock of sheep.

Prior to being put to work Tomas had had it easy. He had been brought up by his mother who hardly left the farmhouse as she did all the household chores for the large family. She had spoken to Tomas in her native tongue, Russian, something she had not had the time to do with the other children and she had taught him ballet dancing. He became quite proficient at both.

Tomas grew up wishing to become a performer and pestered his father who had a magnificent accordion which he would play to the family on special occasions and parties to teach him to play it. His father hadn't taught his other children as they did not have the inclination or talent to learn but Tomas had and his father bought him a concertina which is a small accordion type instrument which was small enough for a young lad like Tomas. Tomas was a keen student and very musically orientated. His mother would call him her little prince and tell him he was special and destined for greater things. He did not wish to become a farmer like the rest of the family.

When the time came for him to start work his father wondered what his job should be. He knew that Tomas was a dreamer and that his mind constantly wandered from the task he was given so he decided that Tomas would be given the task of watching the sheep. He would be their shepherd, a task his brother had performed but had asked to change as it had bored him. Father thought it would suit Tomas as he could go up with his concertina and spend his time playing music if he wanted to. They had the best two sheepdogs in the land and they were well capable of looking after the sheep with little supervision.

Tomas was given a shotgun and the two sheepdogs who were instructed to keep an eye on Tomas as well as the sheep, and that spring they were sent up to the pasture close to the forestry on the edge of Tuchola.

The sheepdogs were named Jerzy and Irena (Now although we would pronounce Irena as Irena, Polish people pronounce it as Iraina, that's because in Europe many languages have symbols above letters like 'e' to show you how the letters are pronounced. This would be useful in English sometimes, especially with words like LIVE which is a word that could mean: To live somewhere or it's a live wire. It's very confusing, isn't it?) to help him herd the sheep and keep them safe from the wolves who lived in the forests which were all around Tuchola.

Now Jerzy and Irena were excellent sheepdogs; they had been taught well by Tomas' father and their parents, who too were both very good sheepdogs. Tomas' father knew Tomas was a dreamer but thought he could rely on the dogs to look after the sheep even when Tomas was dreaming. He tried his best to make Tomas take whatever job he was given seriously and responsibly but it was a hopeless task. He hoped that shepherding was something Tomas could manage without too much bother as Jerzy and Irena would see that everything was in order.

The task was easy; there had been no sighting of any wolves in the area since Tomas' father had seen them off several summers past and if any should return he had a shotgun with which to raise the alarm and the family would come racing to his aid.

So Tomas started his time as a shepherd.

Instead of watching the sheep however, as his father had predicted, Tomas would play his concertina and forget all about the sheep. Tomas was a very good concertina player. Once Tomas started playing, however, the strangest thing happened, Jerzy and Irena would also stop watching the sheep and began to move and jump to the music as if they were dancing; much to Tomas' amusement.

As stated, Tomas didn't really want to be a farmer like his dad; he wanted to be a great showman and travel the world. He dreamt of one day being known as the Great Tomaschevski. He watched the dogs dance and thought to himself, *If I can teach them to dance ballet I would be famous. I could take them to Russia to the great Bolshoi Ballet in Moscow and we would be famous throughout the world. Mother would be proud.*

Dancing is a national pastime in Poland and the great Nijinsky, the famous ballet dancer, had Polish parents. His mother had been a great dancer until a nasty fall had injured her leg and caused a slight limp which had stopped her budding career as a ballerina.

Now ballet is not like the dancing on Strictly Come Dancing. It is much harder and takes a very long time to learn and master, but Tomas, who had heard of the Bolshoi ballet from travellers he had met and stories he had read about ballet, thought he could teach Jerzy and Irena the basic steps and jumps so that he could take them to Moscow to audition for the ballet.

To be a great ballet dancer takes very intensive training and ballet academies were set up to train young ballet dancers and only the very best ever got to perform for the great Ballets.

Every year the Bolshoi ballet auditioned to find new stars in the hope that they would find the best male dancer and female ballerina in the world. Those who did audition were selected from their academies.

The auditions were nothing like the X Factor and Britain's Got Talent auditions, so Tomas knew that Jerzy and Irena had to dance to a very high standard to have any chance of being accepted by the Bolshoi Ballet; it would take much more than just turning in a circle or jumping to the beat of the music. He would have to teach them the disciplines and dance moves such as Adagio, Allegro, Allonge, Arabesque, as well as the Pas assemble, Pas de Deux and Chaines Tournes to name but a few. First to learn was the Pirouette.

First, he would have to teach them balance and posture.

He had read about the importance of balance and posture in dance and how it was even more important to keep everything in balance and retain good posture in ballet.

He taught Jerzy and Irena to balance on their legs and to keep their posture strong.

Both dogs built up their leg and core strength and became fitter and sleeker.

Once they were ready for the next step he started to teach them their moves.

Over the next few months Tomas and the sheepdogs worked harder perfecting their ballet techniques than they did minding the sheep, and the wolves began to take notice.

The sound of Tomas' concertina playing during the night when the sound carried for miles had intrigued a pack of wolves that lived many miles from the Tomaschevski farm. They had heard the music and travelled through the forest to see the source of the marvellous sounds that lit up the night. When they came across Tomas, they were stunned. They stopped in their tracks gawping at Jerzy and Irena who were dancing.

It was the same pack Tomas' father, Jerzy and Irena's parents had seen off years before and they were wary of trying to take sheep from this farm as the pack had been decimated by the farmer and his dogs but now there was a young boy and two different dogs.

Things were looking up for the wolves. Now although they feared the dogs who they knew would defend the sheep, they knew they could outsmart them and the boy shepherd and take the odd stray sheep.

They decided to stay on that side of the forest and watch for any chance to take a sheep or lamb, as it was lambing season, and hope that they would not be noticed. The wolves were good hunters and knew how to stay downwind from the dogs to avoid detection and they made sure that when they howled in the night they were a good distance away from the flock not to cause concern.

At first, they thought that Tomas was giving the dogs fitness training as it was making them seem stronger. Jerzy and Irena certainly looked much fitter and stronger but then they realised that while they were dancing they were not looking after the sheep as they were supposed to and that allowed them to roam and get quite close to the edge of the forest which helped the wolves and they were able to take the odd sheep without Tomas or the dogs realising.

The sheep, however, noticed and began to keep away from the edge of the forest.

So the wolves devised a cunning plan to catch as many sheep as they could when Tomas was well into a session and teaching something new. They would pounce on the unsuspecting sheep, whilst Jerzy and Irena were concentrating on their routines, and drag them into the forest so that they could feed the entire pack, and that's exactly what they did.

One evening Tomas and the dogs had had a very good session and Tomas decided to have Jerzy and Irena learn their coup de grace or finishing move. The grand Jeté which is doing the splits in the air. Tomas was confident that they could do it but the dogs were getting tired. The sheep had wandered towards the forest and were grazing fairly close to the forest's edge where there was still a lot of lush grass. The wolves were lying in wait.

As Tomas was showing Jerzy and Irena what to do, the wolves began to make their move, well some of them were, some were looking at what Tomas was trying to teach Jerzy and Irena.

They were astounded and thought surely Jerzy and Irena would never be able to do the grand Jeté.

It was time for Jerzy and Irena to give it a try. Tomas played his concertina and Jerzy and Irena both leapt into the air performing two brilliant grand Jetés. The wolves who had been watching were dumbstruck. Tomas stopped playing and began to clap loudly as the dogs had done so well. The wolves who had been watching also clapped loudly and began to howl with delight just as the other wolves attacked.

If it had not been for the noise they made, Tomas would have lost nearly the whole flock but luckily he only lost seven ewes and fifteen lambs to the wolves; even so it was a very big loss for the Tomaschevski farm to lose and would make life harder for the family.

Jerzy and Irena despite being very tired did their best to fight off the wolves; Tomas had forgot to load his shotgun and fumbled as he loaded it which took precious time before firing it to signal the alarm They attacked the wolves with a ferocity that no wolf had ever experienced from a sheep dog. Both dogs were spinning and jumping up in the air kicking and biting the wolves with such speed and grace that the wolves were soon reeling and gave up the attack. They had been like ninja dogs and trained in kung fu not ballet.

Tomas too joined in the attack on the wolves and was hitting them with his crook, that's a shepherd's stick.

It was a hard-fought battle and both dogs sustained injuries in the fight. Both required treatment to bites and wounds. The family did not take long to come to their assistance, however, as father and his brothers had trained for such an emergency and had saddled their horses and rode up to the pasture in a flash.

When it was all over they rounded up the remaining sheep, who were scared stiff and Tomas led them limping back to the safety of the farm.

Tomas' father was furious and beat Tomas till he was red raw and he cried himself to sleep that night because as well as being sore he was very ashamed of himself for not looking after the sheep properly and losing so many.

The whole catastrophe had taught Tomas a very valuable lesson, that if you have a job to do, don't start doing something else because you can't look after sheep and practise ballet at the same time.

Tomas had learnt the hard way that multitasking, though it sounds good, does not work because you cannot put all your best effort into two or more jobs at the same time; therefore, your work suffers.

After that Tomas was not allowed to mind the sheep again. The only tasks he was given were to feed the chickens and ducks and collect the eggs, the job his sisters had previously done. Two new sheepdogs were bought and Jerzy and Irena were retired so they were all in the dog house. They were shamed and felt very dejected.

The wolves, however, had a great feast and some of them danced because they had not fed so well in a long, long time. Some even tried the grand Jeté and if you go to the forest around Tuchola today you may be lucky and see some ballet dancing wolves amongst the trees.

You won't see Tomas though.

Tomas, however, still had his dream and he was determined to make it come true.

Chapter 3
The War Begins and Tomas Leaves the Farm

At the start of the 20th century, the Ottoman Empire was weak and the Serbians had defeated the Turks and reclaimed much of its territory thus further weakening its influence in Europe. Serbia became a state in its own right and wanted to expand with its sights on other areas such as Bosnia and Herzegovina etc. The Austrian/Hungarian Empire was also on the decline and feared the expansion of a greater Serbia would eventually impact on their territory too so they tried to block Serbian expansion.

The spring of 1914 saw the seeds of revolution and war being sewn and in June of that year Arch Duke Franz Ferdinand of the Austrian Hungary Empire was assassinated in Sarajevo which was then part of the Austro Hungarian Empire.

This was because young Bosnians, who did not want to be part of the Austro Hungarian Empire or the Ottoman Empire, formed a terrorist group called the Black Hand. They wanted to break free of the Austrian Hungarian Empire and become part of a greater Serbia because of their nationality and they thought that assassinating Arch Duke Franz Ferdinand, who was the heir to the Austrian aristocracy, would help their cause and stir up nationalistic fervour and fuel rebellion.

Now one thing led to another and Austria gave Serbia an ultimatum which consisted of 10 conditions Serbia had to accept and Serbia was in the process of accepting 9 of them and part of the 10th. However, this was not acceptable to Austria and they declared war on Serbia.

The Russian Tsar, Tsar Nicholas, had pledged to support the Serbs, who were the same race as the Russians. If there was to be a war, he was worried as he thought Russia was not prepared for war and would fare badly if it was forced to enter another war. Nicholas wrote to his cousin Kaiser Wilhelm of Germany asking him to mediate between Serbia and Austria to stop a war happening. He proposed that this be part of the Hague Peace Conference, a process that Nicholas had himself initiated at the start of his reign in the hope of preventing further wars in Europe which he saw as a blight to peace in Europe.

This did not stop Nicholas, however, on the advice of his generals, starting to mobilise his army.

Wilhelm, however, was ready for a war and his army were well manned, trained and equipped. He had a treaty with Austria to help them if they were involved in a war.

In fact the German Army was more than ready for war and had a master plan called the Schlieffen Plan, which was a plan to invade France, a feat they thought could be accomplished in a matter of days, then attack Russia before they could mobilise, and defeat Russia in a week, thus making them the masters of Europe.

Wilhelm apparently accepted the role as negotiator but told Nicholas that he had to stop mobilising his troops as they were the threat to peace. The mediation did not work and on 28th July, 1914 Austria declared war on Serbia. Germany followed this up by declaring war on Russia on 1st August 1914.

Germany then invaded France and Belgium, which, due to treaties Britain had with those countries, meant Britain declaring war on 4th August 1914.

The conflict escalated with more of Europe becoming caught up in the conflict which led to different imperial powers joining forces through alliance agreements made earlier. This saw Germany and Turkey ally themselves to the Austrian/Hungarian Empire, and Russia and France ally themselves to Serbia. It did not take long before nearly all of Europe was at war. That one assassination had led to the start of World War One.

At the start of World War One, Britain was neutral but was wary of Germany, as the Germans under Kaiser Wilhelm 2nd (that's Germany's equivalent of our king) had been increasing the size of its navy as well as its army in order to match the British navy in order to create its own overseas empire. Germany, however, as part of its plan to invade and defeat France, needed to attack France through Belgium. They thought that Britain would remain neutral as the Kaiser and British king were cousins, both being grandchildren of Queen Victoria, and would not want to be caught up in another European War. The Germans thought they could conquer France in six weeks on the Western Front and also defeat Russia on the Eastern Front thus creating a greater Germany in Europe.

Britain, however, had a treaty with Belgium to protect its borders in time of war and ensure its neutrality. With this in mind and the likelihood of British interests being threatened, Britain entered the war on the side of France and Russia sending the British Expeditionary Force to Belgium and France with the intention of stopping German expansion in its tracks.

Britain and soldiers from the British Empire such as Australia, Canada, India, New Zealand, South Africa and the West Indies, France, Belgium, Russia, Italy and later America and Japan fought against the German Prussian Empire, Austrian Hungarian Empire and Ottoman Empires for supremacy in Europe and the world.

Britain, as the greatest naval power in the world, set about straightaway in its historical proven strategy of blockade, blockading German ports around the world thereby preventing Germany's fleet from sailing out to confront the British fleet.

Britain also began a strategy of stopping all merchant shipping getting to Germany in an attempt to stop supplies reaching the German military and civilians, preventing vital food supplies reaching Germany which would hopefully stir up civil unrest.

The British also destroyed Germany's overseas wireless (radio) stations to prevent Germany communicating with the rest of the world.

The United States of America, who were neutral and wanted to stay that way, however, granted the Germans access to their wireless station in Copenhagen Denmark, a country that was also neutral, and that was the only way Germany could communicate with the rest of the world. This would prove very beneficial for the British as will be seen later in the story.

The Germans had a fleet of 28 submarines called U-boats which were able to dodge the British fleet and attack ships heading to Britain with the aim of sinking as many merchant ships as they could to prevent goods arriving in Britain. A tactic that proved very successful for the Germans and its effects will also affect the outcome of the War and Tomas' story.

Britain also had submarines which they used during the War but with less success than the Germans, though nine were attached to the Russian navy, a fact that will again play a part in Tomas' story.

The war was fought on two fronts the Western front which was fought in the fields of Belgium and France and involved the British, French and Belgium Soldiers fighting a Trench type of warfare against the Germans which you will learn about in school in greater detail. The Russians fought on the Eastern front, a much more fluid war but still as bloody. Many people on both sides were either killed or seriously injured.

When it was over, they called it the Great War and many thought that it was so bad that it would be the war that ended all wars but unfortunately that was not the case.

This Great War was to affect and take many lives and it was not long before it impacted on the Tomaschevski Farm. Tuchola being in the German part of Poland was stuck in the middle of the fighting with Germany, Austria and Russia, all vying for control.

Tomas' brothers were called up to fight in the German army leaving Tomas and his sisters to share more responsibility on the farm. Tomas' father, however, still did not trust Tomas and he was left to carry out the menial chores around the farm.

Tomas was not happy at all and fearing that he too might be called up to fight in the German army despite being only 14 years old, so he decided to leave the farm with Jerzy and Irena and make his way to Moscow where his mother had lived. He would avoid the fighting and hoped that they could join the Bolshoi Ballet during the war when most able men would be called on to fight in the war. He was going to be a showman, not a farmer or a soldier.

So late one night in late October, Tomas collected what he needed for the trip to Moscow and packed his bags. He picked up his concertina and put all his stuff on an old hand cart, then he called Jerzy and Irena and they said goodbye to the farm leaving a note to his mother and father explaining that he was leaving never to come back. He told them not to worry because Jerzy and Irena would look after him.

Tomas explained that he could never be a farmer and was off to fulfil his dream to become a great showman and he was taking Jerzy and Irena with him because they were the greatest dancing dogs the world would ever see and he had trained them. They would make a fortune and he would send them money to help with the farm when they were rich and famous so that they could restock the flock.

Tomas knew that he would have to endure the harsh Eastern winter so he packed his warmest clothes and blankets for Jerzy and Irena, so that they too could keep warm.

Ballet dancers would not be very good if they got frostbite.

So off they went on what was the start of a great adventure which would eventually lead them to Wales and Abercwmzoo.

Chapter 4
Off to Moscow and the Bolshoi Ballet

Now Moscow is a long way from Tuchola, 804 miles as the crow flies, but that is in a straight line and Tomas could not go in a straight line because there was a war on. Now they would have to take many diversions to avoid getting caught up in the fighting, however, to get to Moscow they would have to travel through areas where there were battles.

Tomas was to travel through East Prussia which was German territory and into Russian territory before reaching Moscow. It would take him much longer than he thought.

There were no motorways or fast cars, although there were trains but Tomas could not afford to use the train. Besides, to go to Russia by train would mean going to Warsaw and taking the train to St Petersburg where the Tsar of Russia (The Tsar was the king of Russia and emperor of the Russian Empire) and his family live. Tomas didn't want to go there; he wanted to go to Moscow and join the Bolshoi Ballet.

Tomas knew this would be difficult because the Russian army was on the move and heading into the Austrian / German parts of Poland. He knew that he would have to cross into Russian territory to get to Moscow and was pleased that at an early age he had developed a keen interest in learning languages and could speak Polish, German and Russian quite well.

Europeans seem to learn languages easily, not like most of us who even struggle with English and Welsh.

Whilst Tomas was still in the German territory, he would entertain the soldiers for food and provisions for his trip to Moscow. He couldn't tell them he was going to Moscow or they might have stopped him going. He told them he was there to help with the morale of the troops who were being overwhelmed by the Russians at first.

The Germans however, although being outnumbered, were far better equipped than the Russians and were better trained. In fact many Russian soldiers did not even have rifles or guns, so despite the early defeats, the Germans were able to mount their own offensive against the Russians.

The route Tomas had to take would take him through the Masurian Lake district which is an area of outstanding beauty with an abundance of wildlife.

This was where the Germans and Russians fought a great battle and the Germans pushed back the Russians who were heavily defeated. This was the first battle of the Masurian Lakes and the Germans called it Tannenberg.

Although this was a win for the Germans, they were still heavily outnumbered and winter was coming.

Now winter in that part of Europe is not like ours; if you think we have it cold and wet, think of what Tomas and the two armies had it like. It was much, much colder and a lot more snow which was great if you are going out to build snowmen or play on your sledge or snowballs but not if you had to stay out in it all day everyday with very little supplies and sheltering only in tents.

So, wanting to defeat the Russians as quickly as they could, the Germans came up with the wicked idea of using poison gas against the Russians and began making different types of gas to use in battle.

Tomas, who could speak three languages, Polish, German and Russian spent Christmas 1914 behind the German lines and would entertain the troops by playing Stille Nacht and Schlittenglocken on his concertina and Jerzy and Irena would dance for them. Can you guess what Stille Nacht is? Yes it is Silent Night. And Schlittenglocken? No, its Jingle Bells.

The German soldiers loved their performances and would shout 'Wunderbar' and 'Zugabe' which means wonderful and encore. Tomas, Jerzy and Irena were loved by the soldiers and were well looked after. They fed well and Tomas was given warm clothes and shelter for the severe winter weather.

On the 31st January 1915, the Germans first used gas against the Russians; they used a type of tear gas against the Russians at the battle of Bolimov but it was so cold that the gas froze and fell to the ground doing no harm whatsoever. Bolimov was only a minor battle in which the Germans wanted to divert Russian attention from Warsaw, which is now Poland's capitol city, but then it was in Russian territory.

They did not give up on the idea of using poison gas, however, and later used a type of chlorine gas at Ypres on the Western front against the French.

Tomas was horrified that the Germans could do such a bad thing and was even more determined to cross the battle lines and get to the Russian side as soon as possible so, despite his relative comfort, he packed as much as he, Jerzy and Irena could carry and they left the German camp. They headed for the Russian border trying to avoid the front line in case he would be mistaken for a spy. He would head for the Masurian Lakes.

It was not going to be easy but The Masurian Lakes were vast and there were a lot of gaps in the lines where Tomas and the two dogs could slip through hidden in the forestry or undergrowth. Tomas' time as a shepherd had taught him how to survive on his own and the dogs who were also well used to staying out for long periods in the cold winters looking after the sheep, knew how to keep warm and would snuggle up to Tomas during the nights and keep him warm too.

They managed to avoid the Russian front line but felt sorry for the Russian soldiers, who had very little in the way of comfort or supplies and when they were close to their positions he could see that their morale was low and discipline, poor. He did not want to get caught there on the front line and the sooner he reached Moscow the better.

Tomas did not like war and he did not want to get caught up in the fighting either.

Tomas lived on his supplies and off the land as best he could but he could not last too long. The winters in Poland and Russia are very cold; sometimes they are under 30 degrees, so not only did they have to keep themselves warm, they also needed to break cover on occasions to scavenge for fresh supplies.

Both Jerzy and Irena were getting thin but because there were so many Russian soldiers in front of them they could not move very quickly and they were running out of food.

One dark night, Tomas, Jerzy and Irena snuck into a small Russian encampment to look for food and anything they could use on their journey to Moscow. Whilst searching through the cook's tent, however, Tomas upset a big iron ladle which fell onto the handle of a saucepan, which was balancing on the edge of a wonky table, making a loud bang; but it did not stop there. The saucepan wobbled then started to fall from the table towards a pile of pots which were on the floor below the table. Frantically, Tomas tried to catch the falling saucepan but tripped over Jerzy who had also seen what was happening and also tried to catch the saucepan. They collided with the pots and sent them scattering, and shattering them all over the ground.

Tomas and Jerzy looked at each other knowing that they must have been heard but luckily for them the Russian soldiers had drunk lots and lots of vodka that night and all but one was fast asleep and dreaming of going back home away from the war.

That one Russian soldier, who must have been the only Russian who didn't like vodka, had been cleaning his boots and writing his own story about the war, stirred. He got up and ran over to the cook's tent and went straight in falling over the sleeping cook as he entered the tent. As he fell to the ground Irena leapt up in the air in front of Tomas and Jerzy performing a perfect grand Jeté crashing into the soldier as he fell knocking him clean out.

The soldier later wrote in his book how he had disturbed a big nasty wolf that had got into the cook's tent and stopped it from stealing all the food. Thanks to his quick action only a small amount of food had been taken, though a few pots had been smashed. When all the others woke up and heard him relate the story, he was treated as a hero.

Tomas, Jerzy and Irena had been lucky. They took only what they could carry out quickly and made their way back into the woods.

They decided that staying in the woods would probably be their best bet to avoid any further confrontation and they headed deep into the forest which lies between Poland and Belarus, heading for Minsk.

Chapter 5
The Białowieża Forest, the Leszi and Bear Cubs

They were in the Białowieża Primeval Forest which is said to be over 7000 years old. It is still very dense and untouched. It is full of wildlife, animals and plant life, and Tomas and the dogs were able to survive on food they scavenged in the forest.

Tomas, Jerzy and Irena were now nearing Minsk, which is now the capitol of Belarus. As with Poland, Belarus has had many changes. It has been known as White Russia, Polesia as well as Belorussia depending on which nation conquered the region at the time.

In 1915 Minsk had a very mixed population with the majority being Russian then there were Poles, Germans and a very large Jewish population who were collecting money for the purpose of buying land and property in Palestine for the Jewish people. Minsk Jews were Zionists and were disliked by all the other races and persecuted by them all throughout their history in Europe.

Tomas was Polish and although he was proud to be Polish, he was careful to keep his Polish ancestry secret as he was now in Russian territory. Luckily he had been well versed in Russian and he could converse with the locals though he tried to remain in the shelter of the forestry around Minsk and live off the land as best he could.

An interesting fact is Minsk is roughly halfway between Berlin in Germany and Moscow in Russia.

One day Tomas was in the forest when he heard a bear growl very loudly as if it was warning something to keep away. Then he heard shots being fired and men cheering. Tomas remained still not wanting to be seen. He heard the men talking; they were

Russian deserters who were desperate, hungry and cold and they wanted the bear for food and for its fur to make coats.

They knew nothing of the forest and if they did they would have realised that they had shot a mother bear and that she would have cubs hidden nearby. Tomas on the other hand had been brought up near forests and knew that the bear sounded as if it was protecting its young. He decided to remain still and investigate when the coast was clear. He would take care of the cubs and motioned to Jerzy and Irena to lie down and remain still.

They would stay on guard, and wait for the men to leave.

The men, however, decided to stay all night before moving on and feast on the bear.

That was a big mistake. They did not know much about the forest and they were not aware that a Leszi had heard the commotion, realised what had befell the bear and was heading towards them hell-bent on vengeance on the deserters.

A Leszi is, in Polish folklore, a male woodland elf who protects wild animals and has a close bond with the wolf. In Russia they are known as Leszi and it is the Forest Lord who carries a club to emphasise his power and status. It is a magical shape shifter that can take the shape of any animal or plant.

The Leszi snuck up on the deserters in the shape of the largest wolf Tomas had ever seen.

Whilst they were hidden from view they watched the wolf carry out a swift and lethal attack on the deserters which left them all dead and mutilated.

Tomas and the dogs were terrified and hoped that they would not be discovered so they lay down as low in the undergrowth as they could.

The Leszi then turned back into his own form and battered each deserter with his club as if he was making sure they would not kill any further forest animal. He then began to dance around their battered bodies, singing a triumphant song.

Tomas waited until all was quiet and then went to see what had happened. He walked into a clearing where he saw a lot of blood and the bodies of the deserters on the ground and signs of something having been dragged away.

He then heard a whimpering sound coming from the undergrowth to his left. Irena went to where the noise was coming from and barked. She then went in to the undergrowth before coming back out followed by three brown bear cubs, who, despite being as big as she was, were still only babies. They were about 12 months old but luckily had been weaned.

Now bears hibernate during the winter and Tomas knew that their lair would be a warm place to snuggle down in and the bear cubs would also keep them warm, and he was cold. First, however, he knew that the cubs must be hungry and he would have to feed them. Tomas had no intention of killing the bear cubs or letting them die. He loved all animals and decided he would look after them and add them to his troop. He would raise the bear cubs to be performers like Jerzy and Irena and they too would be ballet dancers. He knew he was a good teacher and the cubs were young enough to learn. First things first though, they all needed food.

Now the Leszi had been aware of their presence and he had removed the mother bear so as not to alarm the cubs and had watched Tomas and the dogs to see what their intentions were.

He had not sensed any hostility from them towards the cubs and hoped that they would take care of them and when he saw that they would look after the cubs, he confronted them.

Tomas and Jerzy were alarmed but Irena put herself between the cubs and the Leszi and snarled and growled at the Leszi to show that she meant to protect them.

The Leszi laughed out loud and spoke to Irena in dog speak telling her not to be scared he was a friend to animals and would not harm them.

He then spoke to Tomas and asked him what his intentions with the bear cubs were.

Tomas related his dream of taking Jerzy and Irena to Moscow to perform at the Bolshoi Ballet and that he would like to adopt the bear cubs and teach them to perform as well.

The Leszi knew of the taking of bear cubs and turning them into trained bears by humans and he knew how badly those bears were treated but Tomas promised him he would never harm or chain the bears and they would be free to do as they pleased.

This satisfied the Leszi and he was pleased to let Tomas adopt the cubs.

He said to Tomas, "My name is Leonik and I am a Leszy. I was named Leonik because I am as brave as a lion and as strong as a lion; if you go back on your promise I will come looking for you so make sure you take good care of them."

"I won't," he replied.

Now it is well known that when a Leszi befriends a human it will teach him the secrets of the forest magic.

Tomas did not wish to remain in the forest too long as he wanted to get to Moscow as quickly as he could.

The Leszi understood Tomas' haste but imparted to Tomas the ability to learn any language whether it be human, animal or plant before they said their farewells.

He also imparted a gift on the bear cubs.

On their travels Tomas and the dogs had relied on hand-outs from soldiers and peasants for whom they had performed and from what they could catch in the forests or fish from the rivers if they could catch them.

Tomas had struck it lucky when he found the bear cubs because their mother had begun teaching them how to fish the rivers in Minsk and where the best spots to fish were. So when the bear cubs got to the river they all ran up to where the water was shallow and were soon in the river trying to catch fish.

At least two of them were.

One male cub was busy splashing the water and banging rocks together. He was having fun making a loud din and this was sending the fish up towards the other male cub who was catching the fish and throwing up and down just like a juggler.

Then he started throwing them at Tomas, Jerzy and Irena, who stood on the bank.

He was a right little tinker.

The female cub, however, was catching fish further up and putting them on the river bank for Tomas to collect. Soon they had all the fish they needed and they would eat well that night.

The Leszi had improved their fishing skills and given each one a different ability before he had parted.

Tomas couldn't believe his luck; it was the cubs who would be looking after him not the other way round.

Tomas thought of naming the cubs.

He thought as they come from Minsk, *I'll call the female cub Minsky. The cub who likes to make a lot of noise; I'll call Dinsky and the cub who likes to be naughty; I'll call Tinsky and from that day they were Minsky, Dinsky and Tinsky.*

Tomas soon found that although they were sister and brothers, they all had different personalities and liked doing different things.

Minsky enjoyed learning to dance and would get up on two legs and dance just for the fun of it.

Tinsky would also dance until he got bored and he got bored quite quickly. Tomas soon discovered, however, that Tinsky really enjoyed juggling and it soon became apparent that he was an excellent juggler who could juggle almost anything and up to five items at a time.

Dinsky on the other hand didn't like dancing, didn't like juggling but enjoyed making a row. Whether it was banging stones, roaring or bashing things, it didn't matter to him as long as he was making a noise. Dinsky, however, did like listening to Tomas play his concertina and would sit still while the others were dancing and tap the ground or stones whilst doing so.

Tomas at first didn't realise what Dinsky was doing but then began to hear that Dinsky was tapping in time with him. Dinsky had rhythm and was laying down a beat to the music he was playing; he was also making noises as if he was singing to the music as well. Tomas let Dinsky carry his concertina and soon Dinsky started to play it as they were walking. At first it was just a racket so Tomas decided to teach Dinsky how to play the concertina and before long Dinsky was playing polkas and waltzes as good as he could and Minsky and Tinsky would dance to the music Dinsky played.

Tomas now had performing dogs and bears; his dream of being a great showman was looking good.

He now had a show Jerzy and Irena were excellent ballet dancers, Minsky and Tinsky weren't ballet dancers but he taught them to dance a waltz and a polka together. They also danced the kalinka, the Russian folk dance, brilliantly. If you look on the Internet, you can find the Russian Red Army Choir singing the kalinka and there are many videos of it being danced. I recommend that you take a break from reading now and take a look at them. Then you can truly imagine what a marvellous sight it must have been to see three bears dancing the kalinka.

So as well as being dancing bears, Tinsky could juggle and Dinsky could also play a drum, which Tomas had found for him in Minsk; the future looked bright for them.

Tomas decided to give the people of Minsk a show to see if the people liked it. They did, it was a great success and the people of Minsk clapped and cheered making Tomas very proud of his animals. One kind old man gave Tomas a balalaika which is a Russian instrument something like a guitar. He said that he had grown too old to play it and the kalinka was best played on a balalaika not a concertina. He even showed Tomas how to play it and Tomas being a quick learner and very musical, was soon playing it like an expert.

It was now getting warmer. Spring was coming and it was time for them to move on and make their way to Moscow, fame and fortune. They had 426 long miles to go.

Chapter 6
The Tomaschevski Animal Dance Troupe

They travelled now in the open from village to village, town to town performing wherever they could. They became known as the Tomaschevski Animal Dance Troupe and they were applauded and loved wherever they went.

The bear cubs were extraordinary and followed Tomas and the dogs willingly. They loved to perform and the Russian people were amazed that Tomas did not have to beat them or tie them up like other owners of performing bears they had seen.

By the time they reached Smolensk, their fame had preceded them and crowds of people gathered to see their amazing show. They marvelled at the beauty and energy that Jerzy and Irena showed with every performance. They clapped and sang when Minsky and Tinsky did the kalinka. They cheered when Tinsky juggled and danced themselves when Tomas and Dinsky played their songs. Dinsky even did impromptu drum solos, which the audiences loved.

Tomas was the happiest he had ever been and looked forward to entering Moscow to great applause and see Jerzy and Irena fulfil his dream and become great ballet dancers at the Bolshoi Ballet

They now only had around 250 miles to go.

It was May 1915, and reports were filtering through of riots in Moscow. There was already a lot of discontent in Moscow which was Russia's second city. The working classes and the middle classes were unhappy with the Tsar and the conditions they were living under. They were unhappy with the war and riots broke out in Moscow directed against those Germans and foreigners that had settled in Moscow.

Tomas being Polish but from Tuchola, which was under German control at that time, decided that it would be safer for him to remain in Smolensk for a while before venturing on to Moscow. He didn't want to get caught up in the riots and be considered a spy.

It was in May that Britain gained a huge propaganda boost when a German U-boat sank a British passenger liner Cunard's R M S Lusitania off the coast of Ireland on 7th May 1915.

The Lusitania at that time was the fastest liner in the world and had a far greater speed than the German U-boat. The Captain and its owners thought that it could sail back and forth from the United States to Britain without any danger of being sunk by a U-boat.

The Lusitania set sail for Britain from New York on 1st May 1915 without an escort despite an advertisement being placed in the American papers by the German Embassy that the Lusitania would be entering a warzone and would be a target for their U-boats.

This did not deter over 2000 crew and passengers sailing all believing they would be safe as they were travelling on the winner of the Blue Riband, (The Blue Riband is awarded to the world's fastest ship.) and that the Germans would not attack a passenger ship full of civilians.

This did not deter the Germans though who believed that the Lusitania was also carrying munitions for the British army.

On 7th May, the Lusitania was off the coast of Ireland approaching its destination of Liverpool. It had slowed down significantly due to fog and the treacherous coast line so that it was travelling at a speed well within the range of a U-boat and as misfortune would have it they sailed right into the path of a lone U-boat.

The captain of the U-boat could not believe his luck and sent one torpedo at the Lusitania which hit it amidst ship setting it on fire. Whether the torpedo hit the boilers or struck the munitions, the Lusitania burst into flames and began to sink immediately.

It was only a matter of minutes before she disappeared beneath the waves with the loss of over 1100 people with over 120 being American citizens.

President Roosevelt said of the disaster that the British were thieves but the Germans were murderers and their relationship with the Germans was strained.

It did not prompt the Americans to enter the war but the Germans were more wary when attacking merchant ships heading for Britain and they did not attack any further passenger liners.

Meanwhile back in Russia by the end of May, the Military took control and order was restored in Moscow. Discontent was still rife and there was still a lot of tension, but Tomas was impatient and wanted to get to Moscow as soon as possible.

Tomas and his troupe left Smolensk and headed for Moscow. He was pleased to see that they were welcomed and applauded wherever they performed. The people were glad to see them they had little pleasures in life and the chance to see a good show was eagerly anticipated and well attended.

Tomas was buoyed by this overwhelming support and as he neared Moscow, he was optimistic that Jerzy and Irena would be accepted by the Bolshoi Ballet and they would be famous.

When they entered Moscow he was surprised at how big Moscow was. He had never been to such a big city. It was bigger than anywhere else he had been. He saw the devastation the riots had caused with many buildings demolished and widespread damage. The centre of the riots had only been around the foreign sector of Moscow and the Russian suburbs were unscathed.

As it has been throughout history and as it still is, the attitude of the mob is to blame 'Johnny Foreigner' or the Jews for every trouble. The riots were not against the Tsar and the attitude of the regime was that they were patriotic riots against Russia's enemies so reaction to it by the authorities was slow.

Tomas made his way to the Bolshoi Ballet and announced his presence to the director of the Ballet who took one look at him and his troupe and laughed.

Then when Tomas said that he had come all the way to Moscow to audition Jerzy and Irena, his two sheepdogs, to become Bolshoi Ballet dancers, he gave the loudest and longest laugh he had ever laughed in his life.

"That my dear boy is the most ridiculous and outrageous thing I have ever heard in my whole life," said the director.

"Dogs as ballet dancers whatever next. I expect the bears dance as well, do they?"

"Not ballet," said Tomas, "but they can kalinka, polka and waltz."

The director recovering from his laughing fit pulled himself together and said, "What made you think that the Bolshoi Ballet would audition dogs? You should go to the circus and see if they are good enough. Now go away you stupid boy, I'm a busy man." The director walked off in a huff leaving Tomas standing there fuming.

Tomas was devastated he had heard that Muscovites (that's what people from Moscow are called) loved true artists willing to try new things and were always on the lookout for new talent. *Was he wrong?*

Tomas was not wrong; the Muscovites loved Jerzy and Irena and enjoyed Minsky, Tinsky and Dinsky too. They would perform for the public outside the bars and cafés in Moscow to packed crowds and Tomas was welcomed everywhere except for the Bolshoi Ballet. The Tomaschevski Animal Dance Troop were becoming famous.

Chapter 7
Kanga Bruce and the KKK

Although being a tremendous success in Moscow, Tomas still longed for more. He wanted Jerzy and Irena to perform at a proper Ballet.

One day he went to a new bar to perform where he met another traveller, who had also come to Moscow to find fame and fortune, with an animal act.

This traveller had come all the way from Australia, which is the other side of the world, and his name was Rolf Harries. He was Australian but had Welsh parents and he had brought his boxing kangaroo, Bruce, with him from Australia.

Rolf had gone to America with Bruce to box for the middle weight world boxing crown but had not been able to. So instead he had come to Russia hoping that Bruce could box for a title there. They had come to Moscow where he thought he could get a fight, but he too had been disappointed, and was running out of money. He was thinking of going home on his own and leaving Bruce behind.

Tomas had never seen a kangaroo before and neither had Jerzy, Irena or the bears so they stared at Rolf and Bruce who were sitting at a table outside the bar.

"What are you staring at mate, haven't you seen an Aussie and his kanga before," slurred Rolf who was pretty drunk on Vodka.

Tomas thought that's a strange accent and did not recognise the language Rolf had spoken in.

"You going to join me with your animals, or are you just going to stand there gawping. I don't bite but Bruce here throws a mean left hook," said Rolf.

Tomas, who as I have already told you was good at languages and knew just a little English, walked towards Rolf and said in English, "I am Tomas Tomaschevsky and these are Jerzy and Irena, my dogs, the bears are Minsky, Tinsky, and Dinsky. Are you English? I'm sorry but I don't speak English good."

"Not on your nelly, mate. I'm Australian, but my parents were Welsh, not English pommes," said Rolf. "My name's Rolf, Rolf Harries, and the kanga name is Bruce; come and join us but don't mess with Bruce, he's a bit temperamental you know."

Rolf told Tomas how he had found Bruce in the Australian bush when Bruce was a joey, young kangaroos are called joeys, that had lost its mother. Really, Bruce had been abandoned because instead of having a long tail he only had a stumpy tail and for a kangaroo this meant he couldn't hop as fast as the other kangaroos and he had been left behind. Kangaroos hop and with the help of their long tails can travel up to 40 miles an hour. Bruce, however, could not make use of a long tail and could only travel as fast as an ordinary boy.

Bruce would have been surrounded by a pack of dingoes when Rolf came across him and would have been eaten by them if not for Rolf's intervention. Dingoes are Australian wild dogs that roam the Australian outback. Rolf chased the dingoes away and took pity on Bruce who had the cutest smile he had ever seen.

Rolf had raised Bruce and taught him how to box. Bruce had been so good that he became known as kanga Bruce, the Boxing kangaroo, and people began to pay to see him box anyone dull enough to box him. I call them dull because Bruce had a lightning left hook.

Bruce always won and most wins were by way of knockout.

Rolf began to organise events and would travel around Australia with Bruce and organise fights which drew large crowds and he would charge people to watch and bet on the outcome.

Rolf began to make a lot of money from this.

One day Rolf was sitting with Bruce at a billabong, that is a pond that is left after a river dries out, and they were thinking of what to do next when Rolf said, "Bruce mate, you're too good a boxer to be fighting nobodies; you should be fighting for titles. You could be world champion if you were a fella, that's for sure. We've made a load of money we should go somewhere where you can fight for a title. They won't let you in Australia but in

America they might. Things are much easier there; they even have a black man as heavy weight world champion. If they allow that, then surely a kanga can fight for a world title."

Bruce, who understood everything that Rolf said to him, nodded in approval and said, "Yup," which is yes in kangaroo.

So that's what they did.

Rolf and Bruce made their way to Sydney, which is a Coastal city in New South Wales, one of the four regions of Australia, boxing and making money on the way.

When they got there Rolf bought two one-way tickets to America on an ocean liner that was leaving for America the next week.

America is around 9000 miles from Australia and could take up to 60 days to reach the West Coast of America. They were going to cross the Pacific Ocean and they would land in Hawaii.

The trip was quite uneventful. Rolf was sea sick but Bruce was fine; he enjoyed the motion of the ship and had a few boxing bouts until the captain heard about the gambling and put a stop to them.

Finally, they landed in Hawaii and then it was on to California.

They did not have much success in California; nobody wanted to box a kangaroo, and so they made their way across land towards the southern states where they thought they would be more successful.

They were right as Southerners had never seen a kangaroo before and thought Bruce was just an ugly boy with big feet.

Rolf was able to arrange a few fights and Bruce became Kanga Bruce, the Australian prize fighter. After a short while and a few good knockouts Rolf decided it was time to start to fight towards a state title. They had found that prize fighting, which was illegal in some states but legal down south, was very lucrative but Rolf wanted Bruce to be a champion.

Those good old southern boys loved Bruce and soon he was fighting for the Louisiana state championship.

The Southerners saw Bruce as a potential challenger to the Galveston Giant Jack Johnson who was the first Afro American world champion and we all know that down south they don't like coloured champions.

Bruce fought the little known Jed Stonewall for the Louisiana state championship at the Baton Rouge pavilion and won in a knockout.

He then went on to fight the champion of Alabama, Joshia Montgomery, in Montgomery which is the capitol of Alabama.

There was a very large crowd assembled to watch the fight. Montgomery was a local big wig and very wealthy and said to be high up in the K.K.K. which meant nothing to Rolf and Bruce. They had never heard of the Ku Klux Klan which had been quiet for a while.

The fight was very close and often brutal. Montgomery was a dirty fighter and would punch low head butt and bite and the referee seemed to be biased towards him allowing him to get away with it.

Bruce took it all though and in the 9th round hit Montgomery with a haymaker which knocked Montgomery clean out of the ring. The referee counted to ten very, very slowly hoping Montgomery would get up but he did not stir. A doctor was called but he could not rouse Montgomery either. Montgomery did not recover; he had died.

When the crowd realised that Montgomery was dead, the cry went out, "The K.K.K. will get you, Bruce; you'll pay for this." They became an angry mob.

Rolf and Bruce were lucky to escape with their lives.

As they ran, Rolf asked, "What's the K.K.K."

The mob cried, "The Kill Kanga Klan."

Rolf and Bruce ran for their lives and kept running throughout the Southern States. Everywhere they went the K.K.K. was active. They wore white robes and carried flaming torches with which they set fire to coloured people's houses. Luckily they never caught Rolf and Bruce and they made their way to the North. Rolf felt sorry for all the victims of the K.K.K. as he thought it was all his and Bruce's fault that they were terrorised.

Rolf decided to head north up towards New York away from the Southern States and the K.K.K.

They tried to keep away from the main routes and travelled in the wilderness away from towns and cities. They did not want their whereabouts known.

They moved up through the Mid States of America staying away from Alabama, Georgia and Mississippi.

They would head to New York but not take a direct route in order to fool any followers into thinking they were heading east.

They went via Arkansas, Missouri, Illinois, Ohio and Pennsylvania.

On their travels they had many adventures but probably the most rewarding one was when they met an American Chinese man named Kunte Choo Toy who was the son of one of the first Chinese rail workers who were employed by the Central Pacific Railroad Company and was their foreman.

As foreman, he had special privileges that the ordinary Chinese workers, who were treated more like slaves and called Coolies, did not.

He had his own house and had married a former Negro slave and they had a son whom they named Kunte.

Kunte's father was the son of the famous Chinese prostitute Ah Toy who became famous during the Californian gold rush. She had been of noble blood and had trained to be a kung fu fighter but had failed to stay the course and had left China to make her fortune in America.

She had been a keen student of kung fu (the Chinese martial art as practised by Bruce Lee and David Carradine in the television series and films) and had taught her son to the best of her ability, so he too was proficient in kung fu.

He was not a master but he considered himself one and professed to be a master to all in America and this gave him a high standing amongst the Chinese immigrants in America.

When the Central Pacific Railroad Company looked for cheap labour to construct their railroad, Charles Crocker, a head of the company hired Chinese workers and made Toy their foreman with the job of maintaining discipline.

Those Coolies became known as Crocker's pets.

Toy was a ruthless disciplinarian and treated the workers with a fierce regime of harsh discipline which bordered on cruelty.

His wife was not treated much better and when Kunte was born she was determined to teach him civility and humility combined with strength and honour.

Ah Toy had tried to instil humility into her son but failed.

The Chinese have a belief in Yin and Yang which they say are the two opposing forces in the universe and to create order and harmony, must be in balance.

Yin is the passive feminine force while Yang is the active male force and together the two halves make a complete wholeness.

Kunte was taught how to control and use both forces for his benefit and learnt how to control his temper and how to treat people how he would like to be treated.

His mother had abhorred slavery in all forms and would often be beaten for criticising her husband.

Kunte too would be cruelly disciplined if he did not comply with his father's wishes but that did not stop him standing up to his father. He began to champion the bullied which ended up with him being put in jail for assault when he stopped one of the Railroad supervisors beating one of the Chinese Coolies over a minor mishap.

It was while he was in prison that Rolf and Bruce met him. They had been recognised by a bounty hunter who had seen a poster offering the reward of 100 dollars for the capture of Bruce and his trainer and had brought them into the same jail to await the arrival of the K.K.K. for his reward.

Kunte was sitting in the corner of his cell meditating when Rolf and Bruce were brought in and did not acknowledge them for some time.

When he rose to his feet he said to them, "What brings you two strangers to this God forsaken town?"

Rolf explained how they had fallen foul of the K.K.K. and were on the run when they had been captured by a bounty hunter.

Kunte knew all about the Ku Klux Klan, being the son of a former Negro slave and a Chinese immigrant himself, and asked Rolf why the K.K.K. were interested in them.

Rolf replied that the Kill Kanga Klan was set up to avenge Montgomery's death and would not stop until they had lynched Bruce.

"Well I'd better take you two with me when I escape, wouldn't want you to fall into the hands of the Kill Kanga Klan, would we," and he laughed out loud as he said it.

Kunte had studied the layout of his cell and had been meditating on finding a weak spot and a way out.

His meditating had worked out that there was a weakness in the wall below the cell railings window and that a well-struck blow in the right spot would weaken it sufficiently for them to demolish the wall and escape, but they would have to do it when the sheriff and his deputy were occupied elsewhere and it was quiet outside.

He told them of his plan and waited for the right time.

During the early hours of that night the sheriff and deputy had gone out on their rounds believing Kunte and the foreigners to be asleep.

Kunte lined up the spot and kicked it barefoot as hard as he could. The wall shook and cracked but did not break. He struck it again but despite cracking some more and creating a lot of dust, the wall remained intact.

Rolf then said, "Let Bruce have a go; he has a kick like a mule."

Kunte looked at him and replied, "With the size of those feet, I wouldn't be surprised."

Bruce limbered up and took one almighty swing at the wall and it just crumpled in front of them.

They scrambled out and away from the town as fast as their feet could take them.

Kunte found three horses in a coral outside town and saddled them up for them to ride.

Bruce had never ridden a horse before and kept falling off at first. (Can you imagine a kangaroo riding a horse? I bet it was hilarious.) But he got the hang of it as he wanted to get as far away from the town as possible so as not to be taken by the K.K.K.

They had a number of adventures together and Kunte taught Bruce how to meditate and a form of kung fu which Rolf renamed kang fu before they reached New York and went their separate ways.

Rolf had hoped that they would be OK in the northern states; however, the word had got around that the K.K.K. would follow them to Australia if necessary as there was a $100 bounty to bring back Kanga Bruce dead or alive.

They never had another chance to fight for a title.

With the Kill Kanga Klan still looking for Bruce, they decided to leave America and head for Europe, especially

Russia, where they heard that animals were treated well. They daren't head for Australia as they would be spotted straightaway.

That is exactly what they did and they boarded a ship in New York and sailed to Russia leaving Kunte behind and eventually made it to Moscow virtually roubleless.

Rolf was despondent; he was homesick but knew he couldn't go home with Bruce in case the K.K.K. were looking for him there. He had a dilemma: stay in Moscow with Bruce and starve or go home to Australia without Bruce and let him fend for himself, something Rolf did not think Bruce could do.

"What am I going to do?" said Rolf.

Tomas thought for a second or two and said, "You go home. I will look after Bruce; he'll be alright with me. Jerzy and Irena will take good care of him and he can help me keep Tinsky out of trouble."

"Are you sure, mate? That would be great. I really miss Aus," said Rolf.

"If I were you I'd move onto St Petersburg; that's where the royals live and that Rasputin bloke. He's a commoner like us and he made it to the Royal court and is famous throughout Russia. If he can make it, I'm sure you and the animals can too. They say St Petersburg is the best place in Russia for animals; they have a great zoo, a circus and the ballet in St Petersburg is the best in all Russia."

"Is that right?" said Tomas.

"Sure is," said Rolf.

Rolf said his goodbyes to Bruce who was starting to play fight with Tinsky who kept cuffing him.

"I'd best leave now, you take good care of him; he's a beaut," said Rolf with a tear in his eye, "I'm going now before you see an Aussie cry." He picked up his bag and left just as Bruce aimed a quick left jab at Tinsky's jaw and knocked him out.

"You sure pack a punch," said Tomas. "We'll have to make sure we don't annoy you."

Tomas patted Bruce and went to see how Tinsky was. Tinsky was not hurt too badly and was already getting back to his feet. He was dazed and groggy though and decided to keep out of Bruce's way at least for the time being.

Rolf disappeared from view leaving Tomas with another animal to look after but Tomas didn't mind; he enjoyed the company of the animals and considered them as friends. He was sure that Bruce would also be a good friend too.

Luckily kangaroo's diets are vegetarian and Tomas had a supply of berries and goodies for Minsky, Dinsky and Tinsky and as Bruce would eat those too, he had no problem feeding him.

Bruce is a red kangaroo and they can survive without water for ages so Bruce was not much trouble to look after and soon became firm friends with all of them. The only problem for Bruce was he didn't like a lot of noise and being cold. Kangaroos can get pneumonia and colds just like humans and because Bruce came from a hot country, he was more likely to catch cold than the others.

Tomas made some enquiries about St Petersburg and had very favourable reports about the Ballet there, which is called the Mariinsky Ballet and is Russia's oldest ballet. He also learnt that St Petersburg had been renamed Petrograd at the start of the war so that it sounded Russian and not German.

That decided it for Tomas he would make his way to St Petersburg and play the Mariinsky Ballet in front of the Tsar and Tsarina, Nicholas the second and Alexandra.

St Petersburg is around 395 miles from Moscow and they could travel on the Trans-Siberian Railway if they could afford to, but alas they couldn't, so they would have to leave before the harsh Russian winter set in.

The Trans-Siberian Railway linked Moscow to Vladivostok and is one of the world's major railways. It was started in 1891 and was near completion in 1915 and is over 5750 miles long. That's further than from Lands' end to John O'Groats which is roughly 605 miles and that's from the bottom of England to the top of Scotland.

The section from Moscow to St Petersburg was virtually a straight track but for one big bend along its route. This is said to have been done because it was Tsar Nicholas who had drawn up the route and he had used a ruler to draw a straight line between Moscow and St Petersburg and when he joined them up he drew around his thumb which was holding the ruler down and did not rectify it. The builders were too afraid to point it out to Nicholas and built the railway, with the bend, to Nicholas's plan.

Chapter 8
The Influence of Rasputin

Tomas wanted to go some of the way by train to St Petersburg but first they would travel on foot so that they could perform on the way, earning some money, and so he could get to know Bruce better and see what he was capable of.

Tomas tried to teach Bruce to dance but he was hopeless, he had no rhythm at all and could not hold a beat, so he had to think of some other way of incorporating Bruce in their troupe.

Tomas did find out for himself that Bruce had one hell of a punch with both hands when he decided to spar with him one day. Bruce knocked him clean off his feet and out cold. He woke up with Jerzy and Irena licking his face having been drenched by a bucket of water that Tinsky had found and thrown over him.

Bruce was standing close by looking very apologetic; he had a bump on the left side of his head where Tinsky had hit him just after he had punched Tomas.

Tinsky was proud of himself and was happy he had paid Bruce back for flooring him in Moscow.

Tomas decided no more sparring with Bruce; however, Tinsky and Bruce seemed to like playing together and Tomas thought as long as they don't hurt each other they can spar with each other and maybe it can form part of the performances so that Bruce could become part of the Troupe.

Tomas found Bruce an old trumpet and some clothes, which when Bruce wore them, made him look like a clown. The trousers were so baggy they hid his stumpy tail and with a pair of size 22 clown's shoes and the right make-up with which he painted Bruce's nose red, he looked just like a real clown. The clothes would help Bruce stay warm during the hard Russian winter and also disguise the fact that he was a kangaroo so that he would be able to fight for the Russian boxing title.

"Well Bruce, now you look almost human in this disguise. I think you will be able to box for a title. I think we'll still call you Kanga Bruce between ourselves but we'll nick name you Bruce Knockeremov, the knockout clown, in public," said Tomas. "You will also have to stay silent during the performances in case you make kangaroo noises," he added.

And that is how Bruce became known.

Tomas did not take the direct route to St Petersburg as he wanted to stop and perform to the people on the way.

Firstly to make money and keep the animals fit they needed to perfect their performances, especially Bruce who needed the practice as a clown. Tomas did start to teach Bruce some basic vocabulary such as 'yes' and 'no' which sounded like 'yup' and 'nup' when he said them.

Tomas also wanted to see if the people would believe Bruce was a real clown and not a kangaroo, because if they could pull the deception off, Bruce would be able to fight for the Russian title.

Everywhere they played they had standing ovations. Crowds thronged to see the miraculous dancing dogs, the marvellous performing bears and the ridiculously funny clown. They also came to see the end of the show when Tomas would announce that Bruce was an outstanding boxer and could defeat all comers which coaxed all those Russian men who had not gone to fight in the Great War because either they were needed to produce food and manufacture goods for the war effort, they were too young or they had bribed officials not to go.

The contests were always keenly fought, as Tomas did not want Bruce to win too easily or people would always bet on Bruce, and as they made a lot of money out of the betting. Bruce learnt to perfect the art of taking a lot of punches and pretending to be hurt by stumbling all around the ring. This ruse made the punters bet on the challenger who was usually one of their champions and they would be rubbing their hands expecting to win their bets until at the last moment when Bruce would perform his special move.

The move Bruce had perfected was due to his stumpy tail. When he was on the end of what appeared to be a knockout blow from his opponent, he would appear to be falling backwards onto the floor but because his stumpy tail prevented him from going all the way down he would spring back up to his feet and deliver the fastest right or left hook anyone had ever seen and knock his startled opponent clean out.

Which just goes to prove Newton's second law of motion. Newton was a British scientist who lived from 1643 to 1727 and was one of Britain's greatest mathematicians and scientists who developed three laws of motion which some of you may have already learnt. I learnt them in Physics class. Newton's second law states that Force equals Mass x Acceleration and that Acceleration is directly proportional to the net force applied. It is usually shown as $F = M \times A$.

So as Bruce bounced back from the floor he gathered speed giving him extra acceleration and momentum which meant his whole body weight was combined with the punch, hence the knockout blow.

In most sports, there is no substitute for speed and it doesn't matter how big you are; if you are slow, you are going to fall.

No one had any inkling that Bruce was a kangaroo; in fact, no one in rural Russia had ever seen a kangaroo before and just thought Bruce was a funny looking clown.

It was a sensation and word of the amazing Tomaschevski Animal Dance Troupe and the boxing clown soon reached St Petersburg.

Once the people of St Petersburg were aware of the Troupe's intention of coming there it was not long before it reached the ears of one Grigory Rasputin, who was known as the Mad Monk, and was very influential at the court of Tsar Nicholas and his family.

Rasputin was not royalty himself but had been born a peasant in Siberia in 1869 and was about a year older than the Tsar. He was not well educated but from an early age had somehow been able to heal sick animals and then sick people. He had very piercing eyes and was believed to be a hypnotist with very special powers and he was both loved and feared by the Russian people as his fame and notoriety grew.

As he was growing up he went to a monastery where he only stayed for about a year before travelling around Europe preaching and healing along the way. Rasputin, however, was not a monk and he had married and had four children.

It is known that Rasputin also had many women lovers and was extremely cruel to them.

Despite being a commoner, and considered a rogue by the Russian gentry, his name reached the ears of Tsarina Alexandra, the wife of the Tsar, Tsar Nicholas 2nd who was Emperor of all Russia, a vast part of Eastern Europe. They had four daughters, Olga, Tatiana, Maria and Anastasia, the youngest and one son Alexei who, as the only son, was the heir to the Romanov dynasty.

Alexei was a poorly lad who was stricken by haemophilia, which is also known as the bleeding disease as people who suffer from it have blood which is unable to clot. You probably have cut yourself at some point and put a plaster on the cut then waited for the bleeding to stop and form a clot over the cut, and then the cut would soon heal. If you suffer from haemophilia however, the blood would not form a clot and would not heal so easily which could prove fatal to anyone suffering with haemophilia.

Haemophilia is usually an inherent disease which is passed on through generations of families. There was no real history of haemophilia in the Romanov family; however, there were links to Queen Victoria's line, of which Nicholas was a descendant being Queen Victoria's grandson. There was also a history of haemophilia in the Hesse family, which was Tsarina Alexandra's family, and as we know nearly all the royal families in Europe were related by royal marriages. Nicholas and Alexandra were in fact cousins and both descendants of Queen Victoria. Haemophilia, therefore, became known as the Royal Disease and those suffering with it usually died young.

There is no known antidote to haemophilia but nowadays it can be treated by injections and life expectancy is greater. In 1915, however, there were no injections for haemophilia and doctors were unable to relieve Alexei who was very poorly child.

The Tsar had moved the family away from St Petersburg shortly after his marriage as Alexandra did not like the Winter Palace in St Petersburg. The Winter Palace was the Tsar's official residence, but Nicholas and Alexandra preferred the informal nature of the Alexander Palace at Tsarskoe Selo (the Tsar's village) now Pushkin. It is approximately 15 miles from St Petersburg and although it is another grand palace, it is much more secluded and private being away from the hustle and bustle of St Petersburg.

There was also the safety factor to be considered as the Romanov Tsars and family had been the target of several assassinations and attempts over the years and following Russia's Bloody Sunday on Sunday 22nd of January 1905, when over a thousand peaceful demonstrators were killed by the Russian military and police while marching to the Winter Palace to hand a petition to Tsar Nicholas asking him to help them in their quest for better working conditions.

The march had been well organised and the authorities had been informed of its peaceful purpose in advance. It was not a political march or a demonstration against the Tsar and many women and children marched chanting 'long live the Tsar' and singing songs. In fact the marchers thought the Tsar would support and be sympathetic to their cause.

The Tsar however, who was expected to be at the Winter Palace as he had been there that week, had left the night before not wanting to be confronted by the marchers and had left it to his ministers to deal with the march. They in turn left it to the military and the police to deal with and there were a number of incidents where marchers making their way to the Winter Palace were either fired upon and killed, injured or were trampled by Cossacks (Russian cavalry troop) who charged them on horseback trying to disperse them.

The result of this Bloody Sunday was to provoke a wave of strikes across Russia and a lot of resentment against the Tsar which was followed by the first Russian revolution in August 1905. Tsar Nicholas in order to try and repair the damage allowed the setting up of Russia's first parliament which was called the Duma. This legislative body, however, had little power as the Tsar still believed in the Divine Right of the Sovereigns rule and gave little power to the Duma.

Anyway, I digress back to Alexei.

Due to the failure of the medics and clergy to help Alexei, Nicholas and Alexandra looked for other alternatives, such as the supernatural and when Alexandra heard of a faith healer called Rasputin, who was said to be graced by God, she urged Nicholas to fetch Rasputin to the Palace to see if he could help Alexei. Nicholas, against the advice of his advisors and doctors, agreed.

So Rasputin was brought to the Palace and immediately asked to see Alexei who was asleep in bed. Rasputin woke Alexei and looked straight into his eyes and it is said that Alexei was miraculously cured.

He hadn't, but Rasputin did have such an effect on the young prince that he seemed to be much brighter. Nicholas and Alexandra were extremely amazed and happy that Alexei had been cured and Rasputin was put in overall charge of the well-being of Alexei.

Rasputin used this improvement in Alexei's health to ingratiate himself with the Tsarina and the royal children who nicknamed him Ras.

They called him Ras Putin and he would become a spiritual influence to them which gave Rasputin personal access to the Tsar and Tsarina and he became very important in the life of the Romanovs.

It is said he became so powerful that the Tsar and Tsarina took his advice before that of his advisors and other members of the royal family.

It was thought that Rasputin had become the most powerful man in Russia and this made Nicholas' ministers and other family very resentful and the more powerful Rasputin became the more they hated him.

Now that Alexei was looking and feeling better Nicholas had time to pay more attention to the war. Russia was sustaining heavy losses to the Germans but were still fighting bravely and had superior forces.

At the start of the war the army was placed in the charge of Nicholas's uncle the Grand Duke Nicholas Nikolaevich but Tsar Nicholas thought that as he was the Emperor of Russia he should take sole responsibility of the running of the war and against the advice of his ministers he took complete control of the army in September 1915, following heavy losses to the Germans in the Polish territories.

The Grand Duke took over the Russian-Turkish offensive.

His ministers thought that if he was in sole charge and things did not go well for the Russian campaign, the soldiers and people who were weary of the war would sow the seeds of revolution. Dissatisfaction and unrest were in the air and together with the great poverty and famine throughout Russia it would flourish and lead to rebellion.

Their concerns were to be proved right.

Having taken control of the war effort Nicholas spent more and more time at the front leaving Alexandra in charge at home which meant Rasputin's influence over her grew. Alexandra took his council before that of the Romanov family, ministers and royal advisors and this made Rasputin and Alexandra many enemies inside the royal family and government.

Nicholas also made enemies as he made changes in the army hierarchy sacking those he deemed to be incompetent. This also made enemies amongst his own supporters who were angry at his interference.

But I digress again; let's get back to Tomas and the Troupe.

Chapter 9
Babushka and Her Nephew

The animals were finding it heavy going, especially Bruce, who despite having warm clothes, was feeling the cold. As already pointed out kangaroos can catch colds just like we can but as they come from warmer climates like Australia they get worse colds. Even worse than man flu and there's not much worse than that. Geeze, it's almost as bad as pneumonia!

Well Bruce caught a cold. He started coughing and his nose began to run and he became more lethargic day by day. Soon Tinsky was snuffling and even Jerzy started to cough.

Tomas was worried. He was not quite a man yet but he had seen his father suffer with man flu and he did not want to catch it so he decided that they should all stop travelling and take a rest to help them recover and make provisions for the winter.

Tomas was beginning to feel unwell himself so he looked for somewhere to stay.

He looked for rooms in the inns and hotels in the local villages but no one would take him, a funny looking clown, two dogs and three bear cubs but one inn owner said, "My babushka will take you all in and look after you; she has been left with a bit of land to keep with no one to help her, so if you can lend a hand to her she will take care of you, your clown and the dogs if you can help look after her sheep. The bear cubs will behave, won't they?"

Tomas said they would except maybe for Tinsky who could be a little mischievous sometimes but he'd take care of him.

The inn keeper gave Tomas a note to give to his babushka and directions to her home and that's where they went.

I bet you are all wondering what a babushka is, aren't you?

A babushka is an old woman usually a grandmother in Russia or Poland. It is pronounced BA-BOOSH-KA. In English it is sometimes referred to as a head scarf as most old women in Russia and Poland wore headscarves. If you have a babushka doll or a set of traditional babushka figurine dolls which are made of china and each one smaller than the other so that they nest in side each other, you will notice that they get younger and the last one is a baby though they are all wearing head scarves.

In Russia, at that time, the country was mainly rural with the majority of people being peasant farmers. Babushka's husband had been the owner of a small farm and when he died she had no one to help her. She was struggling on her own, the best she could, so when Tomas and his troupe arrived on her doorstep with the inn keeper's note she was glad to take them in and help Bruce recover.

Babushka was an excellent cook and over the years she had learnt and developed many variations of old remedies and incorporated them in her recipes, which had kept her and her husband fit and well into their old age. Her husband had died in a farming accident, not of illness.

When she saw Bruce she immediately knew that he needed rest and put him straight to bed. She boiled up a lovely borsch, which is a beetroot soup, which she fed to Bruce along with some blini which is a type of pancake.

Having seen to Bruce she turned her attention to Tomas and the animals.

"Young man, you should not have let that crooked old clown get so ill. He looks terrible. I wouldn't be surprised if he has caught pneumonia. I will have to take great care of him because if he gets any worse I will not be able to cure him," she said.

Tomas looked distraught. He had grown very fond of Bruce and had high hopes of Bruce becoming a champion boxer.

Babushka told Tomas not to worry as if she was unable to cure him she would send for her nephew in St Petersburg and he would cure him for sure.

She was Rasputin's aunt and that was why no one had tried to take her land when her elderly husband had died of man flu which had turned to pneumonia.

She had been unable to cure him due to his age but then it was due to her care that he had lived such a long and healthy life in the first place.

The peasants thought of Rasputin as a hero and that the royalty were afraid of him, due to his influence with the Tsar and Tsarina.

So while Rasputin was alive and so powerful, Babushka had no worries about anyone stealing her land and animals, not even from the army who confiscated crops and animals from other farms to feed the troops.

This being the case, Babushka had many friends in the area for she was happy to share her produce with the locals who, in turn, looked on her as their saviour and benefactor.

Babushka fed Tomas, Jerzy and Irena and the three bears and showed them to her barn where they could bed down. Tomas did not want to sleep in the farmhouse as he was used to staying with the animals and now preferred to do so.

Babushka told them to get a good night's sleep and they would discuss what they could do to repay her in the morning.

They made themselves comfortable and the animals were soon fast asleep. Tomas, however, took longer to fall asleep as he was worried about Bruce. He eventually fell fast asleep dreaming about their arrival at St Petersburg and starring at the Mariinsky Ballet.

They all awoke quite early refreshed after a good night's sleep and were overcome by the fragrant aroma coming from Babushka's farmhouse and so they all hurried as fast as they could to see what it was.

It was their breakfast. Babushka was preparing a very large pot of something which smelt absolutely divine.

"What's that you are making?" asked Tomas. "It smells delicious."

Babushka replied, "It's only porridge but I add a few secret ingredients of my own to make it sweeter because I have a sweet tooth. I hope you like it. It will give you the energy you need to keep you going through the work I have for you to do."

They all ate heartily and Tinsky even had seconds he enjoyed it so much. They drank berry juice which complimented the porridge so that they all felt wonderfully full and satisfied.

Babushka outlined the jobs that needed doing as she would be tending to Bruce for the foreseeable future. There were the sheep to bring down from the upper pastures and pen to keep them safe from the wolves. The cows had to be milked, the hogs tended to and the chickens fed and the eggs collected and there were fences to be repaired. Then there were the horses to be seen to.

It was lucky that Tomas came from a farming background and he was able to teach Minsky, Dinsky and Tinsky how to feed the chickens, collect the eggs, tend to the hogs and do the general duties around the farm while he, Jerzy and Irena herded up the sheep and brought them down for the winter. This job was long overdue and he could see that the wolves had already taken a lot of sheep.

They all worked so well that the farm was running like clockwork.

Babushka was very happy with the way Tomas was coping; however, her efforts with Bruce were not going so well.

"I am going to have to send a message to my Grigori (Rasputin) and ask him to come and see Bruce, I am afraid that he is not getting any better and will only get worse during Christmas and the coming New Year weather will be harsher than usual," she said. "I will send a wireless message from the town and hope that it is not intercepted by Rasputin's enemies. He will come for me."

So Babushka went to town and sent the message.

Within two days Rasputin arrived at Babushka's farm and he was not alone. He had secretly slipped out of the Palace with Prince Alexei. He told Alexandra that the farm air and scenery would improve his health and that they should go alone so as not to attract attention. Alexei was all in favour of going as he wanted to see the great Tomas Tomaschevski and his troupe of performing animals.

They had travelled by train and Grigori had had to disguise himself with a long hooded cloak so as not to be recognised. Alexei was dressed in common clothes and as he had not been seen in public very often due to his poor health he was not recognised either.

Tsar Nicholas, however, did send two secret service men to watch over them from a distance and go to their aid if necessary. It was not necessary, however, as Rasputin was well capable of looking after himself and Alexei if they encountered any trouble. He was such an imposing figure that just the sight of him frightened off any would-be attackers.

Babushka welcomed Grigori and thanked him for coming so soon.

"My Babushka, your message sounded urgent and when Alexei and I knew you were looking after Tomas Tomaschevski and his troupe, Alexei begged and begged to come as well. We have all heard how wonderful his troupe are," Rasputin said.

Alexei interceded and said, "Ras, introduce me."

"Excuse me my young prince," he said, "this Babushka is Prince Alexei, heir to the Romanov dynasty and future Tsar of all Russia and Alexei, this is my babushka," he announced.

Babushka fell to her knees praising Alexei. She felt honoured that she, Babushka, was being presented to the future Tsar.

"Pleased to meet you, Babushka," said Alexei, "but where is Tomas and his troupe? I can't wait to see them."

"They are busy with their chores and practicing their acts, but they will be back for tea soon; let me prepare something for you now as you must be tired after your long journey."

Babushka made them some tea and got out her special cake and vodka for Grigori making them very welcome. Alexei who was still a little frail was tired and a bed was made up for him to rest in until Tomas and the animals came home. It was not long, however, before he was fast asleep.

Meanwhile, Rasputin asked to be shown the sick clown to start his road to recovery.

Babushka took Grigori to Bruce's room where Bruce was lying in bed looking very dejected and pale. Grigori took one look at him and said, "You are an odd looking fellow, aren't you? I think I will have to examine you thoroughly before I can treat you properly. Leave us, Babushka. I would like to examine him alone."

Babushka left and Rasputin said to Bruce, "What exactly are you, Bruce? You are no ordinary clown; you are an animal of some sort, though I haven't seen one like you before."

Bruce said in his best speaking voice, "Yup Kanga Bruce, Kanga Bruce." At least it sounded like that because kangaroos are not very literate creatures and speech does not come easy to them.

Rasputin took off Bruce's night clothes and examined Bruce from top to toe. He saw Bruce's stumpy tail and big feet and knew he must be some kind of marsupial.

"Ah ha," said Rasputin, "now I know exactly what's wrong and why you are not responding to Babushka's treatment. Don't worry, you'll soon be up and well again but it will take a while until you are your old self again. You've been very ill and would have died if not for Babushka's help. Now lie perfectly still while I manipulate your body and then take away the fever."

Rasputin worked on Bruce's body like a chiropractor and when he finished that he placed his right hand on Bruce's forehead and straightaway Bruce felt light-headed; it was as if the fever he felt was being lifted from his forehead into Rasputin's hand. Rasputin spoke a strange incantation and then lifted his hand away from Bruce's forehead.

Bruce felt as if the weight of the world had been lifted from him and a smile returned to his face.

Rasputin said, "Now you must sleep, my friend, but this time you will awake refreshed and before long you will be out of the bed and clowning around again."

He tapped Bruce's forehead and Bruce immediately fell into a deep sleep during which he dreamt of billabongs, berry orchards and boxing.

Rasputin left him and returned to Babushka. He told her that Bruce would be OK now and all she needed to do was treat him like anyone else who was recovering from a bout of pneumonia. They then sat together drinking vodka and telling each other stories about their lives until Tomas and the others came home.

They carried on their storytelling when Tomas arrived as Russians are great storytellers and can stretch even a short story into an epic. You only have to read Tolstoy, Pushkin, Chekhov and Dostoevsky to see that. (They were great Russian writers whose novels were very long.)

Then it was Tomas' turn to tell them his story and both Babushka and Rasputin were fascinated by the story, and Tomas' dream of Jerzy and Irena dancing at the Mariinsky Ballet. They marvelled at how he and the two dogs had fought of the wolves at his father's farm and couldn't imagine Bruce fighting for the world boxing title but both would love to see it.

They talked well into the night drinking vodka and singing old Russian folk songs before Babushka told them off for being too loud and reminded them that young prince Alexei was asleep and it was best to let him sleep.

They both agreed and Tomas said goodnight and left for the barn while Rasputin gave his leave and headed into town to carry on partying.

He came back bright and early with a big broad smile on his face just as Babushka was serving up her delicious porridge.

Prince Alexei and Bruce were both up and looking forward to helpings of the delicious smelling porridge. Tomas, the dogs and bears were also waiting for theirs.

Alexei, who was four years younger than Tomas, was really excited asking Tomas questions about the animals like what tricks they could do, what dances they could do and would they perform for him.

Rasputin heard him and laughed saying, "All in good time my little prince, all in good time. I will butcher a cow today and Babushka will prepare us a fine beef stroganoff for this evening. Then Tomas and the animals can give you a performance fit for the Tsar."

Alexei was impatient though and said, "Can't they perform now, Ras, I'm sure it would be alright."

"No my little prince, we have things to do this morning and they have their work to do around the farm. Babushka can show you how a farm works and delight you with some of her fine recipes. Tomorrow we must return to St Petersburg before people realise that you are not at the Palace and find us here unguarded. Don't fret Babushka; the Tsar will replace your cow with a bull. I will see to that and then you can mate it with your other cows and have a regal line of cattle."

Babushka thanked him and showed the excited prince around her farm.

He was glad to be out in the fresh air and marvelled at what he thought was the simplicity of the peasant farmer's life.

Later, Babushka prepared the stroganoff from the best cut of the slaughtered cow, showing Alexei her secret recipe, and that evening, Tomas, Jerzy and Irena, Minsky, Dinsky and Tinsky gave the performances of their lives.

Alexei and Rasputin applauded loudly with Alexei shouting, "You wait till my father and mother see you, and my sisters, you will be the favourites of the court. The Mariinsky Ballet would be much more fun with you in it."

Bruce was unable to perform as he was still weak and Rasputin told Tomas that he still needed a lot of care and rest before he would be able to perform as a clown and even longer before he could start to box.

He also told Tomas to stay with his babushka until lambing season in the New Year was over. Firstly to give Bruce time to recover fully and secondly to protect the lambs from the Russian wolves who were much more fierce than Polish wolves. Tomas disputed that but promised to stay with Babushka until spring when they would defeat the wolves and come to St Petersburg to regale the Tsar and his family and join the Mariinsky Ballet.

Rasputin said, "I'll look forward to seeing you and hearing your account of defeating the wolves. I will speak to Rachmaninoff and Tcherepnin both of whom are in St Petersburg and tell them about you. Both were involved with the Bolshoi Ballet and I am sure that if they had been there when you were there they would have loved your performance as much as Alexei and I did."

Rasputin took Tomas aside and said, "Tomas, I think you have been blessed by a Leszy. (In Russian the only difference to the spelling of a Leszi is a 'y' for the 'i'.) It is a great honour, so use it wisely and it will save you in times of trouble. I too have been fortunate to meet and befriend a Leszy. They are truly the most fierce, yet wise, elf ever and if they bestow their magic on you, you are truly blessed but be sure you do not let anyone else know for they will mistrust and fear you which could cause you a lot of trouble in the future."

They all bade each other a good night and enjoyed a good night's sleep waking up early the next morning.

They all ate a magnificent breakfast prepared by Babushka which prompted Alexei to say, "Babushka, I could live this life and stay with you forever."

Rasputin interrupted him saying, "If only we could but you and I have different destinies which require us to live in St Petersburg."

They finished breakfast and Rasputin bade them farewell and he and Alexei returned to St Petersburg on the Royal.

Tomas pondered on Rasputin's advice and vowed to be careful.

Chapter 10
Niels Hans Andersen and the Composers

It was July 1915, they arrived in St Petersburg at the same time as an envoy from Denmark had arrived to consult with the Tsar.

Denmark was neutral during World War One and the war was of no benefit to the country. Denmark was a trading nation and traded with both Britain and Germany and would have benefitted from the war if it wasn't for the British blockades and German submarine activity.

The King of Denmark Christian X and the Danish government wanted peace as war affected Danish trade so King Christian commissioned Hans Niels Andersen, a Danish businessman and shipping magnate, to travel to the warring nations in an attempt to broker a peace deal.

He had already been to Germany and Britain when he arrived in St Petersburg to consult with Tsar Nicholas and his ministers.

Tsar Nicholas was informed of his arrival and the purpose of his visit before meeting Alexei and Rasputin when they arrived back at Tsarskoe Selo.

Nicholas welcomed Alexei and Rasputin back and was eager to hear the story of Tomas Tomaschevski and his troupe.

Alexei was so enthusiastic in his account of meeting Tomas that the Tsar said, "It sounds like a fantastic story. I will have to meet this Tomas myself but first I have matters of state to deal with. An envoy from Denmark has arrived in St Petersburg with a proposition for peace which I must listen to."

Rasputin, who was opposed to the war but understood its importance to Russia, said, "Let us hope that peace can be achieved without any more Russian casualties."

"Let's hope but Russia has responsibilities which must be considered before any decision is reached."

He then left them to resume his duties.

Rasputin left too determined to tell Rachmaninoff and Tcherepnin about Tomas and his troupe.

Sergei Vasilevich Rachmaninoff was a very famous pianist, composer and conductor born in 1873. He was considered one of the finest exponents of what was known as Russian Romanticism. His family had been in the service of the Russian Tsars since the 16th century and they were very well off owning a number of estates. Because of the family ties with the Romanoff's, Rasputin would be able to tell him about Tomas and his dream of Jerzy and Irena performing ballet at the Mariinsky Ballet.

Though Rachmaninoff was not known for ballet, he had studied at the St Petersburg Conservatory and graduated with honours at the Moscow Conservatory. His first operatic work was a one-act opera called Aleko and it was based on a poem, the Gypsies by Alexander Pushkin. Pushkin was a very famous Russian author and poet and Aleko was so successful that it was produced by the Bolshoi Theatre in May 1892. He won the great gold medal for that work and went on to become a famous virtuoso and composed other operas, symphonies and concertos and in 1915 he was in Petrograd where Rasputin could summon him.

Nikolai Nikolayevich Tcherepnin was another very famous pianist, composer and conductor born in 1873. A good year for Russian composers. He too studied at the St Petersburg Conservatory under Rimsky-Korsakov who composed the *Flight of the Bumble Bee*, which I am sure most people have heard many times.

Tcherepnin had a penchant for ballet and in 1902 he became a regular conductor of Russia Symphonic Concerts before writing his first ballet, another one-act performance Le Pavillon d'Armide which was based on a short story by Gautier about a French Viscount in the time of Louis XIV. The ballet was performed in the Mariinsky Theatre.

In 1911 he staged the Ballet Narcisse which was based on the Opera Narcisse et Echo by Christoph Willibald Gluck. It tells the story of Echo and Narcissus, two very famous figures in Greek mythology and a story worthy of telling you right now.

Echo was a wood nymph at the time when the Greek Gods ruled the world from Mount Olympus in Greece. The king of the Gods was Zeus and the queen of the Gods was Hera. Now, Zeus was a randy old-so-and-so and liked to come down to earth to flirt with mortal women or nymphs rather than stay with Hera all the time. This made Hera very cross with him. One day Zeus came down to earth to flirt with the wood nymphs which he did but he got nowhere with Echo who was said to be more in love with her own voice than with anyone else. In fact she is said to have loved her own voice so much that she always had to have the last word of any conversation. (I think we all know somebody like that.) Anyway Hera got to hear of Zeus' whereabouts and came to the wood in search of him. She first encountered Echo who not wanting the other nymphs to get into trouble with Hera kept her talking giving Zeus time to make a getaway. Hera was so angry with Echo that she cursed Echo so that she could not converse with anyone ever again. She did allow Echo to speak but only to repeat the last thing said to her. Hence she echoed what others had said. She became very lonely and longed for someone to love.

This made Echo very sad and she hid herself from the other wood nymphs and mortals until one day she spied the very handsome Narcissus, whom everyone fell in love with, even the Gods. Narcissus was a renowned hunter from Thespiae and the son of a river god named Cephissus and a nymph named Liriope and he loved to tease others who he thought were all unworthy of his love. Echo lost her heart to him and began to follow him afraid to approach him as she could not speak to him and tell him how much she loved him.

Anyway one day Narcissus heard Echo's footsteps in the bushes and called out, "Who's there."

Echo replied, "Who's there."

Narcissus cried out, "Why do you shun me."

Echo replied, "Shun me."

Narcissus called out, "Come out and join me.

Echo replied, "Join me," and ran out of the bushes thinking she was in luck and threw her arms around him in a loving hug.

Narcissus, however, shunned her saying to her, "Hands off. I would rather die than you should have me." But to no avail. Narcissus pushed her off and heartbroken she fled into the woods and from then on she lived on mountain cliffs and in caverns until her body faded and she merged with the rocks until there was nothing left of her except for her voice which Hera had made immortal. So that is how we all have an echo in certain places.

Narcissus, however, carried on taunting and teasing others until one day Apollo cursed him for his cruelty and when Narcissus stopped one day to drink from a pool he saw his own reflection in the water and instantly fell in love with it.

Narcissus was smitten; he thought his reflection was a water spirit living in the pool. He plunged his arms into the water to embrace it but the spirit vanished only to return a short while later. He bent down to kiss it but again it disappeared. Distraught, Narcissus cried out, "Beautiful creature, why do you shun me, surely my face does not repulse you. The nymphs love me, even the Gods love me and you smile at me when I smile at you but when I try to embrace you or kiss you, you disappear." Narcissus tried again and again but each time it was in vain.

In desperation, Narcissus eventually cried, his tears rippling the image in the water and he said, "Stay I entreat you, let me at least gaze upon you if I may not touch you." And that is what Narcissus did, he remained at the pool transfixed on his own reflection until his body faded away. It is said that the only thing that remained there by the pool was a purple flower surrounded by white leaves, which is the Narcissus flower.

Two very tragic figures in Greek mythology whose story has lived on from ancient times.

Just as an extra bit of Greek mythology, have all of you heard of Hercules?

Well, Hercules was a Greek hero and God and he came to be born following another of Zeus's trips to earth. Zeus had seduced Queen Alcemene and made her pregnant while her husband, King Amphitryon, was away fighting a war. Zeus had pretended to be Amphitryon so Alcemene thought it was her husband she was with. Zeus was crafty like that. Again, Hera heard of it and when the baby was born she tried to kill him, even though Zeus had the baby named Heracles, but he survived.

Zeus had Alcemene name the baby Heracles, which means something like Glory to Hera in Greek in the hope that Hera would not hate the boy. We know him better as Hercules but this still did not pacify Hera who remained Heracles worst enemy. I hope you enjoyed that.

Back to Nikolae Tcherepnin now. Tcherepnin was also in Petrograd and working on another ballet, The Masque of the Red Death, about the Great Plague. The Masque of the Red Death was written by the famous horror story writer Edgar Allan Poe. For those who know a little bit about it, the Phantom of the Opera is based on it.

Now Tcherepnin was also someone Rasputin had access to and he promised to put in a good word about Tomas and his troupe to him.

This gave Tomas great hope that he would finally realise his dream, but first they had to get Bruce well again and get the sheep safely through lambing season.

Oh I almost forgot Hans Niels Andersen's peace plan and the chance of peace.

Well, Tsar Nicholas listened as did his ministers and after the meeting they discussed it.

It seemed to them that Andersen's proposal favoured German and Danish interests before Russia's and they dismissed it.

A chance to end the war had gone.

Tsar Nicholas told Rasputin later that to him the proposal sounded more like a fairy story than a genuine attempt at peace.

Chapter 11
Christmas at Babushkas

Rasputin was right although Bruce was recovering it was taking a long time for him to get his strength and fitness back. The winter was one of the harshest on record. Russian winters are always cold and this one was really cold. A lot of snow had fallen and there was still enough work to be done which meant Tomas and the animals were kept busy.

Tomas decided that even though Jerzy and Irena were experienced sheep dogs and had proved themselves more than a match for the Polish wolves in Tuchola, they would need extra training and help come lambing season if they were to defeat the Russian wolves. He knew this because he had gone out into the woods around the fields to see what they would be up against and he was able to spy on them and see how many there were, and how organised they were as a pack.

During these recces he would take Jerzy with him and a rifle in case they got in danger.

They never were though.

The bit of magic he had gained from Leonov, the Leszi, along with the little time he had spent as a shepherd and then staying undercover on his way through enemy lines had taught him how to remain almost invisible, and he was able to avoid wild animals as well as the soldiers.

He knew how to camouflage himself and the dogs and how to use the mud and plants to mask their scents so that the wolves could not smell them. They were able to creep up on the wolf pack and what surprised him most was not how many there were, and he spotted at least 20, but how big they were.

The leader of the pack was a giant of a wolf over five feet tall and must have weighed over 180 lbs. He was the most magnificent wolf Tomas had ever seen and it seemed all the pack were large and healthy. He had heard tales from the local farmers and hunters of this pack making short work of hunting down and killing a fully grown stag. They had also been known to attack bears when they were hungry. Tomas knew they would have their work cut out for them if they were to defeat this pack.

He also knew that they would have their work cut out for them if they were to save most of the flock.

He told Jerzy to remain hidden and snuck up on the leader without it knowing.

When he just appeared in front of him, the leader was stunned; he could not fathom how a human had been able to get so close to him without him sensing his presence and when Tomas spoke to him in his own language he was dumbstruck.

Tomas told him not to be afraid and that he was not there to harm him and that although he had a rifle he would not use it unless threatened.

He told them that he was tasked by the Tsar to look after Babushka's flock of sheep and wanted to avoid any unnecessary bloodshed between wolf and sheep.

He knew that wolves had to feed but hoped that a solution could be reached between them to limit the losses of sheep.

The big wolf, however, would have none of it and told Tomas that it was nature's way for wolves to kill sheep and the land was theirs not the farmers'.

Tomas left knowing that there would be a battle royal ahead.

He decided that when the sheep were released back into the fields in the new year, he would leave Minsky with Babushka to do the chores around the farm and take Dinsky, Tinsky and Bruce as well as Jerzy and Irena if they were to have any chance of warding off the wolves.

So as well as doing their own chores Dinsky and Tinsky also trained to fight wolves. As Bruce was building up his strength he too was training to fight wolves.

Jerzy and Irena taught them some of their ballet moves which became a sort of animal kung fu. Dinsky and Tinsky learnt to fight with long staffs like in kendo and Bruce developed a form of kick boxing which he hoped would avoid close contact with the wolves so that they could not get near enough to him to bite him.

Dinsky soon discovered that if he and Tinsky rattled their staffs together it made a very loud fierce noise which was very scary, and went about making other loud devices aimed at frightening the wolves. However, when he tested them he found that it frightened the sheep as well and would be no good if the sheep all scattered because they too were frightened.

Babushka had a shotgun and a couple of hunting rifles that were her late husband's and Tomas practised with them until he was a crack shot and could hit a potato on a wall from over 50 metres away.

He also made sure that his animals were used to the sound of the guns and shot them close to the sheep pen so that the sheep too became used to the sound of gun fire. He hoped that they would not run when they were fired in the heat of battle.

Christmas came and Babushka started her preparations. In Russia Christmas was not celebrated on 25th December like we do but on 7th January. This is because Russia used the old Julian calendar. (We adopted the Gregorian calendar in 1752 as the Julian calendar was inaccurate and did not reflect the solar year and the earth's rotation around the sun. Russia only adopted the Gregorian calendar in 1918.) Many Orthodox Russians fasted for 40 days before Christmas but Babushka was not orthodox at all as she still liked to eat traditional food over the Christmas period.

She made a special porridge called Sochivo which was even tastier than her normal porridge. She made borsch, sauerkraut and because there was so much beef left she made a special beef stroganoff.

For dessert she made fruit pies, cookies made with nuts and honey, and to drink Vzvar, a drink made with dried fruit and honey boiled in water.

As it was so bitter and provisions were scarce for her neighbours and in the town, because a lot of their harvest and livestock had been requisitioned, Babushka invited all her friends and neighbours to a Christmas party. It was a meal fit for a Tsar and everyone ate and drank heartily before settling down for a night of singing and dancing which Tomas and the animals joined in.

Tomas got his accordion and played many Russian and Polish carols and folk songs which everyone enjoyed and joined in. A lot of vodka was drank (that's one thing Russians or Poles for that matter will never go short of) and there was so much frivolity and merriment that they all forgot about the hardships they faced day in day out during the war. They enjoyed themselves immensely before making their weary and drunken ways to bed. Many just fell asleep where they were; no one minded it was Christmas and despite the hardships the best they had had for years.

Russians do not have Father Christmas like we do. They have Father Frost who delivers presents to the Russian children. That year Father Frost visited Babushka's farm and left a pair of solid wooden clubs for Bruce and a marching drum for Dinsky, a scarf for Minsky, and a pair of boxing gloves for Tinsky.

Tomas and the dogs were not left out and found strong leather gloves and shin guards at the bottom of their beds when they woke up.

Tomas thought even Father Frost is worried about their upcoming fight with the wolves and is helping to kit them out.

Bruce found the clubs a tremendous weapon as he could strike out with the clubs whilst he was in the air kicking out with his feet.

Dinsky struck a beat on his drum with which to march into battle and he could easily carry his staff as well to join the battle when the time came.

Tomas was glad of the gloves as they kept his hands warm which they needed to be to aim the guns properly.

Jerzy and Irena were glad of their shin guards as they had both been bitten on their legs by the Polish wolves but not seriously and the guards would protect their legs.

Dinsky liked her scarf and Babushka showed her how to wear it. She felt like she was now a junior babushka herself.

Tinsky tried his boxing gloves on and thought, *I won't use them against the wolves as my staff is better suited for clobbering wolves, but look out Bruce, because after we've beaten those wolves, it's going to be clobbering time for you.*

He didn't say it out loud just in case Bruce heard him and clobbered him now.

Chapter 12
Preparing for Lambing Season

In the days after Christmas Tomas spent a lot of time thinking about how to keep the sheep safe from the wolves. He did not like using steel traps or poison as that would be cruel and as he liked all animals he did not want to hurt any wolf if he could avoid it.

So he pondered and pondered on how to protect the sheep and frighten off the wolves so that they would never bother Babushka's flock again.

After many days and hours of pondering, probably more than you and I have pondered in a whole month, Tomas came up with a plan.

His plan was for all the sheep farmers to herd their flocks together into one large flock which would graze together and be shepherded together, just like a cooperative. They would have to be able to identify whose sheep was whose but agreement was reached and they formed a collective which was a sort of free market communism as each farmer imagined how much more roubles they would get the more lambs were saved from the wolves.

Tomas decided that in order to safeguard not only the sheep but also themselves they would need to have plenty of room and visibility between the grazing land and the forest. To have this room they would have to cut down the trees and bushes at the edge of the forest and make a barrier or fence to stop the wolves getting near the sheep without being seen. He would also dig holes near the forest, where he thought the wolves would come out, deep enough to trap a wolf without it being able to get out.

And so Tomas got to work. First he got their neighbours to start cutting down the trees and bushes on the outskirts of the forest and place them in bonfires in an arc around where he would herd the sheep during lambing season.

Next he had the pits dug in between the bonfires and covered them with branches so that they would be camouflaged but loose enough that they would not hold the weight of a wolf if one stepped on it.

He then built hides a short distance away from where the sheep were to graze from which he and some of the other farmers could watch for the wolves without being seen or sensed by the wolves when they came out of the forest. From the hides they would have clear shots at them when they attacked the sheep and could catch the wolves in a crossfire.

It was hard work, especially as it was such a hard winter but everyone was more than willing to help and as spring was approaching they were just about ready.

Now the wolves had been watching all this commotion and the pack leader was wise enough to realise that a trap was being set.

He had not lived for so long without having evaded a lot of traps.

He also knew that Tomas was the trickiest shepherd he had ever encountered and that is why he had increased the size of his pack so that there would be safety in numbers.

He knew that with such a large pack they would stand a good chance of getting to the flock when it was let out and was not overly worried by Tomas' traps.

The worrying problem for him and the pack was they were hungry and their source of food was dwindling. They needed the flock to be let out to graze as soon as possible. They had heard the lambs bleating in the farms and were getting twitchy and snappy and fights were breaking out in the pack. It was getting difficult to keep control.

It was a very similar condition in the war. On the Western Front France was being overwhelmed at Verdun and they asked the Russians for help by starting another front in the East, which they hoped would divert German troops away from Verdun and move some to the east.

The Russians were already engaged in hostilities against the Ottoman Empire who had already beaten off a British and French offensive at Gallipoli which was probably Winston Churchill's biggest mistake. (Winston Churchill was British prime minister during World War 2 and his leadership during that war was an example to every British subject. It just goes to show how everyone can make a mistake; the thing is to learn from it and not make the same mistake again.)

The Russians agreed to help; they had been enjoying success against the Turks and had far superior number of troops to the Germans in the east. They had also enjoyed success against the Austro Hungarian army and Tsar Nicholas was itching to have success against the Germans.

The Russians numbered about 480,000 troops whilst the Germans only had around 50,000 troops. This manpower superiority according to the Russian generals was the key to them beating the Germans; however, manpower alone does not win battles, if you like cowboy films you may have seen *The Magnificent Seven* who beat a very large gang of Mexican robbers and saved the town's people from them. (Although it was a cowboy film, it was based on a Japanese legend about Seven Samurai.)

If you haven't heard of them, ask your Mom or Dad and if they don't know, ask your bampy, he'll know.

Apart from the Imperial Guard who were as well equipped and trained as the Germans, the Russian infantry which consisted of mainly peasants were not.

They were hungry, they were not well equipped, many still did not have weapons or experience of warfare and their clothes were not suitable for the conditions. They were not well fed which made them both hungry and cold, whereas the Germans were well equipped and were seasoned soldiers well versed in warfare and although they too were cold they were fed better than the civilians at home.

Many Russians were squabbling amongst themselves and starting to desert. They were cold and fed up and many just wanted to go home; they didn't want to fight in the war and did not have faith in their generals.

The Tsar, however, had increased the supply of weapons for the army and commenced training for the troops which went a little way to restore morale. He also arranged for more food to be sent to the troops but due to the shortages there was insufficient food to go around the troops and civilians at home.

Nicholas had been in the army for 3 years from the age of 19 to 22 and had rose to the rank of colonel, so he had some knowledge of soldiering but nowhere near enough to compare with and turn around the Germans' vast superiority in warfare.

Chapter 13
The Battles of Lake Naroch and Babushka's Farm

In March 1916, the Russians mounted an attack on German lines at Lake Naroch in what is now Belarus, but at that time was part of the occupied Polish territory. It is now part of a national park and is a very beautiful part of that country as you would find out if you ever visited Belarus.

At the same moment, Tomas, Jerzy and Irena led the flocks out to graze. It was a bumper year for lambs; there were so many that Jerzy and Irena had their work cut out for them keeping them all together as they herded them up to the grazing ground. When the other farmers brought theirs up, it seemed that all you could see stretching into the distance were white sheep and a scattering of black sheep. There were so many that they spread further than where they had built the bonfires and the hides.

On the front line of the battle of Lake Naroch the Russian bombardment began, followed by troops storming the German front line, but the Germans held firm. They had set up machine gun emplacements in strategic positions which meant that as the Russians charged their lines they were mown down before they got anywhere near the German front line. The Russian generals did not mind this; they had no respect for the troops' lives and their strategy was to keep the troops charging the German lines in the belief that the weight of sheer numbers would prevail and secure a Russian victory. The reverse in fact happened; the Russians were like lambs to the slaughter and a vast amount of Russian troops were killed or maimed by the relentless German machine gun fire. Compared to the Russian casualties German losses were far less and they did not lose ground.

Back at the farm things were different; there were so many sheep that many could not be herded into the space between the bonfires and the hides so the wolves had a field day picking off those sheep and lambs outside the cordon.

Their attacks reminded Tomas of how helpless he had been in Tuchola when the wolves had caught him by surprise and killed some of the sheep in his care. He was determined not to let the wolves get the better of him this time and he and the other farmers sent their dogs to herd the sheep between the bonfires while they shot at the wolves sending them back into the forest with their spoils.

Not one wolf was hurt during the attack and many lambs were taken but the sheep had learnt not to stray too far from the rest of the flock and they would be easier to keep within the boundaries of the cordon. Again the few had beaten the many.

The wolves fed well that night but that was to be their last good meal for some time.

With all the sheep now protected and night approaching the bonfires were lit and modifications were made to the hides so that they could also fire into the forest as the wolves were retreating. Tomas wanted to teach the wolves a lesson they would never forget and the farmers that the best way to protect their sheep was to work together.

All was quiet that night apart from the wolves howling in delight at the great feast they were enjoying. It was like that for the next few days as the wolves dined on the lambs they had managed to catch on their first attack.

It wasn't that long before all the lambs were gone and the wolves were ready for more but this time Tomas was ready. Every farmer and animal knew what to do, they had practised and practised and were sure that they could lure the wolves into the pits and catch them in their crossfire before they reached the sheep this time.

All they needed to be now was vigilant and they would defeat the wolves and hopefully those remaining would leave the area for good.

The scene was set, the sheep were enclosed in the cordon, the farmer's guns loaded and primed, all was ready for the wolves to attack. The leader of the pack was wary though. He knew that something was not right.

Tomas and Bruce were the only visible shepherds the wolves could see, and they only had two sheepdogs, Jerzy and Irena. This worried the leader as his nose told a different story. He could smell more than just those and the sheep. He sent some of the pack to scout around the outskirts of the flock to see if they could see any more men or dogs. The farmers had done a great job on their hides and had even masked their scents with sheep dip so that they would not be detected by the wolves. The wolves all reported back to the leader stating they had been all around the cordon and the only shepherds there were a young lad, a funny looking man and two sheepdogs.

The leader was still cautious; he told the wolves to be very quiet and they would attack from two directions just before daybreak when the shepherds and their dogs would be tired and hopefully asleep. They were to be very quick and take only enough lambs to keep the pack well fed for a few days in that way the shepherds would not miss any lambs. They could then keep doing sneak attacks without being noticed.

It was a great plan and would have worked if it had not been for Irena who was always alert even when the others were not.

It was 5 o'clock in the morning when the wolves attacked. They snuck in in a circular motion on the left side of Tomas, who was with Jerzy, and to the right of Bruce, who was with Irena. They somehow managed to miss the pits and started to take their pick of the lambs on the edge of the flock.

Now I don't believe sheep ever sleep.

My bampy told me once that when he was on night patrol he used to drive up to Manmoel, Markham Common and Ynys Hywel to see if he could find a sheep asleep. He told me he never saw one asleep. His mates never found any either. He even used to park up away from the sheep and try to sneak up on them but every time he tried he saw that they had one eye open and were watching his every move. He said that although they were watching him they would not move staying put. Bampy said that sheep are not the brightest animals in the world.

Sure enough both Tomas and Jerzy were fast asleep, so too was Bruce who was snoring loudly which was annoying Irena who had moved some way away from him. The first thing she noticed was not the wolves who had come in downwind from the flock but the eyes of the sheep which were all staring at something to her right. They fidgeted but did not move.

She looked around and then saw a large wolf slink past her a few yards from where she was lying. Irena gave a loud woof and immediately sprang into action. She began to spin around on her hind feet in an upright position and performed the best and longest pirouette she had ever performed. In fact she spun with so much power she was like a spinning top which looked out of control but she was not. She was very much in control and attacked the wolf with so much force that when she hit it, there let out an almighty whelp and went rolling along the ground, having sustained several broken ribs.

The noise woke up everyone and the wolves' surprise attack was thwarted. Irena remained spinning and attacked another wolf. Bruce sprang to action waving his clubs and set upon another wolf which had already grabbed a lamb and was making its way back towards the forest. Careful not to hit the lamb in the wolf's mouth he caught the wolf with a mighty blow to its ribs which made the wolf howl in pain and in doing so dropping the lamb which ran back to its mother who was bleating loudly as was the rest of the flock.

Tomas was now wide awake as was Jerzy. Tomas had his gun ready and aimed at the closest wolf to him and shot it dead. Jerzy attacked another wolf and delivered a flying kick to the side of its head which knocked it senseless.

The tables had been turned; it was now the wolves who had been caught by surprise. They had never encountered such fierce resistance and their usual guile and ruthlessness was disrupted. They were in total disarray. The leader seeing his pack in such a disorganised state tried to rally them by calling them to rally around him as he made his way towards Irena who was wreaking havoc with the other wolves with her spinning kicks and blows.

Jerzy saw the leader turn and make huge leaps and bounds towards where Irena was making light work of one of the smaller wolves. He knew what the leader was going to do and tried to warn Irena of the large wolf's attack. Irena could not hear him though, she was too intent on her own attack and was oblivious of the danger that she was in.

Jerzy ran as fast as he could to help her but was not as quick as the wolf that leapt at Irena and caught her back sending her sprawling to the ground in a heap. Irena was stunned and winded. She was unable to protect herself and the wolf confronted her staring at her with his big fierce piercing eyes. Irena had never felt so afraid in her life. She feared that her life was close to ending but her ballet training and tremendous stamina and resilience kicked in and she sprang to her feet and pirouetted to her left just as the wolf pounced, his teeth showing and ready to bite.

Irena just managed to avoid the main blow but the wolf's sharp teeth managed to sink into her right hand shin as she narrowly escaped certain death if the wolf had caught her neck which he had intended to do. Luckily for Irena the wolf could not keep his grip on her shin and Irena fell to the ground to the left of the wolf who could not believe that a mere sheepdog had survived his attack. He had never missed a first attack kill before. He turned to face Irena again; this time he would not miss. Irena was lying on the ground trying to crawl away, her right shin bleeding profusely and in a lot of pain. She did not cry though she was defiant and although very scared, would not show the wolf that she was afraid.

He was just about to make his final attack when Jerzy burst through the wolves that had rallied to their leader's call and were beginning to surround Irena. Jerzy leapt at the big wolf and aimed a flying kick straight at the wolf's head. The wolf was not taken unawares though and dodged the blow butting Jerzy as he sailed past and sending him towards several angry wolves beyond where Irena was down.

The wolf returned his attentions to Irena, he was determined that he would finish off the pesky dog that had scuppered all his plans.

Jerzy was now caught up in his own battle with the other wolves but he was now not alone. Bruce came wading in clobbering the wolves with his clubs and Tinsky had also joined them and was twirling and thrusting his staff with all his might sending wolves reeling but they were so outnumbered by the wolves that they were unable to go to Irena's rescue. They did, however, manage to take out a lot of wolves and stop them from going to the leader's aid.

It looked like Irena's time was up. She was badly hurt and unable to protect herself and she feared the worst.

Just as the wolf was about to sink his teeth into Irena's neck there was a loud bang. It was Tomas; he too had come to Irena's aid and saw that the wolf was ready to strike. He had gone to his knees and taken aim as quickly as he could hoping to stop the wolf in his tracks. The shot was on target. Tomas did not know if it was a magnificent shot or just luck but it hit the wolf right in its head, killing it instantly. The other wolves seeing their leader fall and taking heavy blows themselves from Bruce and Tinsky, faltered. Then came the sound of loud drums and further gunfire as Dinsky led the other farmers towards the battle.

That was enough for the wolves; they up and ran back towards the safety of the forest. This time, however, they were not careful about where they were going and several fell into the pits. The few who made it from the battle did not look back; they ran and ran and never returned to Babushka's farm.

Some say they ran all the way to Siberia where they stayed and prospered. Not all the wolves got away; the farmers followed them into the forest and shot all the stragglers to make sure that there would be no further threat of wolf attacks in their region ever again.

The farmers cheered and rejoiced but Tomas, however, was gutted as both Jerzy and Irena were injured, both had leg injuries with Irena's being serious. Tomas had to carry Irena back to Babushka's farm while Bruce and Tinsky helped Jerzy hobble back.

Babushka treated Irena and Jerzy the best she could. She cleaned up both the dogs' wounds and applied her special lotions and bandaged them up. She told Tomas that Jerzy's leg should heal up in a short time and would be no worse for the injury. Irena, however, was different; her wound was deep and had torn ligaments, she had done her best to repair them but it would need Rasputin's magic to mend them properly or she would never be able to walk without a limp again let alone perform ballet. Without wanting to alarm Tomas, she thought even with Rasputin's help Irena would never be able to ballet dance again.

Things were not going so well for the Russians at Lake Naroch either.

The Germans held out against the Russians attack which mainly consisted of wave after wave of Russian troop attacks. (Remember the Russians had 480,000 men against 50,000

Germans.) The Russian generals called it the human wave but against well organised and heavily armed battle hardened soldiers, they were no match. The German machine gunners and artillery had a field day and thousands of Russian soldiers were killed or maimed in the onslaught.

The Naroch offensive fizzled out in April 1916 having gained nothing. No German soldiers had to be taken from Verdun and Russian morale was at its lowest. Many soldiers wanted and did desert having no faith in the Russian generals at all.

It was a failure and did not put Nicholas' leadership in a good light.

Things were not looking good for the Russians or Tomas and his dream of Jerzy and Irena performing at the Mariinsky Ballet.

Chapter 14
Meeting the Tsar and Finding the Wolf Cubs

Babushka knew that the only chance of saving Irena's leg and dancing career was to get to St Petersburg as fast as she could and let Rasputin tend to it. She went straight to the town and sent a message to Rasputin telling him how Irena had been hurt defending the flock from the wolves and had taken on the lead wolf by herself.

Rasputin was amazed and sent this message back: *This Irena is a dog of great courage and I swear that I will mend her leg as good as new. Babushka, I will go and see the Tsar straightaway and ask him to send the Imperial Train right away. This I promise*

Rasputin was as good as his word. The Tsar was back with the family for a visit and although preoccupied with the war, was approachable.

When he told the Tsar of Irena's injury and the heroism she had shown he immediately ordered the Imperial Train to get ready and told Rasputin that he and Alexei would accompany him to Babushka's home as he wanted to meet Tomas and Irena to see for himself the brave troupe he had assembled.

The Imperial Train was ready in no time as it was always on standby. The Tsar, Prince Alexei and Rasputin boarded and it sped off on the Tsar's order to reach Babushka as quickly as possible

Soon they were at Babushka's and Tsar Nicholas was shown in by Rasputin. Babushka, Tomas and even Bruce bowed low feeling very humbled in the presence of the Tsar of all Russia.

The Tsar told them to straighten up and show him the amazing dog that had taken on the mighty wolf and its pack.

Babushka took the Tsar and Rasputin to her bedroom where she had lay Irena on her own bed. "I put her here," she said, "because of her injuries and because it was down to her that the wolves were defeated and sent packing."

The Tsar walked over to the bed and patted Irena's forehead. He whispered to her, "I hear that you are the bravest dog who ever lived taking on the might of a very large and fierce pack of wolves. I could do with an army of soldiers like you and then we would be winning this war and not losing so many of my people. I will let Rasputin see to you now and hopefully you will be able to show me how well you dance my prima donna."

He left the room telling Rasputin to do whatever was necessary and make sure that she recovered. He then returned to the main room to speak to Tomas.

"I hear that Rasputin told you and your troupe to stay here during the winter and help Babushka in lambing season before coming to St Petersburg to fulfil your dream of dancing at the Mariinsky, is that right?"

"Yes," replied Tomas

"I know Babushka and my farmers must be very grateful but Alexei and my daughters have been awaiting your arrival in St Petersburg and constantly begging for me to send for you."

Tomas felt honoured and told the Tsar that he had been lucky to have such wonderful animals and a friend in Bruce. At that point Babushka came in from the kitchen with an enormous tray of pastries, cakes and a large jug of the most refreshing fruit juice she had ever made. She put it on the table and humbly requested that the Tsar should try some.

Alexei said, "Father, you must try one of Babushka's cakes, they are the best in all Russia and maybe the whole world."

"It all looks delicious, Babushka," said the Tsar, and he took a cake and a glass of fruit juice and told everyone to tuck in as well.

While they were eating, the Tsar asked Tomas to tell him all about the battle with the wolves.

Tomas told the Tsar how he had come up with the plan to tackle the wolves and how it needed proper planning, preparation and performance. He told the Tsar that poor planning and preparation meant that poor performance would follow. There's usually another P word used in this well used saying but it is not

94

suitable for a children's story, but the saying is right and something that you should always remember when you want to do something really well.

Tomas told the Tsar how they had gone out to spy on the wolves to find out their strengths and weaknesses and how he had seen the leader of the pack close up.

He did not tell the Tsar about how he was able to speak to the wolf as he did not want anyone to know that he had been blessed by the Leszi.

He told the Tsar how he had organised the other farmers into a cooperative and how they had cleared a large grazing area away from the forest, dug pits and built hides so that the wolves would not see their strength and would be vulnerable to their guns. The most important thing he said was that everyone, farmers and animals, needed to train beforehand and each be ready and know what to do when the wolves attacked.

They all had suitable weapons and as Tomas had created the battle ground himself by clearing the grazing ground thus giving them a big advantage over the wolves that he had a great admiration for as they seemed so well organised.

The Tsar said, "That sounds like the Germans too. I think my generals and I should take a leaf out of your book, perhaps then they might turn this war around."

Tomas said, "The troops, Your Highness, need proper leadership and the right tools for the job. They also need to be trained so that they know what to expect and is expected of them. A trained soldier is a better soldier and that is why the Germans are so good not because they are better men, they win because they are better trained and equipped and they have better generals.

"Point taken," said the Tsar and he vowed having taken overall charge of the army and the war himself that he would change things. No more relying on the human wave strategy which was in reality just mass suicide; he would order his generals to take account of their troops' losses before commencing any offensive.

Tomas related how they were caught out on the first attack, almost slept through the second attack and that if it were not for Irena's intervention they would have lost more lambs.

The story told, the Tsar was amazed. "You are truly an inspiration Tomas, and I am sure that the people of St Petersburg will be as impressed with you and your troupe as Alexei and I are," he said.

Rasputin came back into the room after seeing to Irena and said, "I think she will be alright in time. It is a nasty wound and the ligaments will have to heal properly but with my care and time I think she will be able to dance again. Babushka, you did a good job of cleaning it up and your sewing is still excellent but we will have to move her to the Palace for me to take care of her. Tsar Nicholas, we must take her back with us on the Imperial Train."

"And can Tomas and the others come with us, perhaps Bruce can teach me how to box?" said Alexei.

"Of course they can," said Tsar Nicholas. "I wouldn't dream of leaving such a gallant troupe behind, but first we must finish Babushka's excellent snack and I must go and see the battle ground for myself and get a feel of the action."

When they had finished, Tomas took the Tsar, Alexei and Rasputin up to the pasture and showed them the clearing they had made, the hides and the pits. There were still the remains of the wolves lying there and the sheep were keeping their distance from them. Their carcasses would be removed later by the farmers, who would use them for meat, as times were still harsh due to the hardships suffered throughout Russia due to the war.

As they were wandering through the pasture towards the forest they heard the sound of a young animal crying. It sounded like a young puppy. Minsky who had gone along to see the battle ground for herself as she had had to stay behind to tend to the farm, went into the forest to see what was making the noise.

When she returned following closely behind her were the cutest looking puppies they had ever seen.

"They are wolf cubs," said Rasputin, "and very fine cubs they are too. But now they are motherless as if their mother were alive I am sure she would have taken them when the rest of the wolves fled."

"What will become of them?" said the Tsar.

"I will take care of them," said Tomas. "No animal deserves to suffer. When they grow up, they can be part of my troupe."

96

Alexei picked up one of the cubs which had sidled up to his right leg.

"Be careful Alexei, they have sharp teeth," said the Tsar. Alexei, however, held it up and cuddled it close to his chest and face. The cub licked him and Alexei fell in love with it.

"Can I keep this one, he is so handsome and look he likes me too?" Alexei asked his father.

"What do you think, Rasputin, is he well enough to look after a wolf?" said the Tsar.

"I think the experience and the hard work it will take to raise a wolf cub will make a man of him and judging by their first encounter I think it will be a good match," he replied.

"Then it is settled. Tomas, you will have one wolf and Alexei will have the other," he said.

The wolf Tomas was keeping gave a little snarl and Alexei's cub yelped joyfully

"You must name them now while they are new to you, so that their names can reflect this first meeting," said Rasputin.

The Tsar said, "I think Tomas' cub ought to be named Ivan after my forefather Ivan the Terrible. He looks as if he is going to be very big and strong. He already has long sharp teeth and has the look of a leader. He will be a bit of a handful Tomas, but I am sure that you will raise him to be a stalwart amongst your troupe, if treated right a wolf can be as faithful and trusty as any dog. And you Alexei, I will leave naming yours up to you as I am sure you will become great friends though I'm not sure that your mother will approve."

Alexei thought for a moment and said, "Father, I will name him simply Wolf and we will be friends forever."

"So be it," said the Tsar, "but I think it is time for us to get back to St Petersburg. Russia needs its Tsar. It's time for me to lead my people."

So they walked back to Babushka's farm and Tomas and the others collected their things.

Babushka prepared a special milk concoction for the wolf cubs to drink and Tomas and Alexei fed them with bottles that they had used to feed the lambs that weren't feeding properly. The cubs lapped it up in no time, they were that hungry.

"Slow down little ones," said Babushka, "they will suffer terrible colic if they drink too fast."

"They are certainly very hungry little wolves," said the Tsar

"Isn't it ironic," said Rasputin, "just hours ago their parents were killing the lambs and now their cubs are drinking from their bottles."

Everyone laughed.

When they had finished feeding and Babushka had filled several further bottles for them for their journey, she handed Tomas and Rasputin her recipe for the milk, telling them that the further ingredients would help the wolves grow strong and contented.

Unfortunately that recipe was secret and has never been revealed so I cannot tell you what was in that special milk. They all said their sad farewells and thanks to Babushka and headed for the station to board the Imperial Train to St Petersburg.

All the town's people had turned out to see them off and they cheered the Tsar loudly and then to Tomas' amazement a loud cheer went up for Tomas and his troupe. Tomas was very proud and felt like a Tsar himself as he made his way to the train and they all acknowledged the crowd.

"May the people always be this happy to see us," the Tsar told him. "There is nothing worse than an angry mob and in these dangerous times the mood of the people can change in the wink of an eye."

Tomas looked back as he boarded the train. "I will miss you Babushka, we all will, you were like a mother to us," he said to himself and with a tear in his eye he joined the Royal party in the conference cabin of the train

The train was a little smaller than he had imagined but there were a lot of gold fittings and it was immaculately furnished.

Fit for a Tsar thought Tomas, which in fact it was.

With everyone aboard and Irena settled in the Tsar's own bed, the train moved off on its way to St Petersburg.

Tomas and the animals sat back and enjoyed the comforts of the train, the Tsar, however, did not settle. He was worried, he knew things were not going well for him and the Russian losses and the hardships the people were suffering meant that his popularity was waning and there were whispers of discord amongst the nobles and revolution in the cities.

He had to turn things around or it would be the end of Russia as he knew it.

He also had to have Tomas and Alexei take better care of the wolf cubs that had started to demolish the furniture and fittings in the conference room as well as not being toilet trained.

"Your mother is not going to be pleased Alexei, if you let Wolf do that in the Royal Palace," he laughed and tapped Alexei on his head.

Chapter 15
St Petersburg and Tsarskoe Selo

The train took them to the Tsar's palace, outside St Petersburg in Tsarskoe Selo.

As we already know Alexander Palace was a far better residence for the family than the Winter Palace and it had acres of grounds where the family could roam in private and enjoy time away from formal affairs.

It was also an ideal sanctuary for Tomas and his animal troupe.

Tsar Nicholas led Tomas and the animals inside where they were greeted by Tsarina Alexandria and Alexei's four sisters, along with a very impatient government minister.

Nicholas greeted his wife and children and then turned to his minister and said, "What is so important that brings you to meet me as soon as I arrive home, has Germany invaded Russia?"

The minister told him that ships with supplies had started to get through to Russia as the Germans had relaxed their indiscriminate torpedoing of merchant ships following the American President Woodrow Wilson having Germany comply with what was known as the Sussex Pledge. This followed a German submarine torpedoing a French passenger steamer in the English Channel in March. The Germans stated they thought it was a minelayer but it was not. It wasn't sunk and managed to limp into port. Fifty people were killed and many injured, several of whom were American citizens.

The Germans bowed to Wilson's demands and pledged to stop suspected merchant ships and give them adequate warning before sinking them if they carried munitions or war supplies. They guaranteed the safety of crew and passengers.

Rasputin then said his goodbyes and left saying, "I must return to my flat in St Petersburg. I have to purge myself and my flock of all of the sin that has occurred whilst I have been away."

"What does he mean?" asked Tomas.

Tsar Nicholas replied, "For a holy man Rasputin is a strange man with strange questionable habits, so my spies tell me, but his advice and treatment of Alexei is invaluable so he is allowed to come and go as he pleases. There are, however, people in the Royal family who only see him as a danger, but I think he is a danger to them not me and I will rue the day that he is no longer around for his help. Now excuse me, I must see this pledge and see if it benefits Mother Russia."

In the meantime, Alexandra and her daughters greeted Tomas and made a great fuss of the animals, especially Irena, who was still very poorly.

The Princesses all wanted Tomas to tell them his story and thought what a handsome young boy he was. Though he was only fifteen years old he was becoming a young man.

Tomas was taken aback by the boldness of Princess Anastasia who, although the smallest, had grabbed him by the arm and was asking him the most questions. She was a year younger than Tomas.

Alexei had kept Wolf hidden behind him whilst they were questioning Tomas and fussing with the other animals until Anastasia spotted him and shouted, "Look, Alexei has a puppy!"

"That's not a puppy, that's a wolf cub," Alexandra said when she saw it. "Alexei, what in God's name possessed you to bring a wolf cub into our home?"

Alexei told his mother the story of how they found it, that Tomas was also keeping a wolf cub and that they would raise them to be loyal and responsible wolves that were no danger to them or anyone else.

"Wolves can be trained, can't they, Tomas," he said hoping Tomas would back him up.

"All animals are safe if they are raised correctly," said Tomas.

Alexandra protested but when Alexei told her that father had agreed to keep Wolf, she backed down and said, "Well I suppose if your father is agreeable then my opinion doesn't count."

Alexei said, "Mama your opinion always counts and Father told me to always listen to you but if I take great care of Wolf you will grow to love him too."

As he was speaking all his sisters were making a fuss of Wolf and he was happily playing with them and letting them stroke his belly.

Alexandra sorted out arrangements for Tomas and his troupe to stay within the grounds of the palace in Tsarkoye Selo and they were given refreshments. Tomas was invited to attend dinner with them that evening.

Tsar Nicholas returned home later having discussed the war and the internal matters with his ministers and they all sat down for dinner.

They had a good dinner and there was much to talk about. Alexandra and the princesses wanted to know all about Tomas' adventures and marvelled at the heroics of Jerzy and Irena, the three bears and Bruce.

"It sounds like a made up story," said Olga.

"But it's all true, isn't it Tomas?" said Alexei.

"It really is," said Tomas.

When they finished it was time for the Royal children's bedtime so their governess was summoned and they bade their parents and Tomas a goodnight and went to bed to dream of adventures of their own. Alexei wanted to take Wolf to bed with him which annoyed Alexandra but Nicholas would have none of her protestations and allowed him to take Wolf with him.

"Rasputin says it will do Alexei good to have a pet and I agree. It may be the making of him. He will learn to take care of another and that will teach him the compassion, feelings and commitment attributes he will need when he becomes Tsar," he told her.

He then said, "Tomorrow I must leave, I must ready the army for battle and organise the generals as well as making sure that our troops are trained and equipped for a bold offensive. We need a victory to rally the troops and this time I intend to make sure we get one."

He bade Tomas goodnight and he and Alexandra made their way to bed.

The next morning Nicholas said his farewells and took the Royal train to the Eastern front where he appointed General Alexei Brusilov as his commander.

He told Brusilov that things were going well against the Turks but they needed a victory on the Eastern front against Austria and the Germans to bolster Russian morale.

He told him that he would make sure that there would be sufficient artillery and weapons for the army and that his forces would be far superior to the enemy, as the new soldiers being sent to the front would have received training.

He told Brusilov to devise a strategy to attack and divide the enemy then press home the advantage in the hope that their offensive would divert German troops from Verdun thus weakening them on both fronts. He also told him that he was working on Romania to get them to join Russia in the war.

Brusilov was wary; he was a great general and commanded the respect of his troops but he was suspicious of the other generals who were not as bold as he was and he wondered if he would have their support when needed.

Nicholas told him, "You have my support and the generals will support you like they do me."

If only that were true, thought Brusilov.

The Tsar then played on Brusilov's ego by saying, "Think of it. If all goes well, you will be a national hero just like Alexander Nevsky who defeated the Swedes and Germans in the 13th century, and he was made a saint."

That clinched it for Brusilov, he was up for it.

While Brusilov was preparing his offensive Tomas was busy too.

With Irena being laid up and out of action it was time to prepare Bruce and train him to fight for the Russian title. There was no shortage of contenders, even though boxing was not a big sport in Russia, and Bruce would have to establish himself as the number one contender in order to be granted a shot at the title.

Rasputin arranged his first fight against a battle-hardened and brutal veteran fighter named Koba who since 1913 had called himself Stalin, the Man of Steel. Now Koba was a revolutionary who had been exiled to Siberia a number of times but had kept escaping. He was a Marxist Communist and a Bolshevik. He was a very dangerous, power-mad man, who wanted to start a revolution and depose Tsar Nicholas and create a communist state. Koba thought of himself as invincible and that is why he had come to call himself the Man of Steel. This riled Rasputin who thought of himself as the invincible one and God's chosen one. He was more a man of steel than Koba and having been of peasant stock and brought up in a religious order surely he was the Man of Steel.

Koba also wanted to ban religion, something Rasputin despised. He was a religious man who saw himself as a devotee of Jesus and whose healing powers came from God.

It was for this reason Rasputin had picked Koba as Bruce's opponent. He wanted Bruce to knock him out and humiliate him. Rasputin thought of himself as the ultimate man of the people and was testimony that a man from humble origins could elevate himself to a position of power if he was strong enough. Although this Koba was also of humble origin having been born Iosif Dzhugashvili in Georgia, he was an untrustworthy bully who dreamt of achieving great power. He was the type of person who would smile to your face then stab you in the back when your face was turned and grab power by any means.

As you grow up I suspect you will meet many of these types who usually rise up to positions in power on the back of other people's hard work.

A very wise man named Edmund Burke who was Irish and died in 1797 wrote, 'All that is necessary for the triumph of evil is that good men do nothing'. He wrote that in his *Reflections on the French Revolution.*

He also said, 'When bad men combine, the good must associate; else they will fall one by one, an unpitied sacrifice in a contemptible struggle'.

I hope all you good young people remember this and watch out for these types as you grow up and not allow them to reach positions of power for as Burke said you will only have yourselves to blame.

Rasputin, however, had great respect for the Tsar and his immediate family and was loyal to them but not to his ministers and other advisors who were mostly nobility themselves. There was no love lost between them.

He was at odds with the Tsar's advisors who were autocratic and did not share the Tsar's more liberal views. In fact they tried to malign Rasputin in order to discredit him every chance they could which wasn't difficult as Rasputin thought of himself as invincible and beyond reproach despite his womanising episodes.

Rasputin thought that if Bruce could humiliate Koba it would destroy the respect his followers had for him and show them that he was not as invincible as he claimed. This in turn would diminish the influence of the Marxists on the people of St Petersburg and Russia.

Rasputin warned Bruce to be very careful against him saying, "Koba, if that's his real name, is a street fighter, he is as hard as nails and is like a man of steel. He may be in his late thirties now but he has a will to match his name and the punch of a mule. If you can beat him, you will go up the rankings. You will have to train hard for this fight or you will lose."

He said to Tomas, "Tomas, this is one fight Bruce must win. Koba is a very dangerous man; if he gets to have his way there will be no future for you or me. I dread to think what will become of our beloved Russia if he and his like get to run this great country. He is agitating the people towards revolution and I fear many people loyal to the Tsar will die if he succeeds. You must make sure Bruce is in tip top condition and ready to cope with any dirty trick Koba will try to win the fight. Koba has a fight on Tuesday next week; if I were you, I would take Bruce to see the fight so that he can see what to expect."

"Thank you," said Tomas. "I will heed your advice and get Bruce in the best condition of his life. It sounds as if he will need to be!"

Tomas started Bruce on fitness training which was overseen by Jerzy who barked and growled at him if he started to flag.

Tomas took Tinsky with him to see Koba fight and told Tinsky to take special note of any dirty tricks or underhand tactics Koba used during the fight so that Tinsky could use them whilst sparring with Bruce. He told Tinsky to make sure that Bruce would be able to predict and cope with any dirty tricks Koba adopted. Tinsky who enjoyed playing tricks himself thought to himself, *I'll use all Koba's tricks on Bruce and a few of my own, so Bruce will be more of a match for him.*

Rasputin went along with them to see the fight.

The fight was not a spectacular one, just a slug fest with both fighters standing toe to toe punching each other as hard as they could. Koba, however, would throw punches below the belt and into opponent's back whenever the referee was blindsided. Tinsky was amazed to see Koba bite his opponent in the clinches and kick and head butt him as well. It appeared to Tinsky that he would use any unfair advantage he could employ to win the fight and that the referee did not warn him about it.

Koba won the fight with a knockout.

His opponent was bruised and bloodied having sustained some horrific injuries.

The crowd was in awe of Koba and they shouted 'Stalin, Stalin, Stalin' in his honour.

Koba saw Rasputin in the crowd and called out, "Look even the great Rasputin comes to see Koba. Perhaps he will serve me come the revolution. What do you say, Rasputin?"

Rasputin said, "You may win a fight by foul means and a weak referee but you are no man of steel or a match for me, Koba. Bruce the Clown will beat you in a fair fight and the people will see you for what you are, just a thug and a bully!"

"We shall see Rasputin you degenerate, look at you, you are unclean and in need of a bath and some new robes. When we are in power, there will be no place for you in Russia. Now go and take your bear with you," he said.

Rasputin said, "Your time is near Koba there is a reckoning coming."

"And it will be yours before mine you Mad Monk," said Koba and he left with his band of followers to celebrate his victory.

"You see the danger he presents, Tomas; Bruce must win and win well, we must not let him become a hero of the people," said Rasputin.

He hoped that by the time of the fight Brusilov would have commenced his offensive and the people would be cheering his victory and have a new hero who would give them hope of winning the war.

Tomas and Tinsky agreed and they pledged to make Bruce's training as demanding and vicious in the hope that by the time of the fight he would be a lean mean fighting machine.

They told Bruce what they had witnessed and started his training immediately. Tinsky sparred with Bruce and took every opportunity that presented itself to bite, kick and rabbit punch Bruce during their bouts. It did not take long for Bruce to wise up and counter the dirty tricks and he devised a few of his own. Soon he was ready for the fight.

Chapter 16
The Brusilov Offensive and the Big Fight

General Brusilov had prepared well. He took the time to have detailed maps of the Austro Hungarian positions, as well as the German troops on the Eastern Front prepared. He knew that their previous losses were due to the superiority of the German army and that the Austro Hungarian troops were much weaker. He also knew that the Germans would be stretched with the battle of Verdun being waged on the Western Front, and this would help his cause.

He was now in overall charge of the Russian forces and had three armies at his disposal, the others under General Evert and General Kuropatkin. They were not as optimistic as Brusilov and did not advocate an offensive and believed that following their dismal failure at Tannenberg and Lake Naroch they should concentrate on defence.

They were now being supplied with superior artillery and better trained troops equipped with rifles which led Brusilov to believe that they would soon achieve parity with the Germans and then become the best troops in the War. He believed that the Russian soldier was far superior to any other if armed properly and that offense was the best form of defence.

He devised a plan to attack the enemy in three stages so that they would not know which was the main offensive.

He would lead the first attack which would start with a heavy bombardment of the Austro Hungarian lines at Lutsk which is now in the Ukraine. The attack which would follow would be by divisions and raiding parties to keep the enemy guessing and cause widespread disruption and draw troops away from other areas, especially the Germans.

Following his success, General Evert was to attack the enemy in the north and General Kuropatkin to follow up with a third attack thus engaging the enemy on three fronts and dividing their forces sufficiently to make a major breakthrough and defeat them in the east. This would give British and French troops fresh impetus making the end of the war inevitable.

Brusilov's plan was a good one and preparations had gone well; if all went well and Evert and Kuropatkin played their part as per script, they would be successful.

General Brusilov commenced hostilities on 4th June 1916 with a heavy bombardment which left the Austro Hungarian troops in complete disarray. This was followed by lightning strikes by Brusilov's infantry divisions and Cossack cavalry. (Cavalry were used extensively on the Eastern front.) Brusilov used raiding parties to spread terror through the enemy ranks. This was helped by the diverse nature of the Austro Hungarian troops who were of various nationalities and beliefs with no common language so communication was almost impossible. (Who says diversity is good older wiser people were taught the adage divide and conquer / united we stand. There appeared to be no unity in the Austro Hungarian troops and that would prove to be their downfall.)

By 8th June, Brusilov had succeeded in taking the heavily fortified town of Lutsk, which was defended by the Austro Hungarian 4th army led by Josef Ferdinand, breaking the Austro Hungarian front and had advanced well into their territory. The Germans were now worried and were sending reinforcements to bolster their defence.

Brusilov was happy and looked forward to a comprehensive Russian victory. Evert was due to attack on 9th June, which would further stretch the enemy and this was the date Rasputin had scheduled the fight with Koba.

General Evert, however, failed to initiate his offensive as planned.

Brusilov was angry but told that they would attack on the 18th. He wondered if Tsar Nicholas was aware of this as he had been promised that the other generals would support him. It was not the Tsar's doing however, but down to the ineptitude of Evert and Kuropatkin in not supporting the offensive.

Brusilov was still advancing but German reinforcements were being rushed to aid the faltering Austro Hungarian troops and despite making massive advances he found himself alone in attacking the enemy.

Back in St Petersburg Bruce was well up for the fight; he had been roughed up by Tinsky who had used every trick he had seen Koba use and others he thought up himself to prepare him, and was raring to go.

Despite the best efforts of Koba's spies he knew very little about Bruce apart from that he was a travelling clown with the Tomaschevski Dance Troupe which had been championed by Rasputin and favoured by the Tsar.

He saw this fight as a way of discrediting the Tsarists and giving the Bolsheviks a great propaganda victory when he won. Defeat was not an option, especially to a clown.

He had been told that Bruce had fought all comers when travelling to St Petersburg but no one of any stature so he was confident of victory. News of Brusilov's offensive was filtering into St Petersburg and to keep up the momentum towards revolution he needed to beat the Tsar's lackey and show him up.

The venue was in a public park on the outskirts of St Petersburg so that a large crowd could witness the fight. However, it was heavily policed and the crowd consisted of mainly people loyal to the Tsar. Known Koba supporters were kept at the back as it was rumoured that Prince Alexei was in the crowd with his sisters. A rumour that on this occasion was true. They were, however, accompanied by a battalion of white guards in civilian clothes, who allowed no one to get close to them, so that they would not be recognised.

The referee for the fight was a captain in the Russian Army who had boxed for the Army and knew all the dirty tricks a boxer could use. Rasputin had briefed him about Koba and so when the two protagonists lined up in the centre of the ring at the start of the fight he warned Koba that he would not tolerate any dirty tricks such as below the belt punches and he showed Koba what he meant by hitting him below the belt. He said there was to be no biting and bit him on his ear and no head butting but when he head-butted Koba it was the referee who held his head.

"What is your head made of?" he asked Koba.

"Steel," said Koba.

"Yes it feels like it," said the captain. "Now back to your corners and when the bell rings come out fighting and let it be a good clean fight."

Both fighters came out fighting but it was nothing like a clean fight but a fight it certainly was.

Koba came out like a lightning bolt and sped towards Bruce launching a haymaker of a right hook straight to the left side of Bruce's head. The speed and power of the punch took Bruce by complete surprise and it knocked him sideways and down to an angle of 45 degrees before springing back upright and catching the oncoming Koba by surprise with a sideways head butt almost knocking him down.

Remember kangaroos with just a stump are like weebles and wobble like a roly-poly so it is just about impossible to knock one like Bruce to the floor.

Both fighters shook themselves knowing that this was to be no easy fight.

They stood toe to toe trading punches but guarding their heads to avoid injury.

For three rounds they pummelled each other neither giving an inch.

In the 4th round Koba was beginning to tire so when the opportunity came he head-butted Bruce whilst the referee was behind Bruce and unable to see it. Instead of Bruce being hurt though, it was Koba who came off worse and he staggered forward and grabbed hold of Bruce and bit his ear.

Bruce yelped at the bite but pushed Koba away and began to bombard Koba with a succession of lefts and rights that had Koba reeling. Luckily for him the bell saved him from being knocked down.

Tomas said to Bruce as soon as he got back to his corner, "You've got him reeling Bruce, finish him off in this round; don't let him get back into the fight."

But he was joined by Rasputin who said, "Good going Bruce, now humiliate him, play with him and hurt him; he must be seen to be weak by all the people here. We must ruin his reputation so that there will be no reason for us or anyone to fear him in the future."

For the next three rounds Bruce kept pounding Koba but not with the power to knock him out. The speed of Bruce's punches keeping Koba at bay preventing him from landing a punch on Bruce. The crowd were now chanting 'KNOYH, KNOYH' which is Russian for clown and pronounced kloun.

Koba was furious and in round 8 summoning every ounce of strength he could muster he caught Bruce with a tremendous right upper cut to Bruce's chin which literally lifted Bruce clean off the floor and up into the air.

From the back of the crowd came shouts of 'STALIN, STALIN' as Bruce tumbled backwards onto the canvas but just as he did in Alabama he bounced back twice as fast and caught Koba with a left hook which sent him clean out of the ring and into the crowd.

Bruce and Tomas were worried that they may have killed Koba and they rushed out of the ring to see if he was OK.

Koba was semi-conscious on the floor but trying to get up.

This surely is a man of steel, thought Tomas.

The referee was counting to ten for a knockout while Koba was trying to get up so Bruce stood on his ankle to prevent him from getting up. When the count reached 10 and he was declared the winner, Bruce put one of his huge feet on Koba's chest and raised his hands above his head in triumph.

The crowd went wild chanting 'KNOYH, KNOYH, KNOYH' and the soldiers lifted him up whilst Alexei and the princesses cheered and clapped.

Bruce was now a legend; he had defeated the man of steel but in doing so had humiliated Koba who vowed to have his revenge. But for now Koba was forgotten a loser who none of the Royals or soldiers present thought would ever become a power in Russia.

They were all wrong.

Meanwhile back at the front, Brusilov was waiting for General Evert to make his move.

Evert then instead of making his own offensive and diverting the aid to the northern front sent his troops to aid Brusilov not realising that that would seal Brusilov's fate and doom the offensive to failure.

This lack of faith and incompetence led to the failure of the Brusilov Offensive. Disloyalty and disunity was its downfall and instead of achieving a great victory it gave the Germans time to bolster the Eastern Front without too much disruption to their troops on the Western Front at Verdun.

Brusilov had managed to advance 25,000 square kilometres into the Austro Hungarian lines and by September he had reached the Carpathian Mountains. About 1.5 million troops were killed in the offensive and he demolished the Austrian 4th and 7th armies in the process. He had to stop the offensive then to go to the aid of the Romanians who had entered the war as promised by Tsar Nicholas, though not until 27th August and were in danger of being defeated by the Germans.

The Brusilov Offensive failed to divert sufficient troops from the Western Front to assist the French at Verdun and the Somme but their effort at least prompted the end of the Austro Hungarian Empire, so something was achieved.

Chapter 17
Winter 1916 – Lloyd George, Sydney Reilly and the Secret Intelligence Service

Bruce had one more fight in 1916, an easy victory over a little known opponent named Vladimir Jerkov.

Irena was on the mend and had begun to exercise and practise her ballet but it soon became obvious that she was never going to return to the nimble elegant ballerina she had been until her injury. She could still perform but the magic was no longer there.

Tomas' dream of Jerzy and Irena dancing in the Mariinsky Ballet was diminishing.

Rasputin, however, was optimistic and told Tomas to be patient saying, "These types of injuries take a long, long time to heal. Irena will dance beautifully again but in her own time. Bruce is close to a title fight but with winter coming, and I think it will be a severe winter again, I don't think there will be much happening before the New Year; though I fear because of the war and the failure of our offensive to deliver the outcome we hoped for that there will be a lot of hardship and discord before things get better. At least we won't have to worry about Koba."

Tomas was dismayed but realistically they were in a good place. Their quarters in Tsarkoye Selo were warm and cosy and they were not hungry.

Rasputin suggested that Minsky, Dinsky and Tinsky could do with a little attention and maybe he could create a ballet for the whole troupe even the wolf cub could be included. "I'm sure with you training him he's bound to be a howling success," he said.

Rasputin had made a joke.

"And if it is good enough I will see if the Mariinsky Theatre will let you show it there," he said.

"Would you?" said Tomas, "You are the best friend anyone could ever have," and he gave Rasputin a big hug.

Rasputin pushed him off and said, "That's it, I'm never ever going to make another joke," and he walked off in a huff.

So Tomas put his mind to writing a ballet for animals.

Rasputin was right, the winter was hard and it brought with it rising costs and food shortages. The people were disillusioned with the war and many soldiers deserted.

The Germans were well aware of what was going on in St Petersburg having many spies in the city and amongst the communist faction that was growing in popularity. In fact their leader, Vladimir Ilyich Ulyanov (He changed his name to Lenin when in exile in Siberia and later became the 1st leader of the U.S.S.R.) was in exile in Germany waiting for a time to return and lead a revolution against the Tsar. He dreamt of leading a workers' revolt and forming a communist state in Russia. His brother had attempted to execute Tsar Nicholas's father, Alexander, and had been executed for it. He had been exiled in Siberia for 3 years before moving to Western Europe and Germany to continue the struggle whilst in exile. The Germans knew that a revolutionary movement in Russia would undermine the power of the Tsar and any resulting conflict would weaken Russia and maybe see the disposal of Tsar Nicholas.

The Germans would support him and saw him as a way of Russia getting out of the war, so they assisted his emissaries in Russia such as Koba and their spies helped the Marxist Bolsheviks fuel discontent.

Many in St Petersburg thought that Tsarina Alexandra was a German spy as she was a German Royal. This was a story spread by the Marxists and enemies of the Tsarina and Rasputin. They included the ministers and Royals who were demoted and had fallen from grace and their views were widely accepted by the Bourgeoisie (the Russian middle classes and academics) who were not informed of matters of state despite the presence of the Duma (the Russian assembly council formed in 1905 following the 1st Russian Revolution). There were many amongst these bourgeoisies who favoured a revolution and the end of the Romanov Dynasty.

Some even held Marxist views of communism but were much more moderate and were known as Mensheviks. They were not as radical as Lenin's supporters and were in the minority of the Russian Marxist movement as their title suggests. (Menshevik means minority.)

The Tsar's popularity amongst the ruling elite was waning because he had not taken the advice of his ministers and had sacked some of his advisors and generals to take command of the war himself. He had left Alexandra in charge because he did not trust his ministers. This made them angry and even more jealous of the power Rasputin was now seen to be exerting, and so they began plotting to undermine Rasputin and take back control from the Tsarina.

The Romanov Tsar was in danger not only of revolt from the Communists but from treachery from his own family and ministers as well as from the German War Machine.

The fact was Rasputin did not exercise power over the Tsarina. He was a help to Prince Alexei and would make observations to the Tsar and Tsarina from a peasant's and religious perspective and it was the power of suggestion he exercised. He was brought up in a religious background and was of peasant stock so he believed he spoke for the people when speaking to the Royal family. The Tsar and Tsarina were quite capable of making their own decisions.

The Tsarina was not pro Kaiser Wilhem, as was thought by the other members of the royal family and ministers who were jealous of her power and influence of Rasputin. Wilhem was a Prussian and a Protestant. She was a Hessian and a Catholic. Hessians had been linked with the British for years and there were many Hessians fighting for the British in the American Civil War. Prussia and Hesse were opposing German states and there was great rivalry between the two so it was unlikely that Alexandra would betray her husband and Russia to aid Germany and even more incredulous to believe Rasputin would.

Alexandra like Nicholas, however, did not share the same views of her advisors and would make her own mind up about policies much to the annoyance of her ministers.

As the winter got worse and Brusilov's offensive floundered, which was down to the treachery of his fellow generals, many deserters flooded back into St Petersburg. There was a great

116

shortage of food and provisions and inflation rocketed and there was widespread discontent. Koba and his Bolshevik brethren used the discontent to stir up as much disruption and civil unrest as they could.

Discontent became unrest and before long the people were ready to riot and Koba was ready to lead the rioting workers.

In Germany the unrest was being encouraged and the German authorities were watching and preparing to allow Lenin to return to Russia to stir further trouble.

It was now December 1916 and in Britain there was a change of leadership. Asquith stepped down and David Lloyd George, a Welsh Liberal, took his place as prime minister. He had been the secretary of state for war and was well aware of the precarious state of the political and social unrest in Russia. He also knew that Lenin was waiting in the wings in Germany and suspected that he would be a German puppet if they sent him back to Russia.

Lloyd George already had spies in St Petersburg as did Germany and France but he wanted someone he could trust to go to St Petersburg and make contact with Rasputin who his spies had told him was the real power in Russia. He decided he would send a delegation of envoys to speak to the Russian government to assess the war effort and a special spy to liaise with Rasputin. His spies also stated that there was rumour of a plot against Rasputin and he wanted to be prepared for any crisis that might impact on Britain's war effort.

Britain had had a spy in St Petersburg for some time; he had been recruited by the Secret Intelligence Bureau before it became known as MI6. His name was Sidney George Reilly who was born Sigmund Rosenblum, near Odessa Russia, of Jewish origin. He had been recruited by a British agent whilst living in Brazil and took the English name Sidney Reilly.

When the war started, there was widespread belief that the Germans had a well-established network of spies throughout Europe as well as in Britain so to match and beat the German threat Britain reorganised its Secret Service and created two separate branches MI5 for internal British Intelligence and at that time was used for the threat of the emergence of the Irish Republicans who were backed by the Germans, and MI6 which dealt with foreign intelligence.

Reilly was like Rasputin, a notorious womaniser, and moved in similar circles as Rasputin but was not a confidante of Rasputin. He had contacts and sources not only in the Russian Government but also amongst the Communists and Koba's circle of friends and amongst the German community of spies so he was thought of as a super spy and had the nickname of Reilly Ace of Spies.

It is thought that he was a great help in identifying many German spies in Britain at the start of World War One, in fact 22 German spies were arrested and 11 were executed which just goes to show that Germany had been planning for war for some time before the war had started.

He had gone to watch the Koba v Bruce fight and sent a report back to London which was of great interest to the Secret Intelligence Service and MI6 Chief Commander Mansfield Smith Cummings who had risen through the ranks of the Royal Navy and may have been the inspiration of Ian Fleming's James Bond.

Mansfield Smith Cummings reported straight to David Lloyd George who was very interested in Rasputin.

He told Lloyd George about Rasputin's apparent interest in boxing and they set about finding a spy with an interest in boxing that could act as his envoy in St Petersburg.

Chapter 18
Johnny Basham (The Happy Warrior)

At this time there were a number of Welsh world class boxers who were able bodied and in the British army.

Lloyd George decided that one would be sent to Russia on a secret mission to meet Rasputin whilst a diplomatic delegation would meet the Russian government.

First there was Freddie Welch (Hall) from Pontypridd who was the world lightweight champion but he was based in America.

Then there was Peerless Jim Driscoll from Cardiff. He was another world champion who had enlisted but was used as a fitness instructor and fought exhibition bouts for the troops.

Lloyd George thought that his role was far too important to use him.

Then there was Jimmy Wilde from Merthyr Vale who became the official World Flyweight champion and was hailed in America as the greatest Flyweight boxer the world had ever seen. He was nicknamed the Mighty Atom, The Ghost with the Hammer in His Hand, and The Tylorstown Terror.

He would have been the ideal candidate but he had a nasty cold which could have been man flu which was upsetting his training regime.

The other contender was Johnny Basham, the Happy Warrior, from Newport, a British and European middleweight champion who was in the Royal Welch Fusiliers and based in Wrexham.

Basham had something in common with Bruce. He too had been involved in a bout where his opponent had died following injury sustained from his blows. In August 1913, he fought Harry Price, a tough South African in Liverpool, and knocked Price clean out. Price never recovered and died later. Basham had been arrested for Grievous Bodily Harm and this was amended. Friends paid for his bail and he attended Price's funeral. At the subsequent inquest it was ruled that Price's cause of death was misadventure and Basham was cleared.

The deciding factor was that Wilde was scheduled to fight a world championship bout that month so it was decided that Johnny Basham would be sent to St Petersburg with the diplomatic delegation.

So it was that Johnny Basham was the most suited and available for such a secret mission.

Basham was summoned to London and told to report straight to the Home Office where he was met and secretly briefed by Lloyd George himself.

Lloyd George said to Johnny, "I imagine you are wondering what has brought you to my attention and brings you to London away from your duties?"

"Yes I certainly am," he replied.

"Well Johnny," said Lloyd George, "I need a boxer for a very special mission in Russia. I hear that they call you the Happy Warrior so I am sure that you will enjoy a trip to St Petersburg even though you'll only see it in winter."

Lloyd George went on to tell him about the importance of the mission and briefed Johnny in secret.

Johnny did not have the chance to tell Lloyd George his nick name was the Happy Warrior and not the Happy Warrior .

I cannot tell you what his briefing was as it was top secret. It was so top secret that there is probably no record of it anywhere, not even amongst the official War Records.

He was going to Russia as part of the delegation and his presence was explained as being part of the security team for the delegation.

He was then summoned to the War Office where he was also briefed by Mansfield Smith Cummings, chief of MI6, the Secret Intelligence Service, and told he would be acting as a spy so not to divulge to anyone the reason for him going to Russia.

"Sorry about telling the P.M. that you are the Happy Warrior old boy," he told Johnny, "but he thought it was a good omen when you were thought of for the mission and I didn't want to upset him."

Smith Cummings briefed him on his role and what he had to do in St Petersburg.

Whilst there he was to liaise with Sidney Reilly who would arrange for him to meet up with a man named Rasputin.

He was issued with a revolver and told that he would be leaving for Russia the next day.

Johnny went back to his lodgings to get some sleep; however, he was so excited that he didn't sleep a wink that night.

Chapter 19
The Ace of Spies and the Plot to Assassinate Rasputin

The delegation set off for St Petersburg the next day by ship. It was a perilous voyage due not only to the weather but also from the threat of the German U-boats which the Germans had a large fleet of.

As we know they were mainly used against merchant shipping carrying supplies and materials from America and the Commonwealth to Britain and France or to Russia but we also know they had also sunk the Lusitania so the crew and passengers were very anxious.

Up to January 1917, German U-boats had sunk over 1.4 million tonnes of merchant shipping as well as many Allied warships and a number of passenger ships, so any voyage was perilous. Luckily for Johnny Basham and the British delegation, the voyage was rough but uneventful and they arrived earlier than expected in St Petersburg on 24th December 1916.

Reilly was at the dock waiting for their arrival having kept watch and receiving updates of their progress through his contacts at the company he had at the docks.

Now, if you remember from earlier, the Russian calendar was different to the calendar in Britain there being some 13-day difference between the Julian and Gregorian calendars. In December 1916, we used the Gregorian calendar and Russia used the Julian calendar so although it was 24th December British time it was 11th December Russian time.

Reilly watched the delegation disembark and identified himself to Johnny. He told Johnny to accompany the delegation to the British Embassy and he would arrange a rendezvous outside the embassy to brief him about Rasputin whom he would organise a meeting with.

Johnny nodded and said, "Mate, but at the moment I'm bloody freezing. They told me it was going to be cold but this is bloody ridiculous."

"You get used to it," said Reilly. "You should go to Siberia then you'll feel the cold, this is just cool," he laughed and said, "Wrap up warm. It will be colder still tonight. Be ready for 7 pm." And then he left Johnny to join his party.

When they arrived at the embassy he was glad to find that the staff there had a stock of winter clothes suitable for Russian winters in all sizes. The previous ambassador had been caught out by the severity of the Russian winter and made sure that all staff and visitors were kitted out and equipped to face the weather.

Reilly sent a taxi to the embassy to collect Johnny and he was taken to a bar in down town St Petersburg where Reilly was waiting. As he was ferried through the city he was appalled by the poverty and desolation away from the finer part of the city and mentioned it to Reilly.

Reilly said, "That's what war does, Johnny."

He ushered Johnny in and took him to a secluded table at the back of the bar where he ordered a bottle of vodka and two glasses. "Have you ever drunk vodka, Johnny?" he asked.

"No," said Johnny, "but I like a drop of whisky whenever I can."

"Well there's not a lot of taste to vodka but it packs hell of a punch," he said.

The vodka was delivered to the table and Reilly began to brief Johnny about Rasputin's rise to power and his preoccupation with womanising and drinking.

Reilly said, "In those respects he's a lot like me but I am no holy man and knowing this man's history and healing powers I think he may have a connection either to God or the Devil which is why he has grown so powerful. He certainly is well connected with the ladies of the court and St Petersburg."

He told Johnny about his involvement with a Tomas Tomaschevsky and his Animal Dance Troupe and their boxing clown Kanga Bruce who was the ugliest clown he had ever seen and was believed to be mute. He told him about Bruce's fight

123

with Koba and how the Tsar's family were championing him. He then went onto the intelligence he had gathered about a plot to kill Rasputin by members of the Romanov family.

He stated that it had come to his attention from a very reliable source that the plotters included a prince related to Tsar Nicholas by marriage with the backing of other Royal family members, including a grand duke, a doctor, a member of the Duma and an army officer. The Prince was Prince Felix Yusupov who had married Tsar Nicholas's niece Irina who was a very beautiful woman. However, Felix was a very promiscuous young man who had a penchant for transvestism and homosexuality which was and still is frowned upon in Russia. The marriage had been a sham, one of convenience, for Felix and Irina did not find out until it was too late. She no longer lived with Felix but stayed at the family retreat in the Crimea to hide her shame.

To say Felix was a bit of a pariah in the Tsar's family was an understatement. Felix, however, had a long standing 'friendship' with Grand Duke Dmitry Pavlovich who was the Tsar's cousin and had been engaged to the Tsar's eldest daughter, Olga, until Rasputin warned him about his relationship with Felix. The Tsar had told him to end his 'friendship' with Felix but it continued and the engagement was broken off.

Then there was Vladimir Purishkevich who had denounced Rasputin as a bad influence on the Tsar and an enemy of Russia. The soldier was a Lieutenant Sukotin, a convalescing young officer under Dr Lazavert who was one of the doctors who were ridiculed by Rasputin; the plan was believed to be that he would poison Rasputin.

Reilly said the plotters were in an advanced state of preparation but he was still waiting for information about the exact plan though he hoped to be in possession of the full details in the next few days.

Johnny said, "Why don't you inform the Russian authorities about the plot?"

"Because there are some in the Secret Service who want Rasputin out of the way and I do not know who, or if anyone is still trustworthy and loyal to the Tsarina amongst the ministry or guard," he replied. "And Rasputin and I are not exactly on speaking terms that is why it is important for you to meet him and warn him about the plot and to be careful," he added.

"This is what I know so far, Rasputin has been referred to Felix by a close friend complaining of chest pains which he states his doctors cannot cure. Of course this has interested Rasputin who always likes to prove that he can heal people who the doctors claim are incurable. Felix has ingratiated himself on Rasputin and befriended him, though I can't see Rasputin being interested in a transvestite like Felix though who knows with Rasputin. Felix does throw some rather exotic parties with some very beautiful girls present. I know I have attended some."

He went onto say, "I believe that whatever they are planning will play on Rasputin's penchant for beautiful women and will be played out at one of Felix's basement parties. Now it is time to finish this fine bottle and for you to return to the embassy."

They finished the bottle and Johnny felt very tipsy; he had drunk more than he was used to and he found vodka had quite a kick. Reilly had a taxi waiting for him and when Johnny got in he told him to keep this information to himself and he would contact him soon to meet Rasputin hopefully at a social event he was organising and that Rasputin would be invited too.

Johnny left in the taxi and returned to the embassy, his head pounding. *What have you gotten yourself in to Johnny Bach?* (That's Welsh for boy) he said to himself.

He arrived back at the embassy and when asked where he had been, simply said, "A Welsh lad like me doesn't get much chance to see the sights of the world. I thought I'd take the opportunity to tour the city at night and try some of that vodka drink you were all talking about on the boat. Well it's not all it's cracked up to be but I've sampled enough of it to know that the best place for me now is bed, so goodnight and I will be ready for duty bright and early tomorrow morning."

He went straight to bed and passed out. The next morning Johnny was up bright and early as he had said and readied himself for his diplomatic duties.

The diplomats were scheduled to meet their counterparts at the Ministry of War to discuss the outcome of the year's war effort, the effect that the change of British government would have on relations between the two countries and what could be done by either side for their mutual benefit.

Johnny was not privy to these discussions but waited outside the closed doors along with his Russian counterparts who looked like man mountains compared to him as he was short, lean but muscular. They did not speak to each other due to the language barrier but did share the refreshments provided.

The Russians kept looking at him and sniggering whispering, "English," and making gestures about his stature.

"I'm not English," he snarled under his breath, "I'm Welsh." Johnny sized up the two Russian guards and thought to himself a good clean uppercut to their stiff chins should sort them out, but God help me if they got me in a clinch.

The meeting seemed to drag on for ages but as soon as the big clock in the hall rang for 4 o'clock the doors flew open and the diplomats emerged from the room clutching their briefcases and hurried out to their waiting diplomatic cars. They hurried back to the embassy where a letter was waiting for Johnny from Reilly.

It was a message telling him that he would meet him again that evening in the same place at the same time with further information. Johnny went back to his room and changed. He had a light meal in his room and then a shower and shave.

He was not needed that evening as the diplomats had to prepare for the next round of meetings the next day. Johnny was waiting by the embassy gates this time for the taxi and this time he was wrapped up warm from head to foot.

Another bottle of vodka was waiting for him on the table and Reilly poured him a glass whilst he took off his hat, overcoat and gloves. "I see you got kitted out Johnny, hope you got your long johns on under there to keep your tackle warm," he grinned.

They then got down to business. Reilly told him that Rasputin was now getting bored with Prince Felix but Felix had promised to introduce him to his wife Irina when she returned home from the Crimea and that was probably the only reason that Rasputin had bothered with him in the first place.

"Rasputin is a lady's man like me, I didn't think that Felix would hold any fascination for him; however, Irina is a very beautiful and elegant woman wasted on a fairy like him. She lives in the Crimea because she feels betrayed and shamed and of course she can't divorce him and is stuck in a loveless marriage. I feel sorry for her," he said

"That's despicable," said Johnny.

"Yes but you'd be amazed how common it is in High Society," said Reilly.

Anyway he went onto explain that Felix was trying to coax Irina into returning to St Petersburg to meet Rasputin. At the moment she is refusing but it looks likely that Felix will try to get Rasputin alone by offering Irina to him and then kill him in private and dispose of his body without anyone knowing what happened to him.

"The only thing is Johnny old boy, I will know and if you can forewarn Rasputin, maybe we can prevent it," he finished.

Johnny had listened to the story wide eyed. He swallowed mouthfuls of vodka as Reilly told him the details.

Although he didn't know Rasputin he started to feel for him and said so but Reilly told him not to be as Rasputin felt no guilt at having other peoples wives and used that well-known phrase 'people who live by the sword die by the sword'. Johnny didn't know what that meant but nodded his head and drank another glass of vodka.

Reilly told him that the British diplomatic party were invited to a ball in the Winter Palace in two days' time and that he had arranged for him to attend. He said he would be there but Johnny was not to act as if he hadn't met him before. Rasputin would be there and he would be introduced to him as a champion boxer and then it was up to him to warn him of the plot against him.

By the time he had finished they had drunk two bottles of vodka and Johnny was getting a taste for it. *At least it made you feel warm inside just the thing for a cold winter's night but I'd better not make a habit of it or it will be the end of my boxing career* he thought.

They said their goodnights and Johnny returned to the Embassy feeling a little better than the previous night.

The next day was filled with another meeting and Johnny took the time outside the meeting room to read a Russian phrase book he had been given by a clerk at the embassy. He engaged the Russian guards in conversation and found that they too were bored and wanted to learn English so between them they looked through the pages of the phrase book and began to speak to each other in broken Russian and English.

By 4pm they all knew 'hello', 'goodbye', 'how are you' and a number of other useful phrases and pronunciations.

The Russians were a great help to Johnny as they explained the Russian alphabet, word and sentence construction to him. He would have been completely flummoxed without them.

Johnny continued to read the phrase book after his dinner at the embassy and asked the clerk who was a fluent Russian speaker to help him. By the end of the night he felt he could hold a limited conversation a little like learning from a foreign language compact disc course.

He knew phrases like: 'My name is Johnny Basham what do they call you?', 'I would like a bottle of vodka please', 'I am the European Light Weight Boxing Champion', 'Who is the clown?' and most importantly, 'I am not English I'm Welsh'.

He also learnt 'the doctor is going to poison you' and 'Beware of Prince Felix' in Russian which he wrote down on a piece of paper and put in the inside pocket of his jacket.

The next morning was the last of the meetings and Johnny took the chance of speaking to the Russian guards and they were not as dour as he first thought.

He gave them an exhibition of shadowboxing which they enjoyed and they in turn helped him with his language lessons.

By the end of the meeting which was 1 pm, he could say 'hello' and introduce himself in Russian and pronounce the phrases he hoped would warn Rasputin about the plot to assassinate him.

They returned to the British Embassy and Johnny readied himself for the trip to the Winter Palace and the function, where he would be introduced to Rasputin.

He was a little anxious as he would be in the company of Royalty, as it was rumoured that the Tsarina and her family would be attending the function as well.

I'd best mind my Ps and Qs and be on my best behaviour, he thought to himself as he prepared. Who'd have thought a poor boy from Newport would be dining in the presence of Royalty.

Chapter 20
The Ballet at the Winter Palace

When they arrived at the Winter Palace Jonny was gobsmacked at the size and beauty of the most elegant building he had ever seen. *I bet even Buckingham Palace is not as grand as this*, he thought. (Johnny had seen Buckingham Palace when he had been summoned to Whitehall.)

He was even more in awe when he saw the splendour inside such as the great halls and antiquities. The statues and the chandeliers were immense. He had never seen so much wealth displayed in one place before.

The rumours were right, Tsarina Alexandra did attend the function and so did her children along with Rasputin and Tomas. In fact Alexandra had arranged for a very special treat for her children and the diplomats, a very, very special performance of the Nutcracker Suite by the Tomas Tomaschevski Animal Dance Troupe.

The evening started with a fabulous banquet followed by drinks and a chance for meeting and talking whilst the main ballroom was prepared for the ballet.

Reilly caught hold of Johnny and introduced him to Rasputin who had been looking forward to meeting the European boxing champion. "I have been told they call you the Happy Warrior Johnny, did you think that boxing would bring you all the way to Russia and a visit to the Winter Palace when you were just a boy?" he asked Johnny.

Reilly acted as interpreter.

"No way," said Johnny, it's like I'm living in a dream,"

"Believe it Johnny," said Rasputin, "who'd have believed a peasant boy like me would be a confidant of the Tsar. Live the dream. I am."

Johnny was just about to warn Rasputin of the plot to kill him when they were all summoned to the main ballroom for a special treat.

Tsarina Alexandra addressed the guests herself and told them of her pride in being given the opportunity to meet and care for the amazing Tomas Tomaschevski and his wonderful animal troupe, who she and her family had grown to love.

She told them the story of saving Babushka's farm and everyone applauded. She finished by asking them to be seated and enjoy The Tomas Tomaschevski Animal Dance Troupe's version of Tchaikovsky's Nutcracker Suite.

They took their seats and Johnny sat next to Rasputin in the second row behind the Royal family.

"You'll like this ballet Johnny, Jerzy and Irena are fantastic dancers and Bruce the Boxing Clown makes a menacing Mouse King," said Rasputin.

They were then beguiled by the most bizarre yet amazing performance of the Nutcracker ever seen. Everyone cheered and applauded Jerzy and Irena and when Alexei and Anastasia booed Bruce, they all joined in.

For Johnny who had never been to a ballet before, it was just like a pantomime. When Minsky came out as the Sugar Plum Fairy, they all laughed and cheered and marvelled at the land of sweets where Tinsky and Dinsky added a bit of mischief which was hilarious.

The ballet was a complete success and everyone gave it a standing ovation at the end.

Jerzy and Irena may not have performed at the Mariinsky but they had performed a Royal Performance at the Winter Palace which was a great feat in itself.

Whilst Rasputin was waiting to introduce Johnny to Bruce, Johnny told him of the plot to kill him. Rasputin said he thought as much but the chance to meet Princess Irina was one he would not refuse.

He said, "People have tried to kill me many times, all have failed. No poison can kill me and Felix hasn't the balls to try. If he has accomplices, I will take care but I will die when God says not these plotters."

He then stunned Johnny and Reilly by saying, "If my time is up and I fear it may soon be, the Royal family will be in danger and I foresee that the writing is on the wall for me and the Romanovs. I want you two to take care of Tomas and Princess Anastasia and his troupe. Get them to England and safety. Oh and make sure Bruce has a shot at a world title fight. He deserves a break, for I am sure that if he stays in Russia Koba will be wanting his revenge on him."

They both promised Rasputin who then introduced them to Tomas and Bruce.

Johnny told them how much he enjoyed the ballet and how he thought the people of Wales would love it too as he was Welsh not English.

Tomas was in awe of Johnny's accent and asked him what Wales was like.

Johnny being a proud Welshman gave such a marvellous and eloquent account of the hills and valleys of Wales he made himself homesick, which left Tomas longing to see it for himself.

Johnny and Bruce had a sparring session and Johnny was amazed at how good Bruce was. "He should come over to Wales for a proper fight and I am sure he will get a title fight before long," he said.

The night flew by and soon it was back to the embassy for Johnny.

He had enjoyed meeting and talking to Rasputin and Tomas, sparring with Bruce had been a joy and he would remember the Winter Palace and the ballet for the rest of his life.

He had the strange feeling, however, that all would not go well for Rasputin and that events in Russia would, as Rasputin had foreseen, not favour the Tsar and Tsarina.

The following day Johnny and the delegation were given time for sightseeing before they set sail for home.

Johnny marvelled at the beauty of St Petersburg but could not fail to see that things there were in a very precarious state.

Johnny returned home and that year he became the first British welter weight boxer to win a Lonsdale belt outright having defended his British championship title three times.

Chapter 21
The Death of Rasputin

It was now 16th December in St Petersburg and although it was extremely cold Rasputin took his daughters Matryona (Maria) and Vavara (Barbara), Alexei and the princesses, Tomas and the animals to the circus where they met Vladimir Durov who was a great clown and animal trainer.

Durov was probably the greatest circus performer in all of Russia and possibly the world at that time. The only one Vladimir had considered as a rival was his brother Anatoly who had died earlier that year of typhus.

Vladimir showed them some of the tricks and stunts he had taught the animals to perform. He too had a wolf like Alexei and Tomas and they all marvelled at the performance.

Bruce was impressed by Vladimir's clown antics which were part of the act and tried to mimic them.

Vladimir saw Bruce and said to him, "My clown is unique to me if you use it, it will not be your act but a copy of mine, please create your own act."

Rasputin had told Vladimir about how Tomas had trained his animals to dance and he was interested to see them for himself. He was amazed at how elegantly and gracefully they performed and wanted Tomas and the animals to join his circus.

Tomas was impressed but wanted to be in charge of his own troupe.

He thanked Vladimir but declined his offer.

Vladimir said to Tomas, "I did not think there was anyone in the world who could train animals as well as me but I think you are a match for me and will look forward to seeing you perform soon."

They all left the circus having had a wonderful day and Anastasia did not leave Tomas' side throughout the day.

Before delivering the Royal children back to the Palace Rasputin took Tomas aside and in a hushed voice said, "Tomas I have seen how you and the Princess Anastasia have formed an attachment and if I am not mistaken I think she is in love with you."

Tomas blushed for he knew he was in love with her.

"But I am just a poor boy whose story is yet to unfold, I will not be allowed to love a princess," he replied.

"But you will Tomas, this I have foreseen. My star is falling and Koba's is rising. You must take care, Tomas, for I see only disaster for the Romanovs and I will be unable to prevent it. Your future is linked with Anastasia's and her future with you."

He left Tomas puzzled and a little afraid.

He said his farewells to the Royal children and took his daughters home.

Matryona, who had inherited her father's way with animals, had enjoyed it so much that she later became a circus performer herself and performed in the Hagenbeck Wallace Circus in America as an animal trainer.

Awaiting Rasputin there was a note from Yusupov that his wife Irina was back from the Crimea and longing to meet him.

The note said that first she had to meet family and friends but would see him after they had left.

He was to stay in and not tell anyone of the meeting and would be collected after midnight, when the guards, who had been ordered by the Tsar to protect him and keep him away from trouble, had ended their vigil. He would then be taken to Moika Palace where the meeting would take place.

Rasputin was ecstatic and began to sing and dance which mystified his daughters and they pestered him to tell them why he was so happy.

When he told them they realised what was going to happen and they begged their father not to go, but Rasputin would have none of it, he could not get the beautiful image of Irina out of his head.

He washed himself, combed his long dark hair and even used a little fragrance, something he never did and dressed in his best clothes.

He then waited rather impatiently to be collected.

It was well after midnight when Rasputin was collected and secretly transported to Yusupov's palace.

It was all done in secret as Yusupov and his co-conspirators did not want to be found out.

When they arrived he was led to the basement where he was told to wait as Irina's guests were still upstairs and not ready to leave. He was given a plate of pastries and a bottle of wine, all of which was laced with poison and told to help himself.

Yusopov left him on his own and went up to join the party which was a sham as Irina would have no part in the plot and had remained in the Crimea.

The only people upstairs were his co-conspirators.

Yusopov kept coming down to see if the poison had taken effect but was surprised to see that Rasputin was showing no sign of being poisoned. He took care to always have a fresh glass of wine with him to give the impression that he was part of the party upstairs.

Rasputin, however, having drunk one bottle of poisoned wine was well into a second bottle.

He was getting irritable and demanding to see Irina and threatened that he would go upstairs himself.

Yusupov calmed him down and told him he would go up and send everyone home and bring Irina down with him.

Upstairs he told the others who were amazed that Rasputin was still alive. He got a revolver, loaded it and went down back to the basement to shoot Rasputin if the poison had not worked.

Rasputin, though a little unsteady, was still alive so Yusupov shot him in the chest at point blank range. Rasputin fell to the floor clutching his chest and Yusupov was certain that he had killed him.

He went upstairs to tell the others so that they could dispose of the body but when they got to the basement they were shocked to see that Rasputin was alive and making his way to the back door to get away through the courtyard.

Yusupov panicked and shot Rasputin another again, first in the back and then in the back of the head.

This time Rasputin had to be dead.

They wrapped and tied him up in an old carpet and his body was taken to the Malaya Nevka River (River Neva) and thrown into an ice hole from a bridge.

The conspirators thought that he would never be seen again and they had successfully killed Rasputin without any chance of being caught.

They were wrong however. A police officer had heard the commotion outside the Moika Palace and had spoken to the conspirators that night.

Also, Rasputin was still alive when they threw him in the frozen river and he had managed to claw his way out of his bonds and had tried to make it back to the bank of the river, but even he with his incredible strength and resolve could not escape the ice and he died in the river not of poisoning or from his wounds but from drowning.

His body was found three days later and the police officer who had heard the commotion and confronted the royal conspirators told his superiors what he had witnessed so they were exposed.

Tsar Nicholas and his family were mortified; they felt as if one of their family had been assassinated and instead of making them more reliant on their cousins and other royal advisors, it had the opposite effect, making them even more insular.

He demanded that the assassins be caught and punished.

Tomas remembered what Rasputin had foretold and worried about the safety of the Tsar, Alexei and his precious Anastasia.

The death of Rasputin was welcomed by the vast majority of the Russian aristocracy and was a fillip for those opposed to the Tsar's Divine Right of power and of the war, such as the Socialist Revolutionary Party and to each of its factions, the Bolsheviks like Koba, the Mensheviks and the other socialists like Kerensky who was in the Duma and they used it as a chance to stir up the workers against the Tsar.

Koba was extremely happy and thought, *Rasputin gone now, all I need is the death of that clown Bruce and people will forget about my defeat by a clown.*

In Britain, the news worried Lloyd George who sent a message to Reilly telling him to keep him informed of the repercussions, especially as rumours were being circulated that British spies were involved.

He called Johnny and the delegation back but not before Johnny saw Tomas again and promised to do all he could to get them to Wales if the Bolsheviks seized power.

In Germany the news was welcomed. They were glad Rasputin had been assassinated and thought the time was right for Lenin to be allowed to return to Russia to help start a revolution to depose Tsar Nicholas and pull Russia out of the war.

Everything was going well for Kaiser Bill.

The conspirators were rounded up but never tried for the murder of Rasputin.

The mood of the courtiers, other royalty, politicians and workers were so anti Rasputin that although Alexandra, Alexei and the princesses called for a trial, Nicholas bowed to the pressure and no trial was held.

Not all Russians were glad to hear of Rasputin's death, the peasantry who loved Rasputin and all the people Rasputin had treated were angry but because they had no political organisation like the Bolshevik workers they could not vent their anger with the same clout.

Rasputin's funeral was a private affair with just the Tsar and his family, Rasputin's family and friends including Tomas and the animals attending.

It was a very tearful funeral and Alexandra placed an icon on his chest as a token of her family's love.

The Tsar's power was on the wane and the path to revolution was now gaining momentum and the popularity of the two opposition parties the Bolsheviks and the Mensheviks was growing.

Chapter 22
Room 40 and the Zimmerman Telegram

It was now January 1917 and the Germans were rueing agreeing to the Sussex Pledge to restrict the use of their U-boats. The Kaiser and his High Command believed that Britain was faring as badly as Russia and Germany through food shortages and if they resumed unrestricted submarine warfare they would quickly starve Britain into submission and end the war.

The breaking of the Sussex Pledge was discussed as were contingency measures.

Germans are in general meticulous planners and they did not embark on any strategy without having examined all possibilities.

They realised that if they were to break the Sussex Pledge it would provoke the United States whose President Woodrow Wilson had insisted on the implementation of the Sussex Pledge.

Wilson was the 28th President, a Democrat and was the leader of the Progressive Movement in America.

He had been elected in 1912 and was responsible for a number of liberal reforms and Acts such as the Underwood Act which lowered trade tariffs and a graduated income tax, the Federal Reserve Act which provided the U.S. with a more elastic money supply and established the Federal Trade Commission to prohibit unfair business practices. He also promised to keep the U.S. out of the war.

He was re-elected in 1916 having kept the U.S, neutral and pledging to remain so.

Don't you wish a Woodrow Wilson was your president?

The Germans decided that it would break the Sussex Pledge in the hope that it would favour them and shorten the war.

They hoped that they could break Britain before the U.S. elected to enter the war on the side of Britain but in the event of being unable to break Britain they came up with a contingency plan enlisting the aid of Mexico and Japan.

Before breaking the Sussex Pledge, Arthur Zimmerman, the German Foreign Minister composed a telegram to the Mexican President elect, the revolutionary Venustiano Carranza offering him financial aid and backing to declare war on the U.S. and the return of the land taken from them during the American Mexican War if they were victorious.

At this time Carranza, however, was still occupied in Mexican affairs dealing, with his Revolutionary counterparts, Emiliano Zapparta and Francisco Villa, who were also vying for power. (Francisco Villa was also known as Pancho Villa.)

In January 1917, Zimmerman sent the telegram via Western Union to the German Ambassador in Mexico to relay to Carranza.

He had to send it through the American Embassy in Copenhagen. (Remember at the start of the war Britain had destroyed Germany's overseas wireless stations and the U.S. had afforded them the use of their wireless station in Copenhagen.)

The telegram was encrypted in a series of numbers and when decrypted, it read as follows:

"We intend to begin on the first of February unrestricted submarine warfare. We shall endeavour in spite of this to keep the United States neutral. In the event of this not succeeding we make Mexico a proposal of alliance on the following basis. Make war together make peace together, generous financial support and an understanding on our part that Mexico is to reconquer the lost territory in Texas, New Mexico and Arizona. The settlement in detail is left to you. You will inform the President of the above most secretly as soon as the outbreak of war with the United States of America and add the suggestion that he should on his own initiative invite Japan to immediate adherence and at the same time mediate between Japan and ourselves. Please call the President's attention to the fact that the ruthless employment of our submarines now offers the prospect of compelling England in a few months to make peace," Signed Zimmerman.

A bold plan indeed but little did Zimmerman know that not only had Britain's Intelligence Service cracked the German codes, it had been monitoring all the transmissions from the U.S. Embassy in Copenhagen and had even cracked the American codes.

Britain was the field leader in monitoring correspondence and encryption and its intelligence analysts were the best in the world.

They were based at room 40 at the British Admiralty and were the forerunner of Bletchley Hall during World War Two.

Britain had started monitoring German messages at the start of the war with the help of the General Post Office and the Marconi Company.

It had already received many captured German code books and by 1917 had extensive knowledge of the German codes and had even cracked the American codes apart from the Red Indian language messages which they were unable to crack.

The interception of the Zimmerman telegram was the coup de grace, a propaganda windfall, but it left the Intelligence Service with a dilemma.

How to inform the Americans that they had intercepted the German telegram without letting them know that they had been monitoring all the transmissions from their Danish Embassy.

It was, however, a pleasant dilemma for Lloyd George and Commander Smith Cummings who knew the propaganda value the telegram would give them.

On 1st February, Germany broke the Sussex Pledge and their U-boats began to indiscriminately sink ships heading for Britain.

On 24th February, the British authorities handed Walter Hines Page the U.S. Ambassador to Britain a decoded copy of the Zimmerman Telegram which they stated had been leaked to them.

The telegram was analysed by the Americans and authenticated and on 26th February was handed to Woodrow Wilson who was mortified and ordered all American shipping to arm against U-boat attacks.

On 1st March, the telegram was published in the American press and many Americans believed it to be a forgery.

Two days later Zimmerman himself was forced to admit it was genuine and accepted responsibility for its leak.

The game was up.

Wilson who had done his best to keep the U.S. out of the war and had been re-elected on his policy of neutrality went to Congress and advocated that they now had no alternative but to declare war on Germany.

Congress agreed and the United States declared war on Germany on 2nd April 1917.

Chapter 23
1917: The February Uprising and Revolution

Before America entered the war, anti-war fervour had spread throughout Russia like wildfire. Following the death of Rasputin the mood of the people in St Petersburg and the rest of Russia, already dire because of the severe winter, the famine and food shortages it caused, worsened.

The Tsar had printed extra cash to pay for the war but that had caused mega inflation which meant that while wages stayed the same, prices soared. Food needed in the cities was being forwarded to the Front for the soldiers and what food did get to St Petersburg was too expensive for the people.

The Bolsheviks and the Mensheviks stirred up anti-Tsarist opinion amongst the workers and the peasants who were hungry were ready to revolt.

In the Duma both upper and lower assemblies were highly critical of the Tsar and his rule.

The Duma was full of those ready to revolt if they were not granted further powers and food, which was being stockpiled, was not released for public consumption.

It was not a happy Christmas for the Tsar and Tsarina or for Tomas and his troupe. They had lost a friend and it seemed that the world was against them. Nicholas' grandfather Alexander 2nd had been assassinated by activists and he worried about the future. He thought that if he could rally his troops they would stay loyal to him and so he rejoined the army leaders at the front leaving Alexandra in charge of domestic matters.

January 1917 was so harsh that conditions in St Petersburg and the rest of Russia were almost unbearable and the reformists in the city knew that time was right for change.

The Socialist Revolutionary Party stirred up trouble amongst the workers, the army and navy.

Their propaganda was distributed in posters and pamphlets like the Pravda newspaper which took the form of periodicals and leaflets before it became the main newspaper of Russia. (Pravda means truth in Russian and was first published in 1912. It was used by the Bolsheviks to spread their Marxist philosophy, it was Lenin's mouthpiece and he had contributed articles even whilst in exile. Trotsky, who was still a Menshevik and also in exile, had been a contributor as well. Pravda had been set up by the Bolsheviks but was now being funded by the Germans to destabilise Russia. It was a follow on from Lenin's first Socialist paper called Iskra meaning the Spark as Lenin said, from a spark comes a fire.)

The troubles brought Tomas and Anastasia even closer together to the dismay of Alexandra who frowned on their relationship, but Anastasia was a very wilful and stubborn child who did very much what she wanted.

With the collapse of the Brusilov offensive and the harshness of another bleak Russian winter, thousands of Russian soldiers were deserting and many headed for St Petersburg where the Bolsheviks and Koba were gaining popularity.

By 31st January 1917, it was reckoned that there was not enough flour left for making bread and despite the freezing weather there were massive queues of women in the streets queuing for the bread that was left. Meat was in even shorter supply.

There was almost a complete economic breakdown in the Russian economy and the system of rationing used was not adequate to satisfy the people and rioting and looting became widespread.

The people, however, were still patriotic and the rioters were protesting about the lack of food, wages and conditions not against the war.

Representatives from the Duma petitioned Tsar Nicholas to give the Duma more powers to avoid further rioting but the Tsar ignored their advice.

In February, Alexander Kerensky the Trudovik in the Duma called for change of government; he was still a Socialist and ready to rejoin the Socialist Revolutionary Party which he had left when he entered the Duma.

Alexandra branded him a traitor and wrote to Nicholas to have him executed for treason.

Lloyd George having been kept abreast of the events in Russia by his ambassador Sir George William Buchanan and reports from his spies feared that a Russian revolution was a distinct possibility.

He sent Sir George to advise Tsar Nicholas of his concerns. Sir George pleaded with the Tsar to grant the Russian people some of the liberties that were granted in Britain but Nicholas dismissed this advice as well.

Koba took great advantage of the civil unrest to organise his Bolsheviks to strike and hold demonstrations to rally the workers and the people of St Petersburg (which the communist Bolsheviks called the Proletariat) to their revolutionary ideas which were gaining popularity, especially amongst the students who were very active in the uprising.

Lenin was anxious to make his way to Russia and canvassed the German government to give him their blessing and funding of the Germans who saw him as their best hope of defeating Russia by causing widespread disaffection and civil disobedience in Russia.

Tsar Nicholas had been in St Petersburg and had refused to heed calls to release stockpiled rations to the public and had dismissed the demonstrations and rioting as the acts of thugs.

He left St Petersburg to return to the front to rally his disgruntled troops ignoring the mounting pressure in the city.

He relied on his support from the army and his Imperial Guard and the Cossacks, the Church, the Nobility and the peasantry whom his father Alexander had given freedom during the reform of serfdom in 1861.

He did not count on the strength of the opposition amongst the new middle and industrial classes, the workers and the poor, nor did he foresee the extent of the desertions from the military that were fed up with the war and did not believe in its cause.

The start of the revolution is seen as the strike at the Putilov engineering factory when workers went out on strike for a 50% pay rise to pay for food. They were refused and locked out of the factory.

A call for solidarity was made by both the Bolsheviks and the Mensheviks to other workers and a widespread strike was called. The Trudoviks supported the call.

Many of the strikers were women who were wives of the deserting soldiers and coincided with International Women's Day.

The Duma was in support of the workers and saw it to their advantage to press for further reforms along the lines of the British Parliament where they had the power to create legislature. The Trudoviks, Liberals and Right Wing in the Duma did not want to see the end of the Romanov's only reform.

The Bolsheviks and Mensheviks, however, did and plotted the Tsar's downfall. They joined with rioters rioting for bread and St Petersburg fell into chaos.

Alexandra wrote to Nicholas that the reports of rioting were exaggerated and all would be sorted; however, she was naive and the trouble was far greater than she envisaged.

On 26th February (Russian time), Rodzianko, the chairman of the Duma, wrote to Nicholas telling him he must return to restore order due to the turmoil and the Tsar ordered General Khabalov to send the city's garrison of troops and the police to secure the city from the rioters; however, many deserted and joined the rioters on the streets leaving the city in complete disarray.

The Bolshevik agitators persuaded the troops to rebel against their officers and by the end of 27th February the rebellion had succeeded.

The Tsar returned by train ordering the army to intervene but by then the army was stricken by desertion and they revolted too. When he arrived at St Petersburg, he was met by a delegation from the Duma, which had taken over the power, representatives from the army and the workers.

He was asked to abdicate and hand the thrown to Alexei. He refused stating Alexei was too weak to be Tsar and he was stripped of power.

The Tsar and his family were placed under house arrest at Tsarkoe Selo. It was a quick coup with very little bloodshed and was to see the end of the Romanov's rule in Russia.

Chapter 24
A Provisional Government and the July Days

A Provisional Government, under Prince Georgy Lvov as its prime minister, was created and Alexander Kerensky, a Socialist, would become minister of state.

As its title suggests it was not intended to be a permanent government but to rule only until an elected government could be formed.

The Provisional Government was made up of many different political outlooks. There were Socialist Revolutionary Party members such as Kerensky, Popular Socialists, Progressivists, who were mainly well-educated moderates who supported the war but wanted social changes to help the people and they were instrumental in forming a ministry of confidence within the government. They had a large group in the Duma and were Liberals.

Then there were the Kadets who were Constitutional Democrats again Liberal in outlook.

Then the Octobrists who supported a limited constitutional government with a monarchy as outlined by Tsar Nicholas and were conservative by nature, and then there were members with no political affiliation.

The Mensheviks joined a little later, and don't forget the Bolsheviks.

There were many different factions vying for power in Russia all with different agendas.

At the same time a Petrograd Soviet was recreated (a soviet is a workers council though it consisted of political activists more than workers) with a Menshevik majority and leader they hoped that it would form part of a dual government and instigate policy.

Kerensky became a member and was elected a vice chairman, so the Soviet could influence the government from outside.

Now in government the Provisional Government abolished the death sentence, outlawed religious and ethnic discrimination and gave freedom to the Press. Kerensky had the high ground and the popularity, so the only part of the Petrograd Soviet with any real power were the Trudoviks.

The Mensheviks who formed the greater part of the Soviet had little say in government neither did the Bolsheviks. It was a government comprising of the Nobility, Rich, Liberals and moderate Socialists, a dual government with the Nobility and Rich, though being in the minority, still holding the power.

They were known as the Bourgeoisie and were very middle class and conventional.

Trotsky, another revolutionary who like Lenin had been in exile, also decided to return. He was not in Europe though, he was in Canada.

Now this revolution had centred around St Petersburg and was not representative of opinion throughout Russia which was a vast country with a population of over 125m people, so the revolt in St Petersburg was seen as a coup by the Tsar and he hoped that there was sufficient support in the country to restore him to power.

The Mensheviks and the Bolsheviks squabbled for power in the Soviet behind the Trudoviks but nothing much changed outside of St Petersburg. There was no love between them and the prospect of them working together in cooperation was unlikely.

Kerensky was in the best position; as minister of state, he had the support of the majority of the people who looked to him to improve their conditions and make food available. Kerensky knew that this would not be easy with Russia still in the war and believed that further revolution was unavoidable unless he could grant universal suffrage and call for an elected government.

Prince Lvov was not sympathetic so Kerensky tried to hold the middle ground between the Right Wing nobility, the army officers and the Left Wing Bolsheviks and Mensheviks. It was a difficult task and he feared both sides.

The Duma supported Russia's role in the war and Kerensky was made minister of war in May. He supported the war as he believed that if Russia pulled out of the war it would stop France and Britain from sending them supplies and make Russia even poorer.

He appointed General Brusilov as commander in chief of the Russian army and ordered another offensive against the Germans and Austrians.

Kerensky was a great orator and told the troops as he visited the front, "There is no Russian Front. There is only one united Allied front." So Russia remained in the war and the food shortages continued.

The soldiers were not entirely convinced and the soldiers committees, which had been set up by the Bolsheviks, were against further conflict but they listened to Kerensky who spoke like one of them. However, there were Bolsheviks spying for the Germans amongst them.

In Tsarskoe Selo the mood of the Romanovs was bleak though not without hope. Nicholas knew that the provisional government did not control the whole country. He knew that they did not want to completely disestablish the monarchy and hoped that a swelling of popular support for him would make them see sense and return him to power.

He also knew, however, that the history of Europe had seen many changes of monarchy with Charles I being executed in England and Louis XVI and the royal family during the French Revolution, but in both countries the monarchies were restored. France, however, abolished the monarchy altogether in 1870 having restored it several times following the revolution of 1792 and created a republic.

Spain had seen the monarchy overthrown in 1873 then restored in 1874 but Portugal and China's monarchies ended in 1910 and 1912.

Therefore, Nicholas' optimism was tempered with doubts. Despite these doubts he did his best not to be too despondent for the sake of his family and did all he could to keep their spirits up.

The Tsar, Tsarina and the children were watched at all times and were not allowed to leave the grounds of Alexander Palace. They could, however, visit Tomas and the animals in their lodgings in the grounds at Tsarskoe Selo and would do so whenever the opportunity arose.

Anastasia, who was the most mischievous of the children and the smallest, managed to visit more than the others. She was able to disguise herself as a servant girl; there was one girl almost identical to her with whom she would swap roles; her name was Greta. Many of the guards believed she really was Greta and would flirt with her making it easy for her to move anywhere in the palace or grounds, without being watched any time she wanted, which was almost all the time.

Nicholas watched and encouraged her to do so thinking that if the worse came to the worst she may have a chance of escaping harm and Tomas might be her best resort.

Tomas and Bruce were not considered to be a danger to the Provisional Government and were allowed to leave the grounds whenever they wished, but were checked in and out. They liked to visit the circuses and the zoo to see and talk to the animals.

Anastasia often went with them disguised as Greta and Tomas would say that she was his girlfriend.

The animals just like the humans sensed that changes were coming and that they would bring great harm to Russia. Animals seem to have a better awareness of danger than most humans. The animals did not like what was happening in Russia and had great reservations about the future.

Tomas told Anastasia about Rasputin's foreboding and they both worried about the Tsar's and their family's future.

Lenin, with the help of the Germans, had arrived in St Petersburg on 3rd April and had taken control of the Bolsheviks. At this time there were no Bolsheviks in the Petrograd Soviet, which was run by the Mensheviks. It was the Menshoviks who at that time were the leading workers' party in Russia, and their leader Nikolay Chkheidze was chairman.

Kerensky, however, was deputy chairman and as such in a very strong position.

There was great rivalry between Lenin and Kerensky. Lenin, as a Bolshevik, was a Communist Marxist and believed in one party rule. He was opposed to Kerensky who was a Democratic Socialist.

Lenin's agenda was to seize power for himself and take Russia out of the war. He had the funding and help of Germany at his disposal.

Lenin, on his return, thanked Koba for his efforts but knew more was needed to stir up the masses and further the Marxist cause. He began making public appearances and speeches to the masses using the slogan 'Peace, Land and Bread', which was exactly what the public wanted.

Trotsky also returned to St Petersburg in mid-May and joined the Mensheviks but he too wanted further revolution and an end to the war. He later left the Mensheviks and allied himself with Lenin and the Bolsheviks.

There followed in July a period of unrest where the people rose up against the Provisional Government led at first by dissident soldiers and then joined by the Bolsheviks. At this time Lenin was not advocating an armed insurrection believing that the time was not right. He was ignored, however, and the streets of St Petersburg witnessed violent clashes again.

This uprising was dealt with severely by the army under General Kornilov who was controlled by the Kerensky and the Provisional Government. Lenin, who was seen as the leaders of the revolt, fled to Finland. Other activists like Trotsky were imprisoned and the Bolshevik press was outlawed.

This period is known as the July Days.

Following the July Days, Llov resigned and Kerensky became head of the Provisional Government. Lvov had been reluctant to take reform any further and had been reluctant to move against the Petrograd Soviet believing that its importance would fizzle out.

Kerensky's promotion was welcomed by Sir George Buchanan, the British ambassador, who saw him as the man to unite the Russian people and stabilise Russia.

This was also the view of the British government but not Lloyd George who preferred to have Nicholas restored to power.

Kerensky stripped Brusilov of his post after the failure of the Kerensky Offensive, which was not Brusilov's fault but due to the Germans having being informed of the Offensive on the City of Lemberg (Lvov) and were waiting for the attack. The Russian planning had been compromised.

Kerensky subsequently promoted General Lvar Kornilov to commander in chief. He did not wish to stop the war but wanted to continue with renewed vigour and defeat the Germans. Kerensky's offensive had started well but like all previous Russian offensives petered out when the Germans attacked. Kerensky's popularity with the workers and soldiers began to wane with it.

Kornilov was an imperial general and very right wing. He wanted to restore the death penalty for desertion something Kerensky was reluctant to do. He also had a vision for restoring Russia to its former glory by taking power for himself.

Kornilov did restore the death penalty for desertion when the Russian soldiers ran from the advancing Germans. They deserted from Kornilov's army which made him abandon Riga and retreat to the Dvina River with the Germans in hot pursuit.

It took a while for Kerensky to realise he had made a mistake in appointing Kornilov and realise that Kornilov might revolt against him and the Mensheviks.

Kerensky began to feel his position was tenuous. His opponents were on both sides and posed a threat to his government. The far left, the Bolsheviks were weakened after the July Days but populous opinion was with their propaganda. The far right were bolstered by Kornilov's control of the army and industrialists and upper classes were beginning to rally to his cause. The Tsar was still in St Petersburg and a counter coup by his followers could not be dismissed either.

He was also under pressure from the allies to keep Russia in the war which was hugely unpopular with the people.

Kerensky had to react positively to secure his position. He pondered whether to move the Tsar and hold free elections to create a government on the lines of the British government.

By the end of July, he had decided to remove Tsar Nicholas and his family from Tsarskoe Selo. He had seen off the Bolshevik revolt but knew Kornilov was critical of Kerensky's Government and wanted the Tsar away from St Petersburg if there was to be a another revolt this time in favour of the Tsar.

Chapter 25
Exile: The Great Deception and a Farewell Party

On 21st July, Tsar Nicholas was informed by Kerensky that he and his family were to be moved from Alexander Palace in Tsarskoe Selo for their own safety. He was not told where he was going to be sent.

Nicholas knew in his heart that he and his family would be safer away from St Petersburg and hoped that if he was away from the seat of revolutionary fervour he might be able to gain support in the country.

Unfortunately for the royal family, support had dwindled and there was no clamour for the return to Tsarist Russia.

Nicholas spoke to Alexandra in private and said, "Alexandra, my dearest love, we are to be moved from Tsarskoe Selo for our own safety. I think we may be going to the Crimea. I do not know what our future holds after that. You surely must have seen, like I have, the growing relationship between our beloved Anastasia and Tomas which I believe is more than mere friendship. It may grieve you to hear this but I believe her future will be safer with Tomas than it is with us and it is with a heavy heart that I will order her to remain at Tsarskoe Selo with Tomas when we leave. She has successfully convinced the guards that she is a servant girl and Greta, your hand maiden, is almost identical to her in stature, age and looks. In fact Anastasia has played tricks on me before and fooled me into believing that she was Greta and if she can fool me, I am sure we can fool the guards into believing that Greta is Anastasia.

Alexandra replied, "I am not blind, Nicholas, I too have seen the way Anastasia looks at Tomas and how he tries not to show his feelings before us. I know that you are right and if our fate is sealed she will be safer with him than with us. If, however, we do survive and our rule restored I am sure Tomas will return Anastasia to us safe and sound."

Nicholas nodded and gave her a big bear hug and said, "I will send for Tomas and you fetch Anastasia, Alexei and the girls. We must brief them all and make sure that there is a plan for them to escape not only Tsarskoe Selo but Russia too, if needs be. For this to work, all the staff must also be briefed and remain loyal through thick and thin."

"There is not one disloyal member amongst our court Nicholas, but no one outside our household must know of this Dear," said Alexandra.

Nicholas replied, "For this to work there is one other person who must know, someone I trust implicitly, Captain Valeri Koshenko of my valiant Cossacks. His help and cooperation will be vital."

Captain Koshenko was summoned and promptly attended. That night and the next week, the Romanov family, staff, Tomas and Koshenko spent planning for the deception and Anastasia's escape from Russia. If all else failed, at least Anastasia would be safe.

Koshenko was given access to the funds and authority to arrange Anastasia's escape if or when the time came. He was given sufficient funds to hire a ship and pay for passage to Britain. Money to bribe officials to turn a blind eye and for any contingencies that may crop up during the escape. He and his men were also to be well paid.

At that time Lloyd George wanted to send a British warship to St Petersburg to rescue the Tsar and his family and bring them to safety in Britain which would save them from having to resort to the deception. King George however, on the advice of his wife, the Queen, refused to help, fearing that if the Russian Royal family were brought to Britain it might spark revolution in Britain. The Queen also reminded him that his presence in Britain would mean further heirs to the British throne.

The plan was scuppered by Royal Command.

Lloyd George was dismayed when King George vetoed his plan to rescue the Tsar and his family and sent the British Ambassador to inform the Tsar personally of the King's refusal to help.

He did, however, send a secret note which the Ambassador was to give to the Tsar unopened which informed Nicholas that Lloyd George wished him the best and offered any other help he could covertly provide.

The Tsar was very thankful that he still had a friend and gave the Ambassador another note which was to be given to Lloyd George personally and also unopened.

Tsar Nicholas sent a secret message to Lloyd George asking him to arrange for the escape of Anastasia from Russia if their position got worse. He trusted Lloyd George who had wanted to help him, but swore him to secrecy and not to inform King George whom he no longer trusted.

Lloyd George agreed to help when the time came and he arranged with Sir Mansfield Smith Cumming to be ready to send Tommy Basham back to St Petersburg to effect the escape if required. He also notified Reilly to prepare for an evacuation at short notice if events warranted it.

By the end of the week the switch was finalised, Anastasia became Greta the maid and Greta became Princess Anastasia.

Tomas and Anastasia were now officially boyfriend and girlfriend with the blessing of the Tsar and Tsarina. They were both extremely happy.

It was not hard for Greta as she and Anastasia had in fact been playing each other for years without their parents knowing and could exchange roles whenever Anastasia wanted.

Captain Koshenko was updated and he set about establishing lines of communication between himself, Anastasia and Reilly.

On 31st July, Tsar Nicholas was informed by Kerensky that they were to be moved the following day and to get his family and household ready for the move. He was allowed to take his servants, physicians and some household staff with him for his exile. Nicholas thanked him and said, "I have staff in the Crimea; it will be nice to stay there in the sunshine," but he was interrupted by Kerensky who countered, "I suggest you take some warm clothes with you. I hear that the weather is not as hot where you are going."

Nicholas was taken aback by this and finally lost his composure.

He glared at Kerensky who carried on saying that there had been strong calls for Nicholas and his family to be jailed at the notorious St Peter and St Paul Fortress on Zayachy Island in the Neva River in St Petersburg. (The Fortress was constructed on Peter the Great's orders to defend the land from the Swedes as he had the city of St Petersburg built on the banks of the Neva and made it the capitol of Russia in 1712 due to its strategic position on the coast and he stationed his navy there at the Kronstadton Kotlin Island at the head of the Gulf of Finland. Peter garrisoned part of the city's troops on Zayacy Island and turned part of the fortress into a high security prison to house political insurgents and traitors. He had his only son Alexei imprisoned there for treason, for which he was found guilty, and executed. It is said he did shed a tear at his son's funeral; what else could a father do? Other famous people imprisoned there were the writers Dostoyevsky and Maxim Gorky as well as Leon Trotsky and Lenin's brother, Alexander.)

Nicholas glared at Kerensky but Kerensky said, "Your safety is at the heart of this decision, rumour has been circulating that you were to be moved and the Crimea was thought the obvious choice. The Bolsheviks are planning to imprison and assassinate you. I do not want that on my conscience so at the last moment I decided to send you to Tobolsk where your safety can be assured but if you let it slip I cannot vouch for your safety."

Tsar Nicholas resigned himself to exile and with a heavy heart thanked Kerensky for his kind regard and told him that if their positions were reversed he would think of him and reciprocate in the same way.

Nicholas bade Kerensky farewell and went to tell his family the unexpected twist.

When Alexandra heard she tried to put on a brave face, knowing that their life may never be the same again but still trying to cling onto the hope that one day they would be saved and restored to the throne.

Alexandra said, "We shall hold a party in the grounds for family, staff and friends. Perhaps Tomas and his troupe can entertain us one last time and we can give Anastasia and Tomas our blessing and farewell.

"That is an excellent idea, my dear," said Nicholas, "and I will give them something to remember us as a keepsake, something which will establish Anastasia's identity if she ever has need of it."

"Oh Nicholas darling, I do hope everything will turn out alright but right now things do not look good for us," she said.

Nicholas said nothing but gave her a long loving hug which spoke volumes in itself.

That night Tomas and his troupe held the saddest yet most poignant concert they had or were ever to perform.

They all knew that they may never see each other again and that their plan could be discovered and their dreams dashed.

Nicholas invited the whole household staff and even the guards to attend a farewell banquet in the grounds of Alexander Palace and had his kitchen staff prepare a leaving meal for all using whatever provisions they still had.

Captain Koshenko also came.

To start the evening off Tomas got out his accordion, Dinsky his drum and trumpet and they played while Jerzy and Irena danced excerpts from the Nutcracker Suite and Irena danced the dance of the Sugar Plum Fairy, which everyone applauded.

They then stopped for the banquet and everyone reminisced about the times they had spent at Tsarskoe Selo and how much they would miss it.

The Banquet was enjoyed by all and after everyone had eaten Tomas and Dinsky played a number of folk dance tunes on their instruments to the merriment of not only the Royal family and the staff but of the guards as well.

They started off with formal dances like waltzes, a polka and a polonez, which are lively Polish dances that Tomas played with such great gusto and enthusiasm that it encouraged all to forget the solemnity of the evening and dance with great abandon.

The Tsar and Tsarina danced together and Alexei danced with Greta. Captain Koshenko danced with Tatiana, Olga and Maria in turn. They also danced with the Captain of the Guard and each other.

Anastasia sat by Tomas while he played but got up to dance with Captain Koshenko when he came over to her, bowed and asked her for the next dance. He winked at Tomas and whispered, "I have a plan when the time comes, we will have to see what happens in the next month or so but I will tell Anastasia while we dance and she can tell you later."

Tomas played a waltz for them and the Captain told Anastasia that he had a loyal band of Cossacks ready to execute his plan if necessary. He told her that they would wait to see if Kerensky could hold onto power and hold elections as he had promised. Then, if he won, would he restore the Romanovs in a government on the lines of the British government which would guarantee the safety of the Royal family. If he lost and the Bolsheviks, who were slowly gaining popularity, won, they would have the Tsar and the family executed. They would have to move quickly if they won. He went onto tell her with a heavy heart that he had heard rumours that Lenin and Trotsky were planning something in secret which led him to believe that they were planning a coup but he could not confirm that. He assured her that he would be ready whatever scenario occurred and that he would make sure that she and Tomas would be taken care of.

The dance ended and he bowed again to her, she curtsied back and went back to Tomas.

Tomas and Dinsky carried on playing a number of Polish and Russian folk dances.

They did a Mazurka and an Oberek followed by a Chechen dance and the Barynya which all present joined in enthusiastically. It did, however, leave some gasping for breath as they are all lively dances.

The Tsar walked over to Tomas and Anastasia and told them he had an announcement to make before the end of the night and as it was getting late, he would make it now.

Tomas called everyone to order and said, "Will you all remain standing. Your Tsar has an announcement to make."

Tsar Nicholas spoke with a heavy heart.

He thanked Tomas for such a wonderful evening and wished him well for the future. He even gave Tomas a big bear hug, which is something Russians do, but not Tsars' so it was a great honour for Tomas. He then thanked all his staff for their loyalty and dedication which was greatly appreciated and to all those present he bade them farewell from him and his family telling them that the Royal family and only certain members of their staff were to accompany them to their exile.

Everyone was sad and apart from the guards raised their voices to shout in unison, "God save the Tsar, God save young Tsarevich Alexei, God save Tsarina Alexandra, and God save the Grand Duchesses Olga, Tatiana, Maria and Anastasia."

Tsar Nicholas thanked them and said, "We must all sleep now for tomorrow brings us all new challenges. I must now leave you and God bless you all."

The family said their farewells too, each one paying special attention to Tomas and Anastasia."

Nicholas spoke to Tomas and said, "Tomas, you take good care of my precious Anastasia and look after her. This you will swear to me on your mother's life and I will know you will be true to your word."

"I will be true for she is now my life and I love her deeply," replied Tomas.

"You must be careful in Britain not to reveal her identity for I am sure that the Bolsheviks will come for her if our fate is sealed and it is revealed that she has escaped," he said.

Tomas replied, "I will take great care to keep our identities secret in fact Johnny has already renamed us for our lives in Wales but he has told me he will reveal those names to me only when we arrive in Wales."

Nicholas hugged Tomas and whispered in his ear, "I hope Wales is good for you and my princess. I have given Koschenko funds to help you which should be available to you in Wales to enable you and Anastasia to fit in. Let us hope Johnny has a cover story which protects your identities and God willing all will be settled and you can return to Russia when this coup is over and life will return to normality."

They both doubted that that would be the case.

Alexandra took Anastasia aside and wept, "I shall miss you my little angel," she sighed, "but Nicholas and I have hidden a few little items for you and Tomas to remember us by. They are in your secret hiding place safe and sound until you collect them."

Anastasia looked puzzled, "My secret hiding place?"

"Little one did you think you could keep secrets from your mother. I have known about it since you were a little devotchka." (Pronounced dey-voosh-ka which means girl.)

Anastasia said her farewells to her brother and sisters and they all parted company with heavy hearts.

Many cried that night including Anastasia who stayed with Tomas and the animals that night.

It was to be the last night she would ever see her family.

Chapter 26
The Tsar Leaves for Tobolsk and the Secret Gifts

Early in the morning the Tsar and his family were roused from their slumber, not that they had slept much. They were all worried about what the day held in store for them.

Tsar Nicholas rallied his family and told them that Kerensky had promised him that they were safe and no harm would come to them. He told them that he believed him.

The Royal staff that had been chosen to accompany them were assembled and with a troop of Russian soldiers they were escorted to the Imperial Train which was ready to take them to their exile in Tobolsk a long, long way from the Crimean.

Tobolsk is known to Russians as the outpost on the edge of nowhere and used to be the capitol of Siberia. The climate there is very different to the climate in the Crimea, which is on the Black Sea and is a holiday destination for many Russians. It obviously is in the opposite direction from St Petersburg.

Kerensky wished for the Tsar's real destination to be a secret and that is why they were packed off early in the morning. It is hard to hide the route of the Imperial Train from anyone not just the Bolsheviks.

Kerensky had assembled a troop of loyal soldiers to escort and guard the Romanovs on the journey which would take them several days through Russia and over the Urals (a Russian mountain range) into Siberia.

Tobolsk is 2550.5 kilometres from St Petersburg. The trip is long but very beautiful as Russia is a vast country full of diverse scenery and it is one well worth taking if you get the chance.

Together with the Romanovs and their domestic staff were Nicholas' advisors and medical staff for Alexei and the family minus Anastasia.

They all boarded the Royal train expecting to be taken to the Crimea but their hopes were dashed when they realised they were going in the wrong direction.

Tomas and Anastasia could only look on as her family were taken into exile. She tried to keep a straight face but could not help bursting into tears at the thought that this would be the last sight of her father, mother, brother and sisters. Tomas did his best to console her but he too had misgivings and had the same feeling.

He said to Anastasia, "Anna my love, we must forget the past. I fear it will never be the same, a new life awaits us in Britain and we must ready ourselves to escape.

Tomas and Anastasia were soon brought back to reality as Anastasia was put back to work as a maid.

Later she and Tomas went to her old hiding place where she found her mother had stashed a few mementos for her to remember them by. There were photographs of the family assembled together formally and informally. A Faberge egg with a small trinket inside and one of her mother's jewels which Anastasia had always liked since she was a little girl and her mother promised to leave her.

There was a note with the mementos in which her mother hoped that they would see each other again but if it were not to be then she wished Anastasia and Tomas a safe, happy and long life together with lots of children.

Both Anastasia and Tomas broke down and spent the night in deep sorrow but both determined to get away and start a new life together.

News of the Tsar's departure from Tsarskoe Selo filtered down to the ears of Lenin's spies and although their destination was meant to be a secret a Royal train is hard to disguise and its route and eventual destination could not be kept secret for long.

Soon everyone knew that the Tsar was no longer in St Petersburg and the intrigue continued.

Capt. Koshenko and Reilly continued to meet secretly and a plan for the escape was taking form whilst Lenin and his Bolshevik conspirators formulated theirs.

Chapter 27
The Struggle for Power

The next plot to seize power in Russia came as Kerensky had envisaged from Kornilov. Kornilov led his troops to St Petersburg but the people of St Petersburg rallied to save the city and the Provisional Government. Kerensky released the subversives like Trotsky and the Bolsheviks under Trotsky were in the forefront of defending the city. The city's own military and citizens beseeched Kornilov's soldiers to defect and many did, rendering his revolt hopeless.

Kornilov was stripped of his position and imprisoned with his fellow officers who had supported him. This was to have further consequences for Kerensky as it reduced the number of good military officers in the army.

Lenin had called for all power to be taken by the Soviets and on 31st August, the Bolsheviks now under Trotsky took the majority in the Petrograd Soviet from the Mensheviks.

This was the spur for Lenin to return and seek absolute power.

There was still an uneasy truce between the Bolsheviks and the Mensheviks but the Bolsheviks were striving for absolute power.

Trotsky was wary of Koba and disliked him intensely. He saw him as an uncouth thug but Stalin was very loyal to Lenin and Lenin told him, 'There are no morals in politics, there is only experience. A scoundrel may be of use to us just because he is a scoundrel.' This is one of Lenin's most famous quotes along with 'One man with a gun can control a hundred without one' and 'When a lie is told often enough it becomes the truth.'

This tells you a lot about not only Russian politics and politicians but all politicians.

What Lenin didn't say and what no politician, king or dictator has ever said is 'People with power can enjoy great riches while poor people can enjoy their poverty.' I think someone else said that.

Tsar Nicholas from his exile in Tobolsk saw that things were swinging in the favour of the Socialists and the power of the Right wing nobility was waning. However, he had been informed by his few loyal friends that the United States had entered the war on their side and that managed to keep his hopes of salvation alive.

Kerensky's coalition government of upper, middle classes and worker's representatives had done nothing to end the war, nothing to allay the peoples hunger for freedom; the economy was still dire and of course bread was still in short supply, even for the rich but he too was buoyed by the news of the United States entering the war and thought that now things were bound to improve.

The United States, however, had been at peace and was not prepared as a nation for war and it would take time for them to make their presence felt the war.

Kerensky had Trotsky, whom he saw as his major threat, arrested and imprisoned but not Lenin, who was widely believed to be an anarchist quack and too radical to be taken seriously.

A grave mistake.

Lloyd George was not totally convinced that Kerensky's government was best for Britain but it was definitely better than a Bolshevik government under the German-funded Lenin.

Lenin's call for freedom, peace, land and bread however was becoming so popular, not only with the workers but with most parts of the St Petersburg population and echoed throughout Russian cities and towns making it the rallying cry of the Revolutionaries.

To combat this call Kerensky proclaimed Russia a republic and promised Universal Suffrage with democratic elections in January 1918.

He hoped this would pacify the public and if he could provide more provisions and a more approachable government, his position would be safe.

The Mensheviks who were also in a strong position welcomed the call for democratic elections and Trotsky was released from prison in September 1917 having only been held for just over a month.

It seemed that further revolution was now not inevitable, however, that October was to see what has become to be known as the Bolshevik Revolution. Free elections were not satisfactory for the Bolsheviks who despite being the most radical faction were not as popular as the Trudoviks and Mensheviks.

They feared that they would not gain much representation in a democratically elected government.

They advocated a one-party state with the Bolsheviks in power.

Trotsky too did not relish the prospect of democratic elections and left the Mensheviks to join Lenin and the Bolsheviks, a move which bolstered the prospects of the Bolsheviks. Together they formed a Military Revolutionary Committee and set about planning an armed uprising to take power before the elections could be held.

Chapter 28
Somerset Maugham and the Plan to Escape

Reilly was still active and working outside his remit with the British Secret Service. His spies told him that the mood in the city within the workers and returning deserters was ripe for revolution. They told him that Lenin was organising and planning a coup to take power from the Provisional Government under Kerensky which was likely to occur in October. He stated that they were being funded and supported by a network of German spies that were active in St Petersburg.

Reilly informed MI6 and Commander Mansfield Smith Cumming, to whom he was contracted, and he reported the information to Lloyd George.

They both knew that if the German-backed Bolsheviks seized power from Kerensky's Provisional Government, it would result in Russia leaving the war and seriously strengthen Germany's position on the Western Front.

They had to prevent that happening and needed a secret agent who could infiltrate the German network and report back to them. Despite having a whole network of spies and informants in St Petersburg, they chose the famous writer Somerset Maugham, who volunteered to go to Russia to help. He was briefed to go to St Petersburg to help the Provisional Government fend off the rising threat of the Bolsheviks. Maugham was fluent in English, French and Germany, having been born in the British Embassy in Paris. He had spent time in Germany too and was fluent in French and German.

Though he spoke very little Russian, he was a quick learner. Maugham was first recruited by The Secret Intelligence Service in 1914 and had spied for Britain in Geneva where he posed as a French playwright whilst spying on the Germans and sending secret messages back to the British, which were encoded in his manuscripts.

He was a gentleman spy and would not accept payment, believing it to be his civic duty. After leaving Geneva, he went to America after finishing his first book, *Of Human Bondage*, which was published in 1915.

Maugham was in America when he was called on again by the Intelligence Service. This time he was to go to Russia following Reilly's report of the rise of the Bolsheviks.

Maugham took the challenge even though he could not speak fluent Russian.

He used the alias Somerville, an American writer who was a neutral but with German sympathies. He would use this to infiltrate the emerging German spy network in St Petersburg and make contact with the Bolsheviks.

He was also to liaise with Kerensky and the Mensheviks and assist them to oppose the Bolsheviks with whatever intelligence he could gather.

He was to keep MI6 informed about the Bolsheviks, who Lloyd George did not want to gain power in Russia.

Johnny Basham was summoned by Sir Mansfield Cumming Smith and ordered to return to St Petersburg, confer with Maugham and be his liaison with Reilly.

When Johnny arrived in St Petersburg he was briefed by Reilly who brought him up to date with the Tsar's exile and Tomas' predicament. He also outlined how the Bolsheviks rhetoric and plans were progressing. Reilly told him that in his opinion the only thing preventing a Bolshevik coup was Lenin's procrastination and that was all that was keeping Kerensky in power.

Johnny was so alarmed by what he was told that he sent a message to Tomas telling him that it was time for him to leave St Petersburg, as further revolution was on the cards and a Bolshevik victory would spell the end of the Tsar and any hope of salvation.

He told him that the Bolsheviks were saying that to prevent any popular counter revolution that it would be expedient to eliminate the Tsar and his family so that there would be no monarchy to restore to power following the coup.

They would also eliminate any friends of the Tsar as well.

He reminded Tomas that Koba (Stalin) was a high ranking Bolshevik and it was common knowledge that he still longed to revenge his humiliation by Bruce. Tomas, however, needed no reminding and knew the danger he faced.

Johnny told Tomas that when he was ready to leave, Reilly would arrange a boat to take him to Wales as they had discussed.

Tomas would have been happy to leave right then but he had others to think of. He would not leave without Anastasia or Bruce, Jerzy and Irena or any of the other animals he loved. And he had plans if he was going to Wales it would be as a showman and he would take with him the greatest animals spectacular Wales had ever seen even if it would take a great risk he was willing to take it. He told Johnny.

Johnny tried to dissuade him stating that in the current situation it would be impossible but Tomas said, "Nothing is impossible Johnny, not if you put your mind to it."

Johnny said, "I think that would be!"

Tomas replied, "I will talk to my animal friends. I'm not leaving without them, and let you know but I want to take my girlfriend with me; can we smuggle her out as well?"

Johnny said, "If you can get her out of Tsarskoe Selo as well then she will be welcome but all the animals that I cannot guarantee." Tomas did not tell him that by his girlfriend he meant Princess Anastasia.

Meanwhile Kerensky knew that Lenin and the Bolsheviks were hatching a plot and tried to stifle their plans by prohibiting the production of the Bolsheviks Pravda newspaper and ordering further arrests.

Lenin though still doubting the time was right for a further revolution, used this to his advantage telling the public that the Provisional Government was not only still oppressing them but was trying to suppress the truth and keep them in the dark about what was happening in Russia and the war. He was winning the propaganda battle and the public and soldiers were joining the Bolsheviks in droves.

Tomas dreamed of going to Wales and to Oakdale with a troupe large enough to form his own Animal Dance Circus and decided he would need more animals to fulfil his plan. His future was no longer in Russia and the dream of performing at the Mariinsky Ballet was no longer viable.

Now when he visited the circus and the zoo he did so with the intention of recruiting other animals to his troupe.

Tomas recruited two elephants who had been nick named Mr and Mrs Truperov. They had adopted two baby hippopotamus, or is that hippopotamae or hippopotamuses? Who thought they were baby elephants. They were called Hippotomas and Hippolena.

Two lions, named Leon and Leona. Leona was pregnant.

Four zebra (he wanted horses but they had all been taken by the army). One male named Zefra and three females named Zeeba, Zuba and Zeela.

A gorilla named Galina and two chimpanzees, Raga and Muffin and their children. Muffin had given birth to two sets of twins named Ras and Cal and Scally and Wag. She was expecting again and the likelihood was that she would have twins again.

This suited Tomas as he thought a large chimpanzee act would be special as chimps were supposed to be very clever.

Tomas thought his troupe was now taking shape.

He went to see Johnny and Reilly and when he told them the size of his party, again not mentioning that his girlfriend was Anastasia, they gulped.

Reilly almost choked. "That many?" he said. Reilly had been ordered to make ready to free the Tsar and his family and have a boat ready to take them to England so although plans had already been put in place to rescue the Tsar and his family they had been scuppered.

That plan was no longer required due to King George's refusal to allow Nicholas to come to Britain. He could improvise though and use it for Tomas and his girlfriend's escape but a group of animals that would take some planning but Reilly was a master at planning.

"Johnny told me he wanted to get you out of Russia and I thought it would only be you and Bruce at first. That would be no problem as smuggling is an art that Russians are masters of. This will be difficult but I will see what I can do. Leave it with me and I will get back to you," he said to Tomas.

Tomas also had a lot to do. He had to work out how he was going to get all the animals from the circus and the zoo, get them to the harbour and aboard a boat without anyone noticing.

Tomas told Bruce and the others of his decision to leave Russia and go to Wales and asked them for ideas as to how to release the circus and zoo animals and get them onto the boat without being stopped.

Bruce and the animals sat in a circle and began to meditate like Kunte Choo Toy had shown Bruce, but it didn't help; they were clueless. Tomas, however, had a plan formulating in the back of his brain and wanted to air it with his co-conspirators. He told Anastasia who after a little consideration said, "Tomas I think it is doable."

A meeting with Capt. Koshenko and Johnny was arranged, as to accomplish an escape of such magnitude it would take an immense piece of planning and a great deal of secrecy and funding. Secrecy could be guaranteed amongst loyal quarters but had to be paid for in others.

Captain Koshenko, Reilly and Johnny were flabbergasted when Tomas informed them of his plans to take not only Anastasia and a few animals to Wales with him but also to take virtually a whole zoo of animals as well.

Tomas outlined his plan to them which was that if they were to escape with a load of animals there would have to be a reason for a load of animals to leave St Petersburg for Britain. That reason could be the pretence of restocking Dublin Zoo which had lost animals during the Easter Rising, a fact that Tomas had learnt about due to his keeping abreast of events outside Russia, an attribute he had learnt from Rasputin and his love of all animals.

The request would have to be official and agreed to by the Provisional Government.

Johnny was sceptical but said he would make the necessary enquiries and Captain Koshenko would make enquiries with his friends in the new Constituent Assembly which had replaced the Duma. He was certain that he had enough influence with the moderates to ensure that if a request was formally made a transfer of animals to Dublin could be arranged and with the right bribes could be done reasonably quickly.

Koshenko went on to say that funds would also be needed for the transportation of the animals to the docks and that reliable people would need to be recruited. Their loyalty would have to be without doubt and more funds would be needed to bribe the dock hands and harbour master to turn a blind eye. Funds, however, were no problem as the Tsar had made sure that all the necessary funds were available if and when required.

Johnny said he would speak to Somerset Maugham and Reilly who he thought could sort out the docks side of the plan and his boss in London who could sort out the request for the zoo animals.

They parted and Johnny went to see Reilly who was also stunned by the enormity of the plan but he also thought it was so audacious that it might just work.

Somerset Maugham was ecstatic. "I could never imagine such a plot, what a great story that would make if we succeed I will turn it into a book; it will be a bestseller," he said. "But best keep it to ourselves. I fear that London will not approve but what a show it will be if we can pull it off," he chuckled.

"Leave it to me. I will sort out the restocking of Dublin Zoo which will go down well in London as it would be a good gesture to the Irish that the British government is thinking of them. I am sure Lloyd George will agree," he said and left Johnny laughing with a wide beam across his face.

Johnny then went to see Reilly and told him of the proposed idea.

"It will take a lot of planning, a great deal of luck and a lot of secrecy; the least number who know the real aim of the transfer of animals the better. It will also take a lot of money to buy a boat and there's the official order which has to be in place. Then there needs to be money for the boat's captain to ensure his cooperation and money left for them to use in Britain," Reilly said. It was a big ask but he would make the arrangements and he wrote a letter for Johnny to give to Captain Koshenko outlining what he would need and how to transfer the funds needed to provide a successful outcome.

"There are a lot of things that could go wrong but if there is to be further riots and chaos in the city we must plan to use them to our advantage," he added.

Anastasia and Tomas thanked Johnny when he told them the next day and Anastasia and Tomas went to see Captain Koshenko with the letter from Reilly. They told him about their plans giving him the letter and the list of animals they wanted to take with them.

He was dubious but said he would do anything to help as the Tsar had commanded him. He told them to leave the logistics and planning to him and come and see him again in a week's time when he hoped that the basics of the plan would be in hand.

He told them to take care that they were not being followed as he felt that there were government and Bolshevik spies everywhere and that he did not want them to see her speaking to him as he was known to be a Tsarist sympathiser. He told her he would get a message to her if things were ready sooner and not to bring attention to themselves.

September went with the plan proceeding at a good pace.

Lloyd George had been contacted by Somerset Maugham and he had broached the subject of restocking Dublin Zoo with the Irish. Lloyd George was as keen to resolve the Irish problem as he was to win the war. He had been instrumental in forming the Irish Convention in June 1917 to try and hammer out a solution agreeable to the Irish people and he offered the idea of restocking the zoo as a symbol of his goodwill to the Irish to its head, John Redmond.

The proposal was to be put before the Convention and an official request was made to St Petersburg for help in restocking their zoo.

The Russian zoos were already aware having been advised by a friend of Koshenko who had brought up the offer in the Assembly.

By the end of September the matter was discussed and the offer was made to Dublin Zoo and accepted.

It was like an interlude in the war when humanity was put first but its significance was not apparent at the time.

A list of animals was prepared by Dublin and it was agreed that the transfer would be made in October. The facts were not kept secret as it had been agreed in the Assembly and it was not seen as important by the Bolsheviks. The Germans also knew of the deal but they too thought it unimportant.

October began and Johnny got a message to Tomas telling him that the offer had been made and things were going to plan. He also told him that the Bolsheviks were stepping up their plans and now had a formidable force by actively recruiting disenchanted soldiers and sailors. If they were to get out, they would have to hurry.

Captain Koshenko sent one of his soldiers to Tsarskoe Selo to see Tomas and Anastasia to tell them that he had secured transport for them and the animals to the dock when required and had bribed the zoo and circus keepers to ensure that the release of the animals when the time was right would go without a hitch. He told them to be ready at short notice as they would have to move quickly and stealthily in order to avoid detection. They had been ready ever since the Tsar had been moved to Tobolsk and wanted to leave Tsarkoe Selo as soon as possible.

The problem would not be in moving the zoo animals, but in moving them without alerting the Bolsheviks. They would use any rioting or marches, when the police and troops would be tied up with keeping the peace, to their advantage.

Johnny told Reilly that everything was in place and Reilly sought out his friend, submarine Captain Francis Cromie CB DSO RN, who was in charge of a number of British submarines in St Petersburg to help in the escapade. Remember, nine British submarines were attached to the Russian navy at the start of the war.

This was partly in response to the receipt of a German naval code book which had been recovered by the Russian navy when they captured the German cruiser Magdeburg which had run aground whilst laying mines during fog in 1914.

Cromie was a gung-ho Irish man born in Waterford Ireland and he had fallen in love with a St Petersburg socialite and beauty, Sonia Gagarin, who was a member of the Russian aristocracy. I do not know if she was a descendant of Uri Gagarin who was the first Russian cosmonaut to orbit the world in space but she could have been.

Cromie was not only a hero to the British but was held in such high regard by the Russian navy following his exploits in joint Anglo-Russian skirmishes with the German fleet. The Russian admirals had mentioned his exploits in despatches to

Tsar Nicholas and he had awarded him the Order of St George medal, Russia's highest military honour.

He was held in such high esteem by the Russian sailors many of whom owed him their lives that they would turn a blind eye to nearly anything he did.

Lloyd George had instructed Cromie to scupper the Russian fleet in St Petersburg and get his submarines away if Russia came under the control of Lenin and the Bolsheviks to prevent them getting into German hands.

He felt sure that Lenin would surrender them to the Germans when the Bolsheviks took Russia out of the war. Reilly had informed Maugham that Kerensky would not be able to withstand the onslaught of Lenin's Bolshevik revolution and that his days were numbered when Trotsky was named as Chairman of the Petrograd Soviet in October.

Trotsky began by organising his army of workers into the Red Guard which would later become the Red Army.

Cromie and Reilly who were both fluent Russian speakers would work together following the revolution in his Majesty's Secret Service, with Cromie being appointed a commander and Britain's Naval Attaché in St Petersburg.

The plan was formulated to act in response to a plea from the Dublin Zoo for animals to restock those lost during the Easter Rising in Ireland, when food was short and the lions and tigers had had to be fed some of the other animals to survive. The Russian zoos were bribed and agreed to supply animals to the Irish zoo.

A boat big enough to carry the increased cargo was chartered and the shipment officially approved.

Reilly sorted all the paperwork and recruited the best smuggler in St Petersburg to transport the secret cargo.

The stage was set, now timing was everything.

The planning did not stop there as preparations needed to be in place for feeding the animals on the voyage and for their arrival in Wales.

Johnny was in charge of the logistics for Wales and had already made contacts with local farmers in Wales and had a man ready to greet them in Wales.

Preparations were well in hand.

Chapter 29
The Time Approaches

Reilly's perception of the situation was spot on. His spies told him that although Lenin was cautious Trotsky and Stalin had proposed an armed resurrection at the Bolshevik Central Committee meeting on 10th October and it was agreed after debate. The Bolsheviks set up their headquarters.

Maugham saw that the Bolsheviks were so far advanced that there was little chance of preventing them from revolting. Trotsky had taken control of the strategy and formed an armed wing from the Red Guard that had protected St Petersburg from the Kornilov revolt. It would later become the Red Army. They were well armed, some of their weapons having been supplied by Kerensky who had given them for the express purpose of defending St Petersburg from Kornilov attack and they had kept them. Kerensky had stated he would not fire on workers and this played into the Bolsheviks' hands.

Kerensky gave Maugham a message to Lloyd George asking for an army to fight the Bolsheviks but Lloyd George would not. Kerensky's Government was on its own.

Lenin had already upped the ante by enticing not only the workers but the soldiers and sailors to join the Bolshevik cause and rebel. An appeal was made to the army and navy advocating that they kill their officers and also to kill the priests. The Bolsheviks were not only anti-Tsarist but anti-religion as their doctrine demands loyalty only to the party and nothing else, (bit like religion really).

Although Trotsky and Lenin were keeping the date of their move to themselves Reilly guessed that as the intensity of their propaganda, the arming of the Red Guard and Koba's activities in the city targeting and disrupting the provincial governments' security, that a probable date would be 23rd or 24th October.

He told Tomas to be ready to move at a moment's notice as it was already 21st October.

Although the paperwork was all in order there was still a delay with the final go ahead; bureaucracy and red tape prevailed in those days as well. In fact even more so as there was a war on, remember.

Captain Koshenko was also aware that a coup was imminent and he had been informed by his troops that attempts had been made by the Bolsheviks to persuade them to kill their officers, but they were a tight-knit troop with strong loyalty not only to each other but to the Tsar as well. They would not join the Bolshevik plot.

Captain Koshenko and his men were ready and the next morning they were on standby.

Chapter 30
The October Revolution, the Great Stampede and a Daring Escape

The call did not come that night but on the night of the 24th of October 1917. The Military Revolutionary Committee had managed to keep the exact time and date a secret despite Kerensky and his government being informed of a pending coup.

Kerensky having been forewarned banned the publication of Bolshevik propaganda and Pravda and tried to raise a force to defend the Provisional Government but he found that loyalty was in short supply.

He did, however, manage to get a company of Cossacks to guard the Winter Palace, which was the seat of government and believed other groups would stay loyal.

Kerensky was a Socialist himself and it was against all the principles that he believed in to order the military to fire on the workers if they revolted.

At 9.45pm that evening the revolution began and armed Bolshevik activists and the Red Guard swept through St Petersburg catching Kerensky and the government unawares. The coup was going well, having been planned by Trotsky and was virtually bloodless until the Bolsheviks reached the Winter Palace, where they met resistance from a company of cadets and women soldiers along with some loyal Cossacks.

Lenin had ordered the crew of the Russian cruiser the Aurora which had positioned itself opposite the Winter Palace to fire a blank shot at the Winter Palace to signal which became symbolic as the start of the Revolution and is known in Russia as Red October.

All ship movement was being monitored by Commander Cromie and his submariners and the Aurora's movement had raised his suspicions.

Cromie informed Reilly and the escape plan was initiated.

The Bolshevik Uprising had started.

Orchestrated by Trotsky, the Red Guard and sailors of the Kronstadt began the military action.

The Kronstadt is a naval base on the island of Kotlin in the Gulf of Finland approximately 18 miles from St Petersburg. They played a big part in Red October and were just as instrumental in the Revolution as the Bolsheviks.

During the February coup, the sailors of the Konstadt had mutinied and killed their officers. They formed their own Soviet and it became a headquarters for fanatical anarchists. They were even more militant than the Bolsheviks and in May 1917, they declared themselves independent from the Provisional Government but in July 1917, when there was a rise in anti-government support, again they came out in support of the Bolsheviks.

The Provincial Government had tried to close it down but they had failed. During the Kornilov Rebellion they had come to the aid of the Bolsheviks but they wished to overthrow the Provisional Government themselves, something Lenin at that time was not ready for.

Lenin did not trust the Kronstadt sailors and he was right not to as later they were to revolt against him during the Russian Civil War.

The Bolshevik Red Guard took control of the telephone exchange to prevent the government calling for help and the bridges to stop any potential support for the Provincial Government arriving by river.

Kerensky tried to muster all the support he had at his disposal which was sparse. Only some of the Cossack units in the city heeded his call and the only other military aid to come to the Provincial Government's aid were the cadets from the city's military academy and one battalion of women soldiers, the 1st Petrograd Women's Battalion who had paraded that morning before they were to be sent to the front.

The Battalion were also known as the Death Battalion and were ferocious fighters. The Provisional Government recruited women as they were more loyal than the men being volunteers and would shame the men by not running away from a battle. That speaks volumes for Russian women soldiers and those who remember still goad their male counterparts when asked what they did in the Great War. Though, to be fair, the Russian men were conscripted and had fought heroically for years at the front line without the proper equipment, many had not even been supplied with weapons and they had not been properly fed and clothed for the winter conditions. No wonder they were unwilling to keep fighting.

Back in St Petersburg Captain Koshenko and his men were ready at the sound of the Aurora's shot and they immediately sprang into action. He had a copy of the order to release the animals from the circus and the zoo, and everything was in place to implement the escape plan.

The trucks were started and they drove off, one to the zoo and the other to the circus to collect the animals.

At this time the roads were still relatively quiet and they made their way without much attention. They could see that swarms of the Red Guard were making their way towards the Winter Palace and took no notice of the trucks going the other way; however, they did not want to arouse suspicion so cheered on the Red Guard when it looked like they might be stopped.

The pick up at the circus went without a hitch but it was a different matter at the zoo where being only a little under a mile from the Winter Palace a detachment of the Red Guard were on standby between the Winter Palace and the rivers.

To create a diversion, the zoo keepers who had been well paid in advance opened the cages of a large number of animals and they ran out of the zoo and into the streets, which caused panic and pandemonium in the streets outside the zoo and amongst the Red Guard. There were lions and tigers, bears and monkeys, giraffes and wildebeest, hippos and rhinos, and numerous other animals fleeing in all directions.

Captain Koshenko's men told the Red Guard that they had been summoned to round up the animals and told them to leave them to them as many of the animals were dangerous. This gave them the permission to drive in and out of the zoo and collect the animals at will. They took the animals they wanted out and some of the escaped animals in, but as it was a long operation, they started to arouse the suspicion of the guards and ended up taking back more animals than was planned for. So the operation took much longer than anticipated.

Tomas and Anastasia heard the Aurora's shot from the grounds of Tsarskoe Selo and rounded up Jerzy, Irena, Bruce, the three bears and Ivan and made their way to the rear of the grounds of the palace gardens and waited for Captain Koshenko who was coming for them personally.

"It's time for us to leave now," Tomas said.

"I wonder if we will ever come back," said Anastasia sobbing. "I do hope Mama and Papa will be OK," she added.

"Let's pray all goes well for them but I think you are doing the best thing," he said.

At the docks Reilly and Johnny were ready.

"Well Johnny Bach," said Reilly, using Johnny's Welsh term, "it's started. Let's hope our little venture goes off without a hitch. The skipper's been paid, the ship is ready but I'm not too happy about how Trotsky's Red Guard have positioned themselves around the city and that the sailors of the Aurora have signalled hostilities."

"Will that affect the plan?" asked Johnny.

"It might if any of the sailors we have paid betray us or Cromie's influence is not enough to let you leave," he said.

Captain Smirnov was nervous but then he always was when he was smuggling despite being an old hand at it. He had been smuggling things in and out of St Petersburg for many years, long before the war started and knew all the crooked dockers and harbour masters. It was how he had come to Reilly's attention and he had been used by Reilly before and was trusted by him.

Smirnov, however, was more used to smuggling things into Russia though than out and as he had only been told that his cargo consisted of animals for Dublin Zoo and a boy and a girl, he was not overly worried. The sound of gunfire and the presence of the Aurora did concern him however.

He knew that he would need his wits about him that night as he would be smuggling out a boy and a girl along with some animals destined for Dublin Zoo. How many and what type of animals he wasn't told and that worried him. The Captain was not an animal lover and was more accustomed to smuggling inanimate merchandise than livestock.

He was, however, in possession of the relevant paperwork, something he was usually short of.

He was not afraid though; he had been well paid and believed the less he knew the less there was to worry about.

Captain Alexander Smirnov was a true smuggler. Smuggling was his livelihood and he liked it. He mostly smuggled spirits and wine in and out of Russia, though he was not averse to smuggling people or weapons in and out as well.

His normal cargo though was contraband alcohol.

He would take vodka out of Russia and smuggle whiskey or wine back into Russia. He would also carry potatoes from Ireland into Russia as some Russian vodka is made from potatoes. (During that time Russian vodka was made with potatoes whilst Polish vodka was made with wheat and even nowadays Russians and Poles will argue till the cows come home over which is the best. They both agree, however, that theirs is better than Swedish or Finnish vodka which is debateable. There's really only one way to find out.)

When vodka was first produced it was believed to be a medicine and to many Russians was known as the water of life, a title that has also been given to whisky.

Captain Smirnov was a cousin of Piotr Smirnov who had built a distillery in Moscow which was the first to use charcoal filtering process to make Russian vodka. He had died in 1910 and his nephew Vladimir Smirnoff now ran the distillery.

Captain Smirnov had sailed back and forth the British Isles for many years avoiding the Royal navy and customs by using remote Scottish, Irish and Welsh ports and not making any unnecessary manoeuvres or noise so as not to attract attention.

Animals were noisy and also very messy and he liked to keep a clean ship so he was dreading carrying a few animals, especially as he had not been told what the animals were. He had been told to stock up with fresh meat, vegetables and grain, and cages had been supplied and put in the hold.

The first animals to arrive were the zebra. They were placed in the hold, without too much fuss, and the lorry left without the captain being told what else was coming.

Tomas was sitting in the front of Captain Koshenko's lorry alongside the Captain who was driving; Jerzy and Irena were alongside him. Anastasia was in the back with Bruce, Tinsky,

Minsky, and Dinsky and Ivan; she was kept hidden just in case she was recognised as the Princess which would put them in greater danger than they were now in.

Bruce was not disguised as a clown as he too would endanger them if he was recognised as the clown who ridiculed Stalin. He was just a plain old kangaroo.

They had over 20 miles to travel to the dock and Captain Koshenko was well aware that they would be stopped at least once before they reached the ship taking Princess Anastasia and Tomas to freedom. (Tsarskoe Selo is almost 15 miles or 24 km south of St Petersburg so it was conceivable that they could be stopped by government troops as well as the Red Guard).

Sure enough it was not long before they were stopped by a small detachment of Cossack troops who were mulling outside the city.

Captain Koshenko spoke to their leader, a sergeant, whom he knew, and told him that he had been informed that the zoos and circus had been ransacked and that animals had been let loose into the streets of St Petersburg and that he had been sent to Tsarskoe Selo to fetch Tomas the animal trainer and his dogs to assist in the task of recapturing those animals.

The sergeant said he had heard that the animals being set free were part of a Bolshevik plot to overthrow the Provisional Government and bring the war to an end. He told the captain to be careful and to avoid the Red Guard who had set up roadblocks all around the city borders. He was not going to enter into the city and did not have the lorry searched but wished Captain Koshenko and Tomas good luck.

They carried on and drove along the road which took them in the direction of the Zoo. The Captain told Tomas it would be better that way because although it was further from the docks it would tie in with their cover story that they had been called to help recapture the animals.

Tomas agreed they would be foolish to jeopardise their escape by heading straight for the dock from the outskirts of the city, so they meandered around the outskirts of the city before heading for the docks.

At the first entrance to the city a Red Guard detachment had set up a barricade to prevent anyone entering or leaving St

Petersburg. Captain Koshenko told Tomas to leave the talking to him and have his wits about him.

The guards, there were twelve of them, all armed with rifles, were alert and were positioned behind the barricade, their guns pointed at the lorry as it approached. One solitary guard stood in front of the barricade signalling them to stop.

Koshenko stopped the lorry a short distance from the guard and got out of the lorry and greeted the guard. "Have you caught any more of the escaped animals?" he asked him.

"What animals?" replied the guard.

"The animals from the zoo," said Koshenko, "That's why you've set up the barricades, isn't it?"

"I know nothing about escaped animals," said the guard, "but the road into St Petersburg is closed, no one in and no one out by order of the St Petersburg Soviet."

Koshenko showed the guard the authority to move the animals to the docks for transportation to Dublin and explained that in the commotion a large group of dangerous animals had escaped adding to the chaos in the city.

"The Soviet must have taken it upon themselves to form roadblocks. I commend them for their quick response. That's probably due to all the dangerous animals that are roaming the streets; we have already caught a few just a kilometre up the road. Luckily they caused us no problem and we can carry a few more back to the zoo before anyone is hurt," he added.

The guard walked back to the barricade and told his commander that the lorry was allegedly carrying escaped animals back to the zoo. The Commander told one of his troops to check if there were any escaped animals in St Petersburg and walked over to Captain Koshenko to question him further and inspect the lorry.

"Comrade, who are you and who is with you in the lorry," he asked Koshenko.

"I am Valdemar Kulczywski, a zoo keeper and I was sent to Tsarskoe Selo to fetch Tomas Tomaschevski to help us round up the wild animals that have been released from the zoo. He can talk to animals and he has his two sheepdogs with him to help round them up," he said.

"My comrade tells me you have caught some animals already, how is that? We didn't see any," asked the Commander.

180

"Animals don't keep to the roads; they try to stay out of the open. We've caught three bears, a kangaroo and a wolf cub," he replied.

"Show me," said the Commander.

Koshenko led him to the lorry and the Commander checked the cab. He looked inside the cab at Tomas and the two dogs and said, "So you are the great Tomas Tomaschevski. Is that clown with you? I know someone who would like to see him again," he said to Tomas.

"No Bruce is at Tsarskoe Selo; he wouldn't be much help to us catching the animals," replied Tomas.

The other guard checked the back and confirmed that there were indeed three bears a kangaroo and a wolf cub in the back of the lorry. He did not get in as Ivan growled at him when he tried to climb on board so he did not see Anastasia hiding behind a cage behind them.

The Commander who had not seen Tomas' troupe and did not know it consisted of three bears let them through the barricade and gave Koshenko a pass and a red flag which allowed them free passage through any further road blocks. He told Koshenko to expect further stops as along with the escaped animals a glorious revolution was unfolding which would free the Russian people and lead to prosperity for all the people. Koshenko thanked him and drove on. "That was touch and go," he said to Tomas. He has high hopes if he thinks that revolution leads to freedom and prosperity," he added.

Koshenko then drove straight to the dock going through several roadblocks without further incidents.

Tomas, Anastasia and the animals met Johnny at the docks and they boarded Captain Smirnov's ship.

The dockers took little notice but some of the militant sailors began to question why animals were being boarded on Captain Smirnov's ship. The lorry carrying the lions brought the wrong lions, one of which was heavily pregnant. It also carried the gorilla and the chimpanzees.

The elephants and hippos were too big to carry in the lorry so they rampaged in front of the lorry in the direction of the docks trampling over the road blocks and scattering the Red Guards and anything else that got in their way.

What the soldiers did not realise was that they had gained stowaways. On the tarpaulin above the lorry were six naughty monkeys by the names of Raga, Muffin, Ras, Cal, Scally and Wag.

They were supposed to wait for the next van but had stowed away on top of the first van so as to make sure they would escape.

Also running behind them was a female giraffe who would not go away when they tried to shoo it away. It stubbornly remained behind them all away to the docks and boarded the ship behind the other animals.

Raga and the other chimps had encouraged it to follow them and it was happy to do so.

Captain Smirnov's face was a picture as was Johnny's when they saw two elephants, two baby hippos, two lions, a gorilla, six chimpanzees and a giraffe climbing aboard his cargo ship, and when the giraffe climbed on and fell into the hold, Captain Smirnov let off the biggest belly laugh that had ever been laughed.

"Alexander you old pirate, this has to be the strangest cargo any smuggler has had to smuggle. If you get away with this, you will be the Tsar of all Smugglers."

The cargo ship lowered a little in the water but was not at a dangerous level so he had sufficient clearance to make the voyage to Wales.

All the commotion had brought some of the sailors over to Smirnov's ship and a heated exchange began with the sailors bearing their weapons and ordering him to let them search his ship.

Reilly and Cromie approached the sailors and managed to placate them with bribes and promises of jobs on the docks if they wished to leave the navy after the revolution. The bribes were enough to placate the sailors and they were free to leave.

Captain Smirnov went to the bridge and ordered his men to cast off. *This is going to be some ordeal*, he said to himself as he sailed out of St Petersburg harbour.

Tomas and Anastasia both had heavy hearts; they loved Russia and St Petersburg, to them was one of the most beautiful cities in the world.

If you were to visit St Petersburg you might agree with them.

They were sad to leave Mother Russia but excited at the prospect of a new life in Wales.

Meanwhile things were not going so well for Kerensky and the Provisional Government.

Trotsky's Red Guard were storming the Winter Palace and despite resistance from the Cadets and some of the 1st Petrograd Women's Battalion, they were winning. Although the defenders would have fought bravely, they were heavily outnumbered and outgunned thanks to Kerensky's own policy of arming the workers and not allowing his troops to fire on them.

By the end of the night the Winter Palace had fallen and the Bolsheviks had won a near bloodless coup d'état.

The Romanov's days were numbered and Lenin and the Bolsheviks were on the rise even though they were still in the minority amongst the Russian Socialist Movement.

You won't find any records of the animal stampede in any official or unofficial account of the October Revolution because when Stalin learnt that Tomas and Bruce had escaped St Petersburg right under their noses, he gave the order that the stampede did not happen and any mention of it would be a death sentence.

Reilly and Cromie who knew of the escape were both killed within a year of the revolution as were the imprisoned Romanov family who Lenin had shot in 1918. Captain Koshenko and his men fought for the White Russian Army during the Russian Civil War which followed the Revolution but that is another story.

The zoo animals, Captain Koshenko, Captain Smirnov, Johnny, Tomas, Anastasia and their troupe knew but they also kept it quiet so as not to alert Stalin of their whereabouts.

Chapter 31

A Spy On-Board and a Lucky Escape

The voyage to Newport meant sailing through some very rough seas in a month when the weather could change at a drop of a hat. They had to sail through the Gulf of Finland into the Baltic Sea then the Kattegat Sea and through the Skagerrak Fjord past Denmark and Sweden into the North Sea.

For the first part of the voyage they would be escorted by one of Cromie's submarines which would stay with them up until they reached the proximity of Copenhagen. They would then be on their own.

Depending on the weather they would then either sail around Orkney and the Scottish Isles into the North Atlantic Ocean and down between Scotland and Ireland on the Irish Sea or sail through the Pentland Firth which is a tricky and hazardous sea voyage in inclement weather and more treacherous due to the patrols of the German U-boats and the British Navy.

St Petersburg to Newport South Wales is approximately 2160 nautical miles and it would take roughly ten days at around ten knots to make it if all went well.

The start went well and they sailed past the Kronstadt and the Gulf of Finland and into the Kattegat Sea without any bother. The British submarine sailed above water alongside their boat between them and the Kronstadt ensuring that no shots were fired at them.

The seas were relatively calm and the animals were no trouble as Tomas would visit the hold and talk to them regularly. He was flabbergasted when he discovered that they had gained a giraffe, six monkeys, a pregnant lioness as well as a pregnant elephant but it did not worry him as he would be able to train them to join his new dancing circus.

What did worry him, though, was that it appeared as if the lioness was ready to give birth at any time and that would require a lot of support and calm for the lions as both were getting more agitated the closer the birth was getting.

The giraffe was also broody and this puzzled Tomas who was at a loss to know why.

On the third day at sea they were approaching the Kattegat Sea and the port of Copenhagen. (Copenhagen is the capitol of Denmark and a major port on the route from St Petersburg to the North Atlantic. It is where Hans Christian Andersen wrote his fairy tales and there is a statue of the Little Mermaid lying on a rock on the waterfront, which is worth seeing if you visit Copenhagen. Copenhagen is another city which is well worth visiting.)

The captain of the British submarine signalled to Captain Smirnov that he was leaving them to resume patrol and they all waved goodbye and watched as the submarine submerged and they were alone.

Lurking around Copenhagen were a number of German U-boats which Captain Smirnov was keen to avoid. He knew that they would be on the lookout for heavily laden cargo ships so he sailed into Copenhagen to stop just long enough for the German spies on the dock to check out that his ship was not carrying a wartime cargo.

Denmark, remember, was neutral during the war but was a place where Germany had many spies. Remember its king had sent Hans Andersen as an ambassador to Russia to speak to Tsar Nicholas to try to broker a peace deal as mentioned earlier in the book in Chapter 13.

Captain Smirnov told the Harbour Master that he was carrying grain to Dublin and had been commissioned to take wild stock there for the Phoenix Park Zoo, as some of the animals had been killed due to the meat shortage following the Easter Rising in Dublin in 1916.

This drew the attention of the German intelligence officers in Copenhagen Docks who hurriedly despatched one of their spies, code named Michael O'Flattelly, to board the ship on the pretence of having been an Irish merchant seaman whose ship had been sunk by the German U-boats but had managed to get safely to shore. He had been unable to get passage back to Ireland.

O'Flattelly was Irish, his mother's maiden name was O'Flattelly but his father was a German intelligence officer named Klaus Kinsky and his real name was Wolfgang Kinsky. He had a broad Southern Irish accent as he had lived in Dublin for most of his early life and considered himself Irish. He was opposed to British rule in Ireland and as the son of a German swore allegiance to Germany at the start of the war.

He was a natural spy and adopted his mother's maiden name to enter Ireland, as Wolfgang Kinsky would have been a bit of a giveaway to the British Intelligence Service if he tried to return to Ireland using his real name.

The Germans wanted more spies in Britain as the British Intelligence Service, though not infallible, had caught most of their spies and after the failure of the Easter Rising a number of their intelligence sources had stopped, so sending Kinsky made good sense.

They saw Ireland as a way to destabilise the British and were keen to aid and finance the Irish Republican Brotherhood and arm the Irish Volunteer Force and Citizens' Army, who wanted to revolt against the British and create an Irish Republic.

The committed Republicans were known as Fenians and saw the Germans as natural allies as they were both enemies of Britain. Fenians were dedicated to restoring an independent Ireland free from British rule altogether.

The two principles of Fenianism are as follows:

First that Ireland has a natural right to independence and second that that right could only be won by armed revolution.

Fenians took an oath to support the cause and Fenian associations spread throughout Britain, especially in London, Liverpool, Manchester and Glasgow where you can still see its presence in the hostility between Glasgow Celtic Football Club (Catholic) and Glasgow Rangers (Protestant).

At the start of the war, however, many Republicans put their opposition to British rule on hold and thousands of brave Irish men enlisted to fight for Britain against the Germans following Prime Minister Asquith's promise of striving for Home Rule for Ireland after the war.

To many Irishmen, the concept of Home Rule was paramount but there were also many who did not wish to leave the United Kingdom.

One such person was Arthur Griffith, an Irish man of Welsh descent, who was a staunch Republican and joined the Irish Republican Brotherhood as a young man. He was a writer and politician who founded Sinn Fein, the political party and newspaper. (Sinn Fein roughly translated can mean 'We ourselves, us ourselves or just Ourselves'.) He did not advocate a complete break with Britain but wanted the Irish to prosper from Irish goods etc. and proposed a dual monarchy, as in the Austro Hungarian Empire, with separate British and Irish governments but still linked to each other.

His ideals were at odds with more extreme Nationalists and he is said to not to have been involved in the 1916 Easter Rising though it has also been called the Sinn Fein Rebellion by some Irish and British press.

After the failure of the Uprising many of its leaders were arrested and shot for treason. Amongst those arrested were Arthur Griffith and Eamon De Valera who was not a native of Ireland but had been born in New York, America, with an Irish mother. His father was Spanish and his birth name was Edward George De Valera. At the age of two his father died and he was brought to Ireland where he was to be raised by his uncle and aunt in Limerick.

In the aftermath of the Easter Rising secret military trials were held and 90 death sentences were issued though through the intervention of the British Prime Minister Asquith; only 15 executions were carried out.

Amongst those 15 executed was Michael Mallin, who had been the leader of the Irish Citizens Army at St Stephen's Green Dublin during the siege of the post office.

Amongst those sentenced to death were Eamon De Valera and Michael Collins. De Valera escaped the death sentence as it was pointed out that he was an American citizen having been born in New York.

Michael Collins and many others were given prison sentences and were deported to Frongoch prison in Wales. Frongoch was a disused whisky distillery on the edge of Snowdonia in Merionethshire in North Wales and was requisitioned by the military as an internment camp for German prisoners of war.

It was not surprising that the Irish Nationalists were held there as they had sought help from Germany who they saw as their natural allies, just as the communists in Russia had been funded by the Germans.

Collins, like Griffith, did not want to break away entirely from Britain. He was a Nationalist though and wanted an independent Ireland Assembly to govern Irish affairs. He made many contacts there and realised that to fight the British for Irish rule they would have to adopt guerrilla tactics.

Collins was released in December 1916 and returned to Ireland and with De Valera, who had not been interned, rose to the top of the I.R.A.

It is important to realise that during the First World War many thousands of Irishmen from both the south and the north, whether they were Catholic or Protestant, were like the majority of people were not obsessed with political ideology. They did not want to align themselves with Germany and had been happy to join the British army to fight for Britain and their heroism is often forgotten in Irish history.

The Royal Irish Regiments included the Royal Irish Fusiliers; the Royal Inn is killing Fusiliers and the Royal Irish Rifles. Republicans and Unionists fought side by side and many brave Irishmen never returned.

The Germans saw the Republicans as a means to divert British troops from the Western Front just as they were financing Lenin and arming the Bolsheviks on the Eastern Front and they had sent arms over to Ireland for the Easter Rising but the British Intelligence Service had been informed of the Rising and although initially caught on the hop had quelled the Rising in six days arrested the leaders and captured the ship leaving the Republicans in disarray though not beaten and the German intelligence cell depleted.

Captain Smirnov agreed to take O'Flattelly to Dublin, but for a hefty fee, on Johnny's recommendation; a little extra money never hurt anyone and they did not want to arouse suspicion even though they suspected him to be a German spy, and when he did not haggle about the fee but paid in cash, Captain Smirnov rubbed his hands in glee.

Johnny would watch their Irish passenger and when the chance presented itself, would inspect his baggage. He was keen to capture a German spy and if O'Flatelly was one it would afford them safe passage to Ireland and be a feather in his cap.

In the meantime he told Tomas and the others not to talk about where they were going in case he could speak Russian.

They left Copenhagen with O'Flattelly aboard and when they sailed on into the Kattegat Sea. Johnny and Tomas took turns to watch O'Flattelly who seemed very interested in the ship's cargo.

When they reached the Skaggerrak Johnny had a chance to look through O'Flattelly's sea bag, while he in turn was checking the animals. He was not surprised when he found a German radio hidden amongst his belongings.

Johnny and Captain Smirnov confronted O'Flattelly who pulled a gun on them ordering them to take him back to Helsinki but he was disarmed by Bruce, who was standing nearby them in case O'Flattelly tried something.

Bruce knocked him clean out with a haymaker of a punch to the side of his head. When O'Flattelly woke up, he was lying down in the gorilla's cage and having his hair preened by the biggest gorilla he had ever seen.

She was a female gorilla named Galina which in Russian means good.

Galina was indeed a good gorilla and had been asked by Tomas to keep O'Flattelly quiet but not to harm him. Galina understood and treated him as if he was her toy. If he made a move towards the cage door, then Galina would slap him and pull him back and scold him which soon taught him to stay still and put up with it.

O'Flattelly was more afraid now than he had ever been.

They were now in dangerous waters. The Skagerrak, which is the strip of water between Denmark and Norway leading into the North Sea, was the location of World War One's most famous Sea Battle, the Battle of Jutland.

The Battle of Jutland was fought between the British fleet under Admiral Sir John Jellicoe and the German fleet under Vice Admiral Reinhard Scheer.

It was fought over two days 31st May 1916 and 1st June 1916 and resulted in fourteen British ships and eleven German ships being sunk with a lot of brave sailors on both sides being killed. Both sides claimed victory. The Germans were forced back to port and Britain still had control of the North Sea and Atlantic because the Royal navy had more ships than the German Navy.

The Germans from that point relied more and more on their U-boats to sink ships taking supplies to Britain and this was what Captain Smirnov was worried about. He knew how to safely navigate the Skagerrak where the mines had been laid and where the wrecks were but he could not anticipate where a German U-boat might cross their path.

They were just leaving the Skagerrak and entering the North Sea when Johnny who was on deck looking out to sea spotted the raised periscope of a German U-boat on their port side. (For those not up on their nautical terms port is the left side of a ship and starboard is the right.)

He did not panic but casually raised his right arm and waved towards the periscope and hoped that they had been informed that a German spy was on board. Although he appeared calm on the outside, his heart was pounding with fear as he had heard many bad stories from British sailors who said that if you managed to survive being sunk by a German U-boat they would surface and shoot survivors in the water and he worried that he might not survive the day. Although widely believed this was not the case; German naval officers were honourable men.

Johnny's fears were unfounded as the U-boat's periscope submerged under the water. Its Kapitan had seen Johnny wave and he said to his Oberleutnant who was standing next to him, "It's the Russian ship with our agent on its way to Dublin; we'll let it pass."

Kapitan is German for captain and Oberleutnant is a Senior Lieutenant.

"Perhaps we'll sink her on its way back," said the Oberleutnant." Then they sailed away leaving Captain Smirnov unaware of how close they had been to being sunk. Johnny said nothing of the incident but his quick thinking had saved them from being sunk that day.

Chapter 32
Stormy Weather, a Difficult Birth and an Unexpected Romance

In the North Sea the weather began to change and the wind became stronger. The sea which had been relatively calm for the time of the year began to get choppy and the ship began to rise and fall in the swells.

Inside the hold, where the animals were kept, the constant rocking of the boat made the animals who had never been to sea before a little sea sick. Tomas and Anastasia were also suffering but Johnny who had made the voyage the December before in much worse weather was fine. He comforted Tomas and Anastasia telling them that these were mild conditions for the time of year and he asked Captain Smirnov for a bottle of his finest vodka with which they drank away their woes.

The animals, however, had to put up with the rolling of the ship without any cure. As they sailed on between the Scottish Isles of Orkney and the Shetlands, Captain Smirnov decided not want to risk the Pentland Firth as the weather got worse as the currents and rocks were North Sea became the Atlantic Ocean.

The waves grew and the ship rocked and rolled as they encountered a force 10 gale.

This made the voyage even more dangerous; not only did the Captain have to keep the ship on an even keel he also had to navigate a safe course through the many wreaks which were littered between the Orkney Islands and Scapa Flow.

He plotted a course between Fair Isle and North Ronaldsay keeping the Fair Isle South Lighthouse on his starboard side. (In nautical terms starboard is the right side of the boat and port is the left.)

Captain Smirnov and his crew had their jobs cut out keeping the ship on course and even Johnny was worse for wear. He had been wrongly nicknamed the Happy Warrior ; he was not a Happy Warrior during this storm, nor was he a Happy Warrior.

However, he knew a way how to make it more bearable. He got some more bottles of vodka from the hold and shared them with Tomas and Anastasia and soon instead of dreading every high wave that sent them up and down in what felt like they were in a barrel going over a waterfall, they looked forward to each roll and cheered every motion as if they were on a rollercoaster.

They were soon very drunk and Tomas came up with the idea of giving the animals vodka to soothe their nerves which really was not such a very bright idea at all.

Have you ever seen a drunk animal, I have. Bamp used to let Willow drink some of his beer. Willow loved beer and would knock over people's beer bottles at barbeques, if they left them unattended, and he would drink what was split holding the bottle in his paws swigging as much as he could.

One evening at one of my bamp's barbeques everyone kept giving Willow swigs of their beer without Bamp realising and it was not long before Willow was bumping into things and howling to the music which Bamp always played during a barbeque. To those silly people who gave him beer it was hysterically funny and they laughed at him. It was not funny though and could have seriously harmed Willow so don't try that at home.

Holly Bamp's other dog however, who had also been given swigs of beer was not so funny. She didn't like it and was very sick. Holly never drank beer again. It did not stop Willow though, even though he had a hangover in the morning. Willow became known as the Alchy dog, as he liked his beer so much.

Anyway ignoring common sense, Tomas and Anastasia filled the animals' bowls with vodka, even giving some to Galina and O'Flattelly.

Some animals lapped it up, others spat it out when they tried it and others turned their noses up at it.

Now alcohol does different things to different people. Some become boisterous and rowdy, as did the chimps Ras, Cal, Scally and Wag. They were even more mischievous than normal. Ras,

Cal, Scally and Wag ran amok. They began to throw everything and anything they could get their mitts on.

They smashed bottles and threw things at the lions that were in their cages making Leon the male lion extremely angry as Leona the lioness was expecting cubs. He roared and snarled at the monkeys between ducking the flying objects.

Raga and Muffin did not join in as Muffin had found a safe corner away from the others and was about to give birth.

Raga just froze and covered his eyes. He knew that they were going to be in trouble. Big, big trouble with a capitol T but was concerned for Muffin.

He managed to pull himself together and went to Muffin's aid supporting her head and body as best he could against the rolling of the boat.

It was not Muffin's easiest birth and she was very sick during the birth but she managed to give birth to another set of twins of which the first, a male, was the roughest and Muffin screamed and screeched very loudly.

Raga was petrified as he did not know how to help her.

Luckily Jerzy, Irena and Bruce had not drunk any vodka and when they saw what was happening, came to their aid.

Jerzy kept Raga calm and together they tried to stop the little tearaway monkeys from causing any further mayhem.

Whilst they had their hands and paws full doing that Irena and Bruce helped with the delivery which because of the rolling and disposition of the boat had become a breech birth. (A breech birth is when the baby's legs or bottom are the first parts of the baby to emerge from the mother's womb, leaving the head to be the last part to come out. This can be very dangerous for both baby and mother.

Irena had seen lambs being born breech whilst back on the farm and how the shepherds had assisted. Though not many lambs had survived without having to be cut out she instructed Bruce who with a great deal of difficulty but surprising gentleness managed to coax and pull the little chimp out; and although it was not breathing he turned it upside down and slapped it's back until he gave out a large gasp and began to cry loudly.

He was alive and kicking.

Raga and the dogs were relieved and congratulated Irena and Bruce. Oh and of course Muffin who was also relieved not only that her baby was alive but because the pain of the breech birth had been intolerable.

The second was a female who just popped straight out thirty minutes later without a problem.

They named the male Ruf as his birth had been so difficult and the female Fian, meaning fine, as her birth had been much easier.

Now there were eight monkeys.

Despite all the noise, Minsky, Dinsky and Tinsky fell asleep as did the giraffe and the zebra.

Alcohol makes some people sleepy.

Now alcohol makes others amorous and that is exactly what it did to O'Flattelly and Galina.

The more O'Flattelly drank the more he enjoyed Gallina's fondling and he began to reciprocate.

It wasn't long before he was whispering sweet nothings in Galina's ears and declaring his love for her.

Sweet nothings are words of affection.

When the mayhem had calmed down and the monkeys had been suitably chastised, Bruce went to find Johnny to show him what Tomas and Anastasia's stupid idea had caused.

Johnny was up in the cabin with Captain Smirnov who was struggling to keep his boat afloat.

They were in the worst storm the Captain had ever sailed in. The swells of the waves were over 30 feet high and they were in a force 10 gale.

Bruce's stumpy frame helped him keep his balance but it was hard for the others.

He managed to get up to the cabin and get Johnny's attention.

Captain Smirnov told Jonny to go with Bruce but to be careful.

He said, "Johnny, I have seen some nasty storms but Poseidon has really blown his top this time and it will be a miracle if we get through it in one piece."

When Johnny saw the mayhem at first he was dumbstruck but then he had a brilliant idea. A plan to take full advantage of what he saw as an amazing turn of events. That was if they made it through the storm.

The mess could be cleared up and things did get broken during stormy weather on board boats, but a love-struck German spy and a female gorilla, that was an opportunity waiting to be exploited.

He decided to keep O'Flattelly drunk and infatuated with Galina so he topped up O'Flatelly's vodka, just enough to keep him amorous.

They coaxed the young monkeys back into their cages and locked them up so that they could cause no more trouble and tidied up the best they could.

He then spotted Muffin in the corner with her new babies and provided them with blankets and secured them as best he could to shield them from the debris which was flying around with every roll of the boat.

He left Bruce in charge and went up to see Captain Smirnov to tell him his plan, and that they would have to dock in Belfast before going on to Newport and Dublin.

When Captain Smirnov heard that O'Flattelly was getting amorous with Galina he let out the loudest belly laugh he had ever laughed and said beaming, "A love-struck German all lovey-dovey with a Gorilla. This I have got to see but not until we are safely through this storm. Johnny, keep them sweet and I will head for Belfast."

Johnny then went to the wireless room and called the Irish Port Authorities in Belfast to tell them that they had a medical emergency, suspected rabies, on board and would need a doctor, a vet and quarantine facilities ready for when they arrived at Belfast.

In 1917 the radio was called a wireless as radio signals were sent without the use of wires.

Captain Smirnov told his crew and the yellow flag was hoisted from the ship's mast to indicate that there was a medical disease on board.

Flags are used as signalling devices by sailors not only to show which country they belong to but also as a way of passing messages. The yellow flag which represents Quebec in the phonetic alphabet means quarantine showing there is an epidemic or other contagious disease on board and warns others to stay clear. It was decided to use yellow, as yellow fever and cholera were prevalent during early voyages.

Johnny also sent a coded message to Commander Smith Cumming using Morse code.

He knew that Room 40 had a number of listening stations known as Y stations to monitor wireless transmissions and knew that his message would be picked up by them and taken to the Commander with great haste as it was of great importance.

I can't relay the message as it was sent as a secret code was used but this is basically what it said.

Have German spy on board. He has been captured and is being held in a compromising position. Need cinematic equipment and gramophonic equipment to film and record spy in compromising position. Must be ready at Belfast when we dock. Have informed Belfast authorities of need for quarantine facilities so spy can be interrogated and turned in secret. I believe he could be of great use in Southern Ireland. Happy Warrior .

Johnny was right; the message was picked up and immediately relayed to Commander Smith Cumming.

"Jonny never ceases to amaze me," he said out loud to his operators. "What equipment do we have available in Belfast to facilitate Johnny?" he asked.

"Get me the head of military intelligence at Belfast dock on the phone now," he added before anyone could reply.

The number was rung and a young man answered.

"Belfast Dock, Lieutenant Bond," he answered.

"Lieutenant Bond, this is Commander Cumming; can you put me through to your commanding officer?"

Bond was flabbergasted to find himself speaking to the head of British Intelligence but he kept his composure and replied, "I am sorry sir my commanding officer is away at Dublin Castle in a meeting with Sir Matthew Nathan." (Nathan was second in command of Irish Intelligence and Dublin Castle was its headquarters.) "What can I do for you sir?"

Commander Cumming explained the situation to Bond who responded by saying, "I like this Basham's thinking; he sounds like a devious agent. Leave it to me. It will take me a little while but I know a few people who may be able to supply the stereophonics we'll need and I will organise the cover for the quarantine and arrange that what needs to be done is done on board the boat without any inkling of what is happening getting ashore, sir."

"It's in your hands now Bond, don't let me down."

"I won't let you down. Now if you'll excuse me I'll get right on it," and he hung up.

Cumming was impressed. *Let's hope he is as good as he thinks he is, but what are stereophonics*? he thought to himself.

Bond had made a slip of the tongue, an anomaly as the stereophonics were not around in 1917. They were formed by Kelly Jones, Richard Jones and Stuart Cable in Cwmaman in 1992 and only mono sound was recorded then.

Meanwhile Captain Smirnov was battling the waves around the Isle of Lewis and the Outer Hebrides on their way to Belfast.

Chapter 33
Quarantine at Belfast Dock

Lieutenant Harry Bond was busy. He had been involved in the confiscation of film equipment used by the Republican movement from the rapidly emerging Irish film industry, which had publicised their cause during the 1916 Easter Rising.

The Irish were and still are the most avid filmgoers in Europe and in 1909, James Joyce, the Irish author, opened the first Irish cinema in Dublin called The Volta.

In 1910, Sidney Olcott and his film company, The Kalem Film Company, came to Ireland from America to make films and the first Irish silent film was *The Lad from Old Ireland*. It was a nostalgic film made for the new Irish settlers in America.

In 1916, Henry M Fitzgibbon and James Mark Sullivan formed the Film Company of Ireland, which was based in Dublin near the centre of the 1916 Easter Rising and some of their films, crew and equipment were lost in the fighting.

Bond knew what had happened to the equipment, his enquiries had been centred on the filming of Nationalist Propaganda films and he had seized and stored many film cameras and also sound recording equipment, which he used for his own purposes when the showing and making of the films were banned by the British Government.

He had brought the equipment with him to Belfast and had been experimenting himself with the motion cameras and sound equipment to see if he could coordinate pictures and sound.

At the start of the 20th century, filmmaking was in its infancy. The first real motion picture was made in 1872 when a photographer named Eadweard Muybridge began experimenting with moving images.

He placed twelve cameras at a horse race track and spread thread across the track attached to each camera's shutters so that

198

when he had a horse run past them, the horse's legs would break the threads causing the cameras to operate in sequence. This resulted in twelve photographs showing a horse's gait.

With his own invention, which he called the ZOOPRAXISCOPE, he was able to quickly project the images, creating what was to become motion photography and as such the first movie to be shown.

It wasn't until 1885 that George Eastman and William H Walker developed the first film reel.

Sound recording was also in its infancy in 1917.

In 1877, Thomas Edison filed his first patent in Great Britain on a sound recording and reproduction of sound. He was the first pioneer and with his associate, John Krusel, they constructed their first phonograph, which recorded and reproduced the sound of a voice.

In 1880, Alexander Graham Bell and his cousin, Chichester Bell, began experimenting with sound in Washington DC and in 1881, they developed their own system called the Graphophone.

They wanted to cooperate with Edison but he wouldn't and they competed against each other on further innovations.

Competition grew from other inventors and by 1897, Emile Berliner, a German immigrant to America, had developed the first gramophone and a disc record.

Thomas Edison and William KL Dickenson worked with the French Lumiere brothers and made further developments on merging film and sound, and in 1894, Dickenson invented the kinetoscope and made a kinetoscopic recording of a sneeze.

The first synchronised talking movie was not produced until 1927. It was *The Jazz Singer* starring Al Jolson. Short talkie films had been made prior to *The Jazz Singer* but this was the first full feature film and film and sound were in sync.

So in 1917, a synchronised sound and picture film, like we have today, could not be made, but Harry Bond believed that one day it would be possible and was trying to merge his film with the phonograph equipment he had.

Back to the stereophonics, stereophonic sound was not invented until 1931 when an English inventor named Alan Blumlein, working with EMI, patented stereo records, films and surround sound.

Bond contacted the port authority and arranged for Captain Smirnov's boat to be docked as far away from prying eyes as possible.

He recruited a local vet, who was a loyal British subject and two of his secretaries to act as nurses and requisitioned the equipment and uniforms necessary to facilitate their deception.

It was November 16th when Captain Smirnov landed outside Belfast dock with the yellow flag prominently displayed. A medical delegation was sent to assess the situation on board by a rowing boat.

The delegation returned and confirmed that there was a suspect case of rabies on board and that the ship would have to be quarantined but it could be brought to the end of the dock, where it would be isolated for further investigation.

Bond was waiting on the dock with a stack of equipment loaded on a cart hidden under covers so no one could see what was being taken onto the boat. There were a lot of curious eyes watching the proceedings, some of which were Fenian and disloyal to the British Crown.

They had been alerted due to the secrecy involved in the unexpected docking of a Russian merchant ship with suspected rabies on board.

Now rabies is not a disease that is common in Britain but it is fatal if not diagnosed and treated in time. It affects animals such as dogs including wolves and cats. It has an incubation period of two to twelve weeks and early stages mimic the early stages of the flu. In 1885, Louis Pasteur and Emile Roux produced the first treatment for rabies, so a cure was available if caught early.

However, no matter how much they tried, they could not get close enough to the boat to see and the noise of the animals coming from the boat disturbed them.

The military was guarding the dock and imposed a strict long distance between the public and the boat with signs being displayed warning of suspected rabies outbreak on board the boat.

The dockers were told that the boat was carrying wild animals destined for Dublin Zoo and there needed to be a long quarantine zone due to the danger the animals might present.

This satisfied the majority of the dockers, but when word got back to the high level Fenian Council and Sinn Fein, they were not so easily convinced.

A meeting of the high command was convened and Eamon De Velera suggested that one of their top men in Belfast go and investigate.

They knew that a German spy was on board the boat and Michael Collins, who was at the meeting, was the man who was going to meet him in Dublin and be his handler. Collins was suspicious of the sudden change in plan and the boat docking in Belfast. He also questioned the authorities' motives in quarantining the boat on its unscheduled arrival and wanted to clarify that their spy was not compromised in any way as it would affect his own safety.

De Valera and Collins both agreed that urgent action was required, and they immediately designated that their top man in Belfast, Shaun O'Connery be sent to investigate and spy on the dock. He was to report directly to Collins, who would make his way there directly.

There were no mobile phones in 1917 and the message had to be sent to O' Connery by telephone, a landline telephone which was transmitted from the Dublin Exchange to the Belfast Exchange so, just like today, all calls could be and sure enough were being monitored. Secrecy is something one can only keep to their self.

So when O' Connery was tasked to investigate the arrival of Captain Smirnov's boat at Belfast Dock, the British Intelligence Service and Bond were made aware.

Collins set off to Belfast Docks immediately with great haste to meet up with O'Connery itching to find out what was happening himself.

He must have broken the 1917 land speed record because he arrived and rendezvoused with Connery at the entrance to the dock in next to no time.

His suspicions were further fuelled when O'Connery told him that a medical team had arrived with a load of equipment which was mysteriously hidden under wraps and that it was being treated as a suspect outbreak of rabies and that he could not get close enough to the boat to see what was happening.

However, Johnny too had anticipated that the Nationalists would be suspicious and had Tomas brief the animals to make a din like they were sick and in pain so that the racket coming from Captain Smirnov's boat gave the impression that all was not well aboard.

Bond and his party, which included the vet, had been escorted to the dock by a troop of soldiers and boarded the Russian boat away from prying eyes which also added to Collins' suspicions.

He told O'Connery not to leave the dock and make a note of anything that seemed wrong; he would go to a safe house and disguise himself so as not to be recognised by the port security before re-joining him at the dock and taking a look for himself.

Back at the boat, Bond introduced himself to Captain Smirnov and Johnny Basham as soon as he boarded.

"There's a lot of Irish eyes watching us out there and they're not all smiling," he said to them. "I hope this subterfuge will be worth it."

Johnny understood but Captain Smirnov was a bit bemused.

"Oh I think it will," Johnny said, "they'd all be laughing if they were to see what I'm going to show you now. Have you got all the recording equipment I asked for?"

"Yes, and I've made a few modifications of my own so that the speech and film can be coordinated to make it almost in sync," he said. "What have you got for me?"

"Come down with me to the hold and I'll show you," said Johnny.

Johnny and Captain Smirnov led Harry Bond and his team down below deck to the hold past the other animals to the cage holding Galina and O'Flattelly.

When they looked in the cage, they were all dumbstruck, no one spoke and their eyes almost popped out of their sockets. For a moment, even Harry, who was never at a loss for words, was speechless.

What had rendered them this way was the sight of O'Flattelly stark naked in a fond embrace with Galina and whispering in her ear in a very slurred Irish accent.

Johnny broke the silence and said, "There's your German spy, Harry Bach, as you can see he is ready made for turning; all you need to do is get all this on film while he is still drunk and I think he will do anything you ask."

"I couldn't agree more," said Harry, shaking his head in disbelief.

"Everyone start setting up and get this farce on record."

Bond's team began to set up their equipment which set off the troublesome monkeys, who thought as they were acting, they should give a command performance.

They started to rattle the bars of their cage and chatter as loud as they could; there were oohs and eees, bangs and aaahs in abundance, which in turn led to sssshs and shut ups from Bond and his team.

Tomas had to tell them to calm it down.

All the commotion set off Galina, who became very agitated and began to beat her chest and roar at Bond and his team.

The vet stopped and thought then said to Johnny, "Have you any sheets to cover the monkeys' cage and Galina's cage I think you will have to film them in secret."

"Will that be a problem?" Johnny asked Bond.

"It shouldn't and it may be even more steamier if they think they are away from prying eyes," he replied.

Covers were placed over the cages and the camera and sound recorder were set up in peace.

A hole had been made in the cover over Galina's cage and the lens of the camera poked through it.

When everything was set up and ready, Bond took his place behind the camera and said, "Sound, camera, action," and clapped his hands.

"I always wanted to say that," he said.

They started recording.

The recording only lasted fifteen minutes but Bond was extremely happy with what he had captured on film.

The sound recording was in sync and Bond said to Johnny, "This must be the most compromising blackmail film ever recorded; if it were to get out, O'Flattelly would be devastated.

I can't tell you what was recorded as it was kept so secret that it doesn't even appear amongst the items listed under the Official Secrets Act.

So officially, no such recording was ever made.

Galina and O'Flattelly were weaned off their vodka diet and separated.

Both Galina and O'Flattelly were full of remorse and surprisingly both pined for each other.

They were so stricken that the vet had to sedate both of them.

Bond was flabbergasted when he interrogated O'Flattelly to discover that O'Flattelly did not regret his love for Galina but begged to be reunited with her.

He had to change his tact from compromising O'Flattelly with exposure to promising him a picture of Galina and assuring him that if he worked for British Intelligence, he would be reunited with Galina after the war.

Bond gave him a pocket size picture of Galina he had drawn, he was a good sketcher, and O'Flattelly thanked him and divulged what he knew of the German's network of spies in Ireland, which had been depleted after the Easter Uprisings failure.

He also promised to report to Bond when he made contact with the Irish Republicans in Dublin.

Bond and Johnny were extremely satisfied with the result but wondered how a love so strong had developed between a man and a gorilla.

Whilst Bond was interrogating O'Flattelly, the vet checked the health of the other animals and gave them a clean bill of health.

He did however warn Johnny and Captain Smirnov that the lioness and the elephant were both close to giving birth, and it would be best if it could be done in port on terra firma.

He also said that the giraffe was acting very furtively and that he had been unable to examine it due to it pushing him away every time he got near it.

He advised them to keep an eye on it.

Tomas told the animals that they could now act normally like healthy animals, which was just as noisy but totally different to the sound of sick animals.

Bond and his team disembarked the ship on the night of November 19th.

They took with them large body bags which were filled with what looked like dead animals.

Bond waved to Captain Smirnov, Johnny and O'Flattelly, who were on deck to see them leave. He made a point of verbally giving them the all clear to allay any prying eyes that were still around, saying, "We'll dispose of the carcasses and inform Dublin that there is no further chance of infections, you've all been vaccinated. *Bon Voyage.*"

Sure enough, O'Connery was not far away and noted the exchange.

He had been given O'Flattelly's description and recognised him as the spy.

He thought O'Flattelly looked very pale and ill.

Was he genuinely ill or had he been discovered and put on deck for show?

He couldn't tell but due to the nature of their docking at Belfast and the show, he doubted that O'Flattelly was genuinely ill.

The medical team took down the posters declaring it to be a quarantine zone and informed the Harbour Master that it was a false alarm and that the outbreak on board had not been rabies, but it was better to be safe than sorry when dealing with suspect outbreaks.

Britain and Ireland were still rabies free, a new double agent had been recruited and the Republican spy Shaun O'Connery had witnessed the medical team leave.

He had watched their farewells but his suspicions were not allayed.

He would tell Michael Collins to be careful when he would return and meet the spy in Dublin.

O'Connery made his way to the dock entrance for Collins, who arrived just in time to see Bond and the veterinary wagon leave and they both missed a small, two feet tall man like creature sneaking aboard Captain Smirnoff's boat, who hid himself under some tarpaulin on deck.

They both looked at the boat which was preparing to set sail with grave suspicion.

Chapter 34
Mumbles Bay

Captain Smirnov did not waste any time in leaving Belfast and sailed out almost immediately after Bond and his team left.

Bond had told Johnny that it would be unwise to sail straight to Dublin as they had already aroused republican suspicion. He suggested that they drop off their passengers in Wales first but not to use a large port like Newport, as there was every chance that there would be republican sympathisers in Newport and that their consignment would be compromised.

He also urged them to make good speed so as not to arrive in Dublin too late to arouse further suspicion.

Johnny remembered an old boxing friend of his that he had sparred with before the outbreak of the war and enlisting in the army. Johnny had found him employment as a night watchman on the pier at Mumbles Bay Swansea as he was no longer fit enough to enlist.

Johnny knew the area as he had fought in West Wales as an up and coming future Welsh champion and had fallen in love with the Welsh coastline and in particular, the Gower Peninsula around Swansea.

He asked Bond to send messages to the lighthouse man at Mumbles Bay and to Ivor Storey, the Mumbles pier night watchman, to look out for them and make sure that it would all be plain sailing for them.

Bond told him that he would update Sir Mansfield Cummings Smith as soon as he got back to the office and request that the messages be delivered ASAP.

Bond and his party left as swiftly as they had arrived, and Captain Smirnov had set sail almost immediately catching even the Harbour Master out, who frowned when he saw them leave.

Their swift departure took Collins and O'Connery by surprise as well, and Collins cursed that he had not had a chance to slip on board to speak to O'Flattelly face to face.

Collins had hoped to slip on board the ship to speak to O'Flattelly but their sudden departure just added to his suspicions. He wished he had followed the medical team instead as when he tried to pick up their trail, it was as if they had left the face of the earth. Neither O'Connery nor any of his fellow Republicans on the dock had seen where they went, but O'Connery did confirm that he had seen the vet before and knew that he was from Belfast.

Collins stayed in Belfast a while but returned to Dublin unable to answer what had happened on board the ship at Belfast, but he did manage to establish that a local Belfast veterinary surgeon had boarded the boat but that he was a staunch Ulsterman and Unionist, so he would be unable to glean any information from him other than sight of the report he had submitted stating that he had been sent to investigate a suspected outbreak of rabies on a ship heading to Dublin with animals for the zoo and that the animals were inspected and an outbreak of rabies had been ruled out and that it was safe for them to proceed to Dublin.

Collins learnt a valuable lesson from the debacle though. He believed he had been hoodwinked by the British Secret Intelligence Service and that if he was to win independence for Ireland, he would have to up his game and become a master at intelligence. He vowed then and there to recruit and develop more spies and infiltrate not only the docks but the army, police and the secret service itself starting at Dublin castle. He eventually established a strong network of Republican spies and had spies spying on the spies.

Cummings Smith and Bond though were no mugs themselves and had spies spying on his spies.

Espionage is a funny old game.

Johnny told Captain Smirnov that he was now directed to head for Wales first as if they were to land in Dublin with Tomas, Anastasia, Kanga and all the other animals on board, it was highly likely that their ruse would be discovered.

He had chosen Swansea to be their destination. He knew someone he could trust in Swansea and the coast there, although

207

treacherous in bad weather, was suitable for a boat to land there at night unnoticed and as soon as he was out of sight of the Irish coast, he was to sail around the Isle of Man between the island and the English mainland.

Captain Smirnov agreed and that ducking out of sight between the English coast and the Isle of Man made sound sense. He had sailed those waters many times on his numerous smuggling trips to Wales, where he exported his contraband vodka.

They had one problem however, which could put a spanner in the works. Both Ilsa the lioness and Mrs Trumperov the elephant were close to giving birth and then to top even that, another storm was brewing.

If they had not rushed out of Belfast dock, they would have received a storm warning from the Harbour Master which warned of an imminent Category 10 Storm.

Storms are categorised using the Beaufort Scale, which is an historic means of measuring wind speed and force. It was developed by Admiral Sir Francis Beaufort in 1805 to aid sailors to estimate the strength of pervading winds which would affect their voyages and to aid their seamanship. It was a great aid to the British Navy and its use became wide spread by seamen of all nationalities.

At the time, it was of great use to the British Navy, which was engaged in fighting the French during the Napoleonic War and maybe it was put to use and an advantage to Lord Nelson and the British fleet in their victory at the Battle of Trafalgar that year.

The Beaufort scale is still used today and ranges from 0 to 12 with 0 being calm with no wind and a calm sea and 12 being a hurricane. There is another scale to measure hurricanes and if you want to be a meteorologist, you can look them up after reading this story.

Captain Smirnov was an experienced sailor, and he had spotted the signs that a storm was brewing as he had witnessed many sudden storms whip up in the North Sea without much warning.

Captain Smirnov was lucky he managed to sail between the Isle of Man and the Scottish coast before the storm hit and proceeded down the English coast towards Swansea.

The Isle did not offer a lot of protection from the storm though, as it was a northwest wind that howled down the channel and buffeted the boat from the stern, which put Captain Smirnov's seamanship to the test. He was determined not to be caught out by this storm and was not going to let a little wind and a few waves stop him from getting to Mumbles Bay safely with his cargo. He would weather the storm and boo-hooed Johnny's suggestion that if the weather was too perilous, they should forgo secrecy for safety and land at Douglas until the storm subsided.

Douglas is the capital of the Isle of Man and is a coastal town with a port of its own.

For you younger readers, and it may interest some of you older readers, the isle of Man was the island the Reverend W (Wilbert) Awdry used as an inspiration for the fictional Island of Sodor, the home of Thomas the Tank engine. The Island is part of the Church of England, Diocese of Sodor and Man and its Bishop's office is in Douglas.

The Isle of Man is a bit of an anomaly within the British Isles as although it is under British sovereignty, it is the original devolved state and has its own parliament and its own laws and tax raising powers. It has never been integrated into the British parliamentary system and has no representation in Westminster nor in Brussels and the European Union. What about the Customs Union you may well ask? Who knows?

The Isle of Man has an elected president and two legislative houses just like in Britain. The upper house is known as the Legislative Council and the lower house as the House of Keys. The parliament is named the Tynwald and the Tynwald Court is where its business is conducted.

The Isle of Man has flourished for centuries right on Britain's doorstep and perhaps British politicians, if they had an ounce of common sense, could have used the Isle of Man system to devolve power to Ireland, Scotland and Wales, keeping both the Nationalists and Unionists happy whilst maintaining the integrity of the United Kingdom. To my knowledge there has never been a Republican revolutionary party in the Isle of Man. They hold elections every five years and you don't hear of far right and far left ideology coming from Douglas. Perhaps they are educated on the Isle of Man to realise that both the far right and far left are as dangerous as each other.

I think Michael Collins would have settled for a government like the Isle of Man with links to Britain and if he had had his way, there may never have been the 'Troubles', which as we know are politically motivated and not religiously motivated, though the politicians have used religion as propaganda for their own ends as have rotten religious leaders, who bend their teachings to suit their own ends.

Politics, a funny old game.

The situation on board was worsening. The animals were again seasick and the expectant mothers were both showing signs of imminent delivery, in fact Mrs Trumperov's waters broke and flooded the lower deck, prompting the monkeys to fly into a rage squealing that the boat had sprung a leak and was sinking.

Tomas and Anastasia calmed them all down but the constant buffering did not help; they were in a force 10 gale and they went up to the bridge to inform Captain Smirnov and ask whether it was suitable for them to give birth on board a ship during a storm.

Captain Smirnov shrugged his shoulders and said, "Babies have been born in storms before. What will be will be but I will soon be landing in Wales; if they can have their offspring on dry land, if they can't, so be it but you children will have to be midwives for the livestock again."

Johnny interceded, "At least we have a following wind which will give us good speed, Captain Smirnov. How long do you think it will take us to reach Mumbles Bay?"

Captain Smirnov replied, "With this tail wind, we are making good time. We are nearing the Gower Peninsula and I think within the next couple of hours, we will be landed and the livestock disembarked at your friend's pier, Johnny, and then it's on to Dublin to deliver the rest of our cargo."

This satisfied Johnny, who said, "And when we land, Ivor will be waiting for us."

Now the Gower Peninsula has a spectacularly beautiful coastline and on May 9th, 1956, it was designated Britain's first area of outstanding natural beauty, and when you visit Mumbles, you will see that it hasn't changed much since 1917.

If you have the chance to visit Swansea and the Gower peninsula, you will see for yourself. In fact, the whole Welsh coast is outstanding and the Welsh coastal path is a joy for ramblers and there are many beautiful bays to enjoy.

With the storm still raging, Captain Smirov sailed down the coast of Carmarthenshire, past the Burry Port and Whiteford lighthouses, around Worm's Head and Rhosilli, passing and on to Mumbles Bay, which is a very dangerous passage, especially in bad weather, but he was at his best in stormy waters and with a bottle of vodka in his hand, he navigated into the bay with apparent ease, despite the fact that many a ship had been wrecked in bad weather along the Gower Peninsula.

There was also the danger of lurking U-boats to contend with, and they had sunk ships in those waters too.

So Captain Smirnov had to be at his sharpest and alert to all dangers as they presented themselves.

He placed his first mate at the bow of the ship to look for any signs of wreckage in front of them.

The Whiteford Lighthouse, which stands off Whiteford sands, is made of cast iron and is quite unique. It was opened in 1865 and only stands 44 feet high, and is an attraction in its own right.

Captain Smirnov navigated through the bad weather and obstacles with a smile on his face; he loved the challenge of rough seas and was in his oils during storms, singing Russian ballads and sailors' songs whilst drinking from his bottle of vodka.

When Johnny was alarmed and asked him to stop drinking, he laughed at him and said, "But Johnny, I am at my best when I am merry."

Johnny left him to it and as they reached Mumbles Bay, Captain Smirnov pointed to the bay and towards the Mumbles Bay lighthouse, which was shining its light directly towards them.

Johnny said, "Good, the lighthouse man has got my message."

The Mumbles Bay Lighthouse was opened in 1794 and stands on the outer of the two small rocky islands in Mumbles Bay. It alerts sailors of the perils they face at the bay. The two perils are Mixon Sands and Cherry Stone Rock. The massive undersea sand banks there had wrecked many ships over the years and their wrecks were still ahead of Captain Smirnov.

Captain Smirnov was aware of the danger and had navigated his way past them and docked at Mumbles before but this time was different.

The Mumbles Lighthouse keeper had received the message from the Secret Service to expect Captain Smirnov's boat and to make sure that it landed safely at Mumbles Pier and as he had spotted it approaching the bay, he frantically signalled them to alert them of further dangers in the bay.

The signal was directed towards the ship and went on and off at different intervals.

Johnny said, "That's not just an acknowledgement signal Captain, that's Morse code. He's sending us a warning."

"Oy, oy, oy," said Captain Smirnov, "what's he saying Johnny?"

Morse code is a code in which letters are represented by long or short lights or sounds. Each letter has a different duration and was invented by Samuel Morse, Joseph Henry and Alfred Vail in 1836 to send messages over long distances using electrical impulses through the telegraph system. It was then adapted to light signals, the most famous Morse code message is SOS. it means 'Save Our Souls' and is the international distress call for sinking ships. It consists of three dots, three dashes followed by three dots, or in light signals, three short beams of light followed by three long lights and then three short lights.

Johnny was glad he had asked Bond to not only relay a message to Ivor on Mumbles Pier but also to the lighthouse keeper as his timely message alerted them to a new danger in the bay.

Now I bet you are thinking Mumbles is a funny name for a bay in Wales, and it does not sound very dangerous. The shore is beautiful and safe but the sea isn't.

The bay is called Mumbles Bay due to its distinctive features.

At right angles to the promontory of the bay (a promontory is a high headland or cliff, which juts into the sea and there are high cliffs around Mumbles Bay), are the two small rocky islands which look like women's breasts and stand out like sentinels. Remember the lighthouse stands on the outer one. In Latin, breasts are called *mamma* and in French, they are called *mammelles*. Now the Welsh language is, in my opinion, a mismatch of Latin French and English words and thus, the bay's name became Mumbles rather than Mambles.

You can see where the terms mum and mam come from; the odd part though is that the English call their mothers mum whilst the Welsh call their mothers mam. Strange.

The islands are really more like large rocks and affect the currents. Along with the sandbanks, the waters were tricky enough, but the lighthouse keeper informed them of a new danger.

On October 24th, a steam hopper named The Franklin, had capsized whilst at anchor in Mumbles Bay with the loss of four of its crew, which shows just how dangerous the bay can be. The wreck of The Franklin still lay in the bay and was a danger to Captain Smirnov, which he had not foreseen; so what Captain Smirnov had thought would be a relatively straight forward docking for him, was potentially very perilous. If it was not for the lighthouse keeper's signal, he might have sailed straight in and hit it in the dark.

Captain Smirnov heeding the warning, sent Johnny to ask Tomas to send his wolf out into the storm and onto the bow to assist the first mate in looking for the wreck, and Tomas went out to with Kanga, who with his big feet could keep his footing and anchor Ivan and Tomas so that they would not be washed overboard.

His judgement proved sound as it was Ivan who spotted the wreck as his keen eyesight in the dark was better than any sailor and he let out a loud howl when he spotted it.

Captain Smirnov was able to avoid it and sail on up to Mumbles Pier without mishap.

Mumbles Pier was opened in 1898, just under twenty years ago and it has a boathouse and a lifeboat slipway to aid ships in the perilous waters.

Mumbles Bay had become a popular holiday destination for Victorian vacationers and the pier was an added attraction.

There was another piece of good fortune, which they weren't even aware of, for that day, Sir Mansfield Cummings Smith himself had intervened by having the foresight to have the Admiralty to recall the HMS Saxon, a converted trawler, which was tasked to patrol the Bristol Channel and guard the Welsh coastal waters from the threat of German U-boats for an overhaul.

The HMS Saxon usually docked at Mumbles Pier and patrolled the channel between Mumbles and Ilfracombe in Devon, but that night it was in dry dock at Cambrian Dock Swansea so Mumbles Pier was free for Captain Smirnov's boat.

Their concerns for the expectant mothers were unfounded and they docked at Mumbles Pier just after nightfall, neither elephant nor lion had given birth.

Mumbles became a holiday destination for the Victorians and the pier was erected in 1898 for the pleasure and amusement of the visiting public, who would really have been amused to see the cargo that was due to be unloaded there that night.

Just to show how important the lighthouse keeper's due diligence was helpful; on December 5th, just days later, the steamship, Seaforth, carrying coal from Barry to St Malo, France, struck the wreck of the Franklin and sank adding another wreck to the perilous waters.

Mumbles and the Welsh coast was also protected by sporadic air patrols.

Captain Smirnov sailed into Mumbles Bay and made his way to the pier. "Well Johnny, we made it in the end and your forward planning made the difference," he beamed.

"You know what they say," replied Johnny.

"No, what do they say?" replied the Captain.

"That p---poor preparation and planning means p---poor performance," Johnny said sternly.

Captain Smirnov let out a loud belly laugh that rang out in the night air and said, "I'll remember that, that just about sums up everything."

I blanked out the last three letters of one word because it is not suitable for young children but for those older readers it rhymes with hiss.

As Captain Smirnov was laughing, he misjudged the distance he was away from the pier and he collided with the pier with a bump.

Johnny was perturbed as Ivor was not on the pier to meet him and muttered, "Maybe the planning was not as good as I had hoped."

Captain Smirnov thinking it was directed towards him for bumping the pier, replied, "Mishaps will happen when the wind blows, Johnny boy."

The bump woke up the sleeping night watchman, Ivor Storey, who was supposed to be their welcoming committee but he had not received the message as he had been out buying his bottles of beer, which he drank to help him see through his night's watch.

He had been recommended to Swansea Council as a suitable night watchman by Johnny, who had always found him reliable.

In his day, Ivor had been a useful boxer and had been a challenger for the Welsh Lightweight title. He never got any further, though he had fought some very good boxers in his day and had always given a good account of himself. Johnny had fought him on his way to his British title and thought so highly of him that they became friends.

Ivor had kept fighting far too long as he had no other skills and had become cannon fodder for the up and coming young boxers. Johnny took pity on him and hired him as a sparring, but towards the end, he was more like a punch bag and all the blows that had landed on him during his boxing career eventually caught up with him, taking their toll and leaving him punch drunk. Too many of those blows had been to his head and they had caused brain damage and the term used for it is being punch drunk, so Johnny caring about his welfare, only used Ivor to practise on his body shots.

Now that night Ivor was not just punch drunk, he was completely and utterly drunk. In fact, he was in a bit of a drunken stupor as they say in some parts of Wales; he was completely snobbled.

In Polish, he would be *Badzo pijany ot pijany jak bela,* and if he was Russian, he would just be considered as merry. Russians don't admit to getting drunk, though those in Russia who abstain from drinking have a term for very drunk which is *ochen' p'yen.*

He had just fallen asleep sitting on his chair whilst drinking from a bottle of pale ale, which was half-finished on his lap and his head was resting on his chest.

He had fallen asleep having looked out of the window and thinking he had seen something on the sea approaching the pier, but then it had disappeared from view having been swallowed by a swelling wave.

He dismissed it as a mirage and promptly dozed off.

Ivor awoke with a bump spilling his pale ale over his lap and trousers.

"*Darro du,*" he uttered, "what's occurring here, Ivor bach," he added busily wiping off the spilt beer off his lap.

Then he jumped up shouting, "Ivor, the Germans are landing and the Saxon is not here to repel them. It's up to you Ivor bach; time to be a hero and ward off a German invasion," and he stumbled over to the wall where he kept his trusty old shotgun, which he kept loaded and ready just in case of emergency and this was such an emergency.

He would do his duty tonight and defend the pier and alert the town of the German landing.

The people of Mumbles, however, were used to the sound of Ivor's shotgun as he had used it frequently to frighten any would-be-thief or noisy seagull which landed on the pier roof and disturbed his sleep.

Ivor picked up the shotgun and made his way to the door, knocking over his pile of empty beer bottles as he stumbled towards the door. Ivor had taken his shoes off to be comfortable and he tripped over the rolling bottles and cracked his head on the door just as Captain Smirnov's first mate was securing the bowline rope and mooring on the pier.

Ivor opened the door and confronted him. He shouted in the best commanding voice he could muster, "Oy, who goes there now then, friend or foe?"

The first mate, who could not speak English, looked at Ivor and saw the shotgun pointing at him and froze then he put his arms up and shouted in Russian, "*Ya podychinyayus!*" which means I surrender.

Ivor could not speak Russian and did not recognise the phrase, for all he knew, it was German as he could not speak German either, though he knew it was not Welsh.

The sight of the shotgun did not frighten Ivan and Kanga though, who jumped onto the pier to join the first mate and Ivan growled the most fierce and nasty growl that any wolf had ever growled at any man.

216

Ivor stepped back and was just about to shoot at them when Johnny appeared having heard the commotion and when he saw Ivor standing on the pier pointing a shotgun at the first mate with his hands up and Ivan and Kanga confronting Ivor threateningly, he ran over to them and shouted to Ivor, "Sergeant Basham, Royal Welsh Fusiliers. Is that you Ivor?"

"Ivor Storey night watchman at your service. Johnny bach, is that you? Let me see you in the light. What brings you to Mumbles Bay on such a dismal stormy night?"

Johnny replied, "Ivor you old codger, didn't you get my message. I'm on a top secret mission for King and country and you were supposed to have been informed as you are my point of contact in Swansea."

"Well, no one tells me anything," he slurred and lowered his weapon as he recognised his old friend, "but why are you in the company of a German, an Alsatian dog and whatever he is," pointing at Bruce, who was wearing sailors' oilskins.

Johnny replied, "They're not German, they're Russian and the less you know the better. It is top secret Ivor, so what you see and hear here tonight is to be kept that way, OK?"

"OK Johnny, my lips are sealed, you can trust me," he replied.

Johnny was not impressed, not only was Ivor drunk but he had blood gushing from a wound to his head.

Johnny took hold of Ivor and took the shotgun off him placing it on the deck without removing the cartridges.

"Now let's get that head wound seen to. How did you manage to cut your head?" Johnny enquired.

"I bumped it on the door as I came out, it's only a graze," he replied.

Johnny took him inside and sat him down carefully, avoiding the litter of beer bottles strewn across the floor.

As he sat him down on the chair, he asked Ivor if he had arranged for the supplies he had asked for to be delivered, but Ivor just stared at him blankly.

Stupid question, thought Johnny and he told Ivor to sit there and stay put while he got someone to look at his head wound.

Johnny returned to the boat and asked Anastasia if she would take a look at Ivor's head and patch it up for him.

Anastasia said she would be glad to get off the boat and look after Ivor. "Tonight, I am a midwife and a nurse," she told him.

Tomas too was glad to get off the boat and while Anastasia went to tend to Ivor, he supervised the disembarkation of the animals, who were to accompany him as his dance troupe in Wales.

Captain Smirnov and his crew made the boat ready for its onward journey whilst the animals disembarked.

Galinda was supposed to travel with Tomas and the troupe but she was so enamoured with O'Flattelly that she refused to leave him and told Tomas that she would travel on to Dublin so that she would be able to see O'Flattelly and O'Flattelly pleaded with him to let her stay with him.

Tomas reluctantly agreed knowing that Johnny had already made arrangements for Galinda to be received at Dublin.

The monkeys however, were to go with Tomas and they were really excited to get on to terra firma. They did not listen to Tomas's instructions and ran onto the pier and climbed all over the pier roof. Scalley picked up the shotgun and looked down the double barrels of the gun.

He played with the trigger and pulled it, fortunately just after pointing it upwards towards the sky. The left cartridge discharged and the shot narrowly missing Wag and Ras, who were swinging from the lamp post on the side of the pier.

Tomas rushed over to him and snatched the shotgun off him, throwing it onto the floor but this triggered the other barrel and it shot off out to sea, spraying the pier fence.

Ivor jumped up and ran to the deck to find out who was firing his shotgun, and so did Johnny and Captain Smirnov.

Scally scampered off chuckling to himself, he thought it was hilarious.

Ivor invited Johnny and Captain Smirnov in for a chinwag, and Johnny asked Captain Smirnov to fetch Ivor a bottle of vodka to celebrate their safe landing in Wales.

Ivor and Captain Smirnov were both drunk and Johnny thought that he may as well join them. Tomas and Anastasia also fancied a drink as did the boatswain and first mate, so Captain Smirnov broke out, not one bottle of vodka, but a case.

Johnny introduced Ivor to everyone and reminded them though, that they could not stay long as they had to make all haste to Dublin so as not to arouse any more suspicion than they already had.

Johnny introduced Ivor as a Swansea Jack, which was a bit of an anomaly as Swansea folk were not called Jacks until after 1937, following the death of the famous Swansea dog known as Swansea Jack.

Swansea Jack was a retriever dog built more like a Newfoundland dog and he lived on Swansea docks. Swansea Jack became famous for heroically saving many sailors and people from drowning in the waters of the dock. He died from eating rat poison in October 1937, and was sadly missed by the folk of Swansea as he was seen as their hero. They revered him so much that Swansea folk were nicknamed Swansea Jacks and the nickname stuck.

A monument celebrating Swansea Jack was erected to remind the people of Swansea and those visiting Swansea of Jack's exploits and stands on Swansea Promenade by St Helens Rugby ground Swansea.

In 2000, Swansea Jack was awarded the title of dog of the 20th century, beating the likes of Lassie and Rin Tin Tin.

Johnny asked Ivor why the floor was littered with so many empty beer bottles as they were obviously a health hazard as Ivor's cut to the head testified.

Ivor replied, "They're my deposit and refund collection, Johnny."

In those days, they operated a system whereby if you bought a bottle of beer, soft drinks or milk etc. you would pay a deposit which was included in the price. The deposit was an incentive to return the bottles when they were empty so that they could be cleaned and reused. It was the ideal form of recycling and its use was the norm for most people as when they returned their empties, they would be refunded their deposits.

As bottles in those days were made of glass; plastic bottles and cartons had not been introduced in 1917, though the first plastic called Bakelite, made from phenol and formaldehyde, was invented by Leo Hendrik Baekeland in America in 1907; it was an entirely sensible and practicable thing to do. It encouraged the return of the bottles, thus reducing the amounts of litter we see today and we all know the extent of broken glass bottles and plastic waste we see littered around our cities, towns and countryside.

So all you youngsters who think your grandparents were relics would have learnt more from them about respect for the world, morals and decency than the modern teachings of consumerism, the throw away culture, multi-tasking, which involves doing many things, usually less than adequately, instead of doing one thing at a time and doing it right before going onto the next thing.

They may have been involved in a World War, which was the making of the ruling classes and not the ordinary folk but if not for the war, their lives were more straightforward with less stress and diversity was not even thought of.

My Bampy did not live in those days but he told me that refunds for returning bottles of beer, cider and soft drinks were still paid when he was a young lad growing up in Oakdale and he learnt of it from his older friends, who would go hunting for any discarded empties left lying around by the new breed of litterbugs that were bred in the 1960s. He remembered it prompted the posters and public information film to keep Britain tidy, though it didn't work as more and more kids, grownups too, thought nothing of throwing away their empties rather than using a litter bin. Standards were on the decline and have declined ever since.

Litter bins, you don't see many of them nowadays.

My Bampy said he would hunt for bottles too and take them to the off sales hatch at the Half Way house in Gelligroes, Pontllanfraith, where the landlady would sell beer cider and spirits to be consumed off the premises. She would pay refunds for the returned bottles including soft drink bottles such as Corona Pop and Tizer bottles, and you could use the refund to buy flagons of beer or cider.

Bampy was 13 years old the first time he went up to the hatch with a bag full of empties and nervously in his deepest voice asked the landlady for a flagon of Bulmer's cider. The landlady stared at him and in a menacing voice said, "Are you 18?" – you had to be 18 years of age to purchase alcohol – and my Bampy, just about holding it together, stammered, "Yes."

She sold him his first flagon of cider; he was just 13 going on 14 and years of underage drinking had begun. Not hidden but that had given him the courage to drink in the pubs outside Oakdale, where he was not known but later to be thought of as a member in Oakdale Miners Institute, which we shall learn more of later in the story when he played rugby for Oakdale at the young age of 17.

Anyway, I digress again.

They just had a few tots of vodka and Johnny introduced everyone to Ivor.

Ivor said, "What have you gotten yourself into now Johnny bach?"

"Nothing that concerns you Ivor, it's all on His Majesty's Secret Service and the less you know about it the better. Now let's drink to old times and we can be on our way. I'll just want you to get these supplies for Tomas in the morning and he will be on his way," Johnny said handing him a list of supplies. Tomas would need for his march to their meeting point outside Newport en route to Oakdale.

He had given Tomas the directions and told him he would meet him outside Newport on his return from Dublin.

They were saying their farewells when Ivor spotted another animal run off the gangplank of the boat and gallop off up the beach away from the rest of the animals, who had been told to wait quietly under the shore side of the pier.

The animal was the giraffe and it made its way along the beach until it found a cave in the rocks big and deep enough for it to hide from prying eyes.

"Cor, that giraffe was sure in a hurry to get off," said Captain Smirnov rubbing his head.

"Did anyone see where it went?" asked Tomas.

"I did," Ivor said pointing towards where the cave was.

Tomas said, "We'll have to find it we can't let a giraffe run amok on its own."

Johnny agreed saying, "We'd better find it before we leave, we don't want to leave any trace of our landing behind or we will endanger our entire operation."

As he issued his warning, Mrs Trumperov gave birth to a baby daughter under Mumbles Pier. She was the first and only elephant calf to be born under Mumbles Pier but she would not be the only animal baby to be born on Mumbles Bay that night.

Chapter 35
The Birth of Taff the Giraffe and Bleddyn the Bwca

The giraffe had certainly been in a hurry as it was keeping a secret from the others, which was that it was a female giraffe and she too was pregnant.

She was not only pregnant, her baby was also due to be born and she felt that the birth was imminent.

A female giraffe is called a cow and a male giraffe a bull, so I bet you've guessed it. A baby giraffe is therefore called a calf just like a baby elephant.

A female giraffe pregnancy can be up to fifteen or sixteen months long and it is not unknown for females to hide their pregnancies, as in the wild, they would be seen as vulnerable if they showed signs of being pregnant. So the giraffe had hidden the fact that she too was pregnant.

In January 2011, zookeepers, at Paignton Zoo in Devon, England, were stunned when their female giraffe, Sangha, gave birth to a five-foot calf giraffe, which they subsequently named Kito (Kito means jewel).

The birth came as a complete surprise as Sangha had hidden it so well.

Unfortunately, Kito only lived a couple of weeks as it had health problems and was shunned by her mother Sangha, who did not feed it.

That may seem cruel but animals are wild and Sangha may have known that Kito would not survive so abandoned it.

Sangha is still at Paignton Zoo, and in May 2015, she gave birth to another calf in front of an excited bank holiday crowd of lucky visitors to the zoo.

Two weeks later however, the calf had died, again having been shunned by Sangha, who had fed it for the first two weeks but then stopped.

Both times the zookeepers tried to feed the calf and keep it alive but were unsuccessful. This second calf also died.

The stowaway female giraffe had indeed run down onto the beach and headed west as Ivor had said. It was looking for a good sheltered spot away from the others so that it could give birth to her calf in secret. She wanted to go to the zoo in Dublin and did not wish to settle in Wales (What a Stupid Giraffe). Who wouldn't want to settle in Wales?

Like Sangha, she too did not want a calf and was going to abandon it there on the beach and return to the boat after the birth.

The giraffe had found her sheltered place amongst the rocky cliff face. She was just in time and delivered her baby without any complications. It was a male calf almost six feet tall, very handsome and strong. The mother looked at her offspring without showing any remorse, pushed the little giraffe calf into the small cave which was behind her.

She was about to leave it when it began to bleat loudly. Young giraffes are very talkative and noisy. She looked at it again and instantly regretted being so callous and decided to feed it before leaving. She let her calf nuzzle, giving it enough milk so that it would survive long enough for it to either be found or it would have to fend for itself, something baby giraffe calves can't do. She still intended to go to Dublin Zoo on Captain Smirnoff's boat and did not want to bring up a baby calf.

She fed the baby and when it had had its fill, it lay down and it fell asleep in the cave, which was warm and safer than the cold windy beach. When it was fast asleep, the giraffe left and headed back up the beach back to the boat.

Now Ivor was not the only one who had watched the giraffe run down onto the beach. Remember the little man who had stowed away, well he had stayed hidden until the boat landed at Mumbles Pier and had got off after the other animals had disembarked and taken the opportunity to leave the boat without being noticed when Johnny and the others had gone for a drink with Ivor. The giraffe had almost knocked him over in its haste to get down onto the beach when she too had seen her chance to get off the boat without being seen.

The little man knew at once that it was pregnant and about to give birth for he was not an ordinary short guy, he was a bwca and his name was Bleddyn.

I bet you are wondering what a bwca is, aren't you?

A bwca, pronounced booka, is a Welsh type of fairy folk like a leprechaun in Ireland or a leszy in Poland, remember Tomas meeting the leszy. All these fairy folk are related and though similar in some respects, they have different quirky characteristics. They all like to remain hidden from humans and are very secretive. They are all only about two feet tall with gnarled features and are a sort of dwarf.

The bwca, like the dwarf, is an underground dweller that lives in underground caves or mines and they love to play tricks on those who like exploring caves, potholes; especially miners.

In Wales, many new coal mines were being developed much to the annoyance of the Welsh bwcas. Their homes were being invaded and though they were not malicious folk, they enjoyed their privacy and did not like people entering and destroying their homes.

Would You?

No, of course you wouldn't.

The bwcas began to steal the miners' helmets and lamps. They would hide their picks and shovels. They would even steal their sandwiches and packed meals, eat them and leave the leftovers near other miners, which made the miners extremely cross. The bwcas would make it look as if the other miners had stolen them and this would cause squabbles and fights amongst the miners whose jobs were dangerous enough without the interruptions and inconvenience the bwcas would cause.

As the mines got deeper, the bwcas felt more and more threatened, and what started as pranks, became more serious as their homes were endangered. They stole the miners' explosives and began to ignite them in places away from their homes and the rich veins of coal the miners were looking for. They did not do it maliciously and did not wish to put the miners in danger, so they would knock on the mine walls with their shovels to warn the miners of any imminent explosion or danger. They would create false trails for the miners to follow, sending them away from their homes.

Now as everyone knows mining is a very dangerous occupation, and mining disasters costing the lives of many miners were not uncommon. They could be caused by collapses, flooding or by the escape of coal gas which is common in coal mines and is very toxic and lethal to humans. Coal gas is a mixture of hydrogen, methane and carbon monoxide. It is not only lethal when breathed in but is also very inflammable and when exposed to a naked flame can cause an explosion, if present in large amounts.

The mine owners were businessmen and most put profit before human lives. They employed many children to work in the mines as they were small enough to crawl into the smaller crevices to explore for seams of coal and dig them out, putting them in great danger. It was not unknown for children as young as five years of age to be used in the mines and they would be used to dig for coal alongside their parents and siblings. They would be used to open the air doors for the miners to keep the air fresh or push the carts and direct the pit ponies, which were used to take the coal out of the pit. Mining was a family occupation with sons following their fathers down the pit at an early age and the mine owners encouraged and profited from the practice, paying the miners poorly and their children even less.

The mine owners did not like disasters. Disasters not only cost lives but also delayed production, which cost them deep in the pocket and we all know rich people do not like being hit in the pocket. Just look at those bankers, company directors, politicians, council bosses, entrepreneurs and all those individuals who exploit religions and doctrines for their own self-interest, as their only motivation is self-interest and importance. It's not tough at the top.

Have you ever known those people take a pay cut or have to struggle like the rest of us?

But I digress. I must remember to stop getting on my soapbox when I reach topics which show the worse in people like thirst for power and extreme wealth to the detriment of others. I keep hearing that voice again, letting me know that injustice is all around us, even today.

Mining disasters devastate not only communities but also families; as a whole generation of a family could be wiped out in a big disaster. Such a disaster occurred in Senghennydd Colliery near Caerphilly on October 14th, 1913, killing 439 miners, leaving hundreds of grieving wives and mothers.

The bwcas did not like mining disasters either and they did not like injustice. They did not wish to harm the miners or their children and would make a loud knocking sound in the mines to warn the miners of any impending dangers such as collapses or flooding. Their warnings saved many miners lives.

They were however unable to warn the miners about the presence of coal gas as they were unaffected by it and therefore only thought of it as just a funny smell.

The Senghennydd mine had been Bleddyn's home and he had been powerless to prevent the disaster and was lucky to escape himself. He had left for Ireland, distraught, having lost his home and so many miners and sought solace from his cousin, Shaun the leprechaun.

As the miners got further into the mines, the children, who were small enough to go into the smaller spaces, began to spot the bwcas who would frighten them away. Rumours of their existence grew.

The children, like their elders, wore helmets with a naked flame on it for light and if the air was bad, with coal gas, the flame would flare up indicating the presence of coal gas. Some children however, did not realise the danger and were either asphyxiated or caused explosions which in turn led to collapses.

The miners began to use canaries to probe for the presence of gas and this proved successful at first but the bwcas found the canaries a tasty snack and began to eat them.

So the miners began to leave food in the mines, especially for the bwcas, even though they weren't sure of their existence. It didn't hurt to have fairy help on their side and it was thought that they were good luck, as some sightings coincided with the detection of coal gas and collapses.

It took a Cornish scientist and chemist named Humphrey Davy to come up with the solution for a safe way for detecting coal gas, following his experiments with air and gasses. He identified the toxic effects of some gasses early in the 19th century and invented the safety lamp which was widely used throughout the world for mining. It was named the Davey lamp and became widely used in the mining industry.

And now back to Mumbles Bay, where the giraffe has given birth to a baby son.

Now where had we finished, oh yes, Bleddyn the bwca; he had heard about the new mine being dug at Oakdale and had decided to make it his new home, having been revitalised after his stay with Shaun. Bleddyn had almost been knocked over when the giraffe had run past him on to the beach. He instantly realised that the giraffe was pregnant and about to give birth and pondered whether to let Tomas know.

He had observed everyone on the boat and deduced that Tomas was somehow different to the rest of the humans on board as he had heard him talking to the animals and the animals talking back to him. That was an amazing feat which he had never witnessed before. (He had not heard of Dr Doolittle, who was a fictional character created by Hugh John Lofting, who had the idea of a doctor who could talk to the animals whilst serving in the trenches of Flanders and France. He had joined the Irish Guards during the start of World War One and had witnessed the suffering of the animals during the war and had devised the doctor, who would not treat humans, only animals, which sounds like a vet to me. Anyway, Lofting was wounded and invalided out of the army and went on to publish books about the adventures of Dr Doolittle, unaware that his idea was not as farfetched as it appeared, for Tomas could do it and he wasn't fictional.)

Bleddyn had then decided not to let Tomas know and let nature run its course and stay out of sight.

He knew that Tomas was heading for Oakdale and that there was a new big colliery being mined there and he wanted to make a fresh start there too. He had gone to Ireland to visit his cousin, Seamus the leprechaun, when his old mine had been flooded before the war and was eager to return to Wales.

He would tag along with them out of sight but close enough to scavenge food from them along the way.

Chapter 36
Brion the Lion and the Odd Adoption, Oh Yes, and Dylan Thomas

Johnny was organising a search party before he and Captain Smirnov set sail for Dublin when the giraffe came bounding back along the beach towards them.

"It looks like we don't need that search party," said Anastasia, who was looking down the beach. "Here comes the giraffe now."

The Giraffe joined the party and ran straight back onto the boat.

"Looks like it's coming with us," said Captain Smirnov. Now let's get back on board and cast off we can't delay any longer."

They all said their farewells and Captain Smirnov gave Tomas a bottle of his special vodka, which he told Tomas to keep for a special occasion. He winked and said, "Like a wedding maybe."

Johnny gave them the directions to Newport, telling Tomas and Anastasia that he would meet them at his friend's farm at High Cross after he had delivered the other animals and O'Flattelly to Dublin.

The boat set sail, leaving Tomas, Anastasia and the animals ashore to contemplate their new life in Wales.

As they stood pondering their next move, a little gruff voice said, "Before you go anywhere you'd better find that baby giraffe before someone else finds it or worse, it dies."

"Who said that?" asked Anastasia.

"I did," said Bleddyn and he stepped into sight.

Tomas stared at him not in disbelief but in wonder and said, "Are you a leszy?"

So that's how he can talk to the animals, thought Bleddyn, *he's met a leszy and lived. He must be a very special lad indeed. I'm glad our paths have crossed, I will look after this special one.*

Bleddyn answered, "No, I am not a leszy; they are woodland fairies and are very dangerous, they don't like humans. Me, I am a bwca, a mine fairy, but I can be a little menacing when I want to be. You must tell me about your brush with the leszy later but now you must go find the baby that flighty giraffe gave birth to before the daybreaks and people arrive on the beach. Oh, and the lioness is about to give birth too."

"I nearly forgot about the lions," said Tomas. "I'd better stay with them, lions get pretty temperamental at births, so I had best be there when the cub is born to calm Leon so he doesn't go on a rampage."

Bruce said, "I will go look for the baby giraffe Ivan, Jerzy and Irena can help, I'm sure with their sensitive noses they can sniff it out."

Ivor who had been watching and listening, was fascinated even though he couldn't understand everything that was happening; he sensed that he was witnessing an historic moment and that this story would make him the most famous person from Swansea of all time. At least that is what he thought.

He watched the funny looking man and the three dogs walk off down the beach in the direction that the giraffe had taken and wondered whether he should follow them. *No*, he thought, *I'll stay and see what happens next; I am still on guard and must keep the pier safe.*

The sun was rising when Ivan caught the scent of the young baby giraffe and he bounded over to the cave where the baby giraffe was sleeping. Bruce and Irena followed him but Jerzy's attention had been drawn to movement further down the beach.

That morning, David Thomas had been woken up early by his son, Dylan, who had woken up several times in the night and disturbed not only his older sister, Nancy and their dog, but his parents as well.

"Dylan bach," his father had scolded him, "if you don't go back to sleep this instant, your mother and I will lock you in the cwtch with the dog, and you will have no breakfast or dinner till supper time. Now go back to bed and leave your mother and me in peace." (In this case a cwtch is a small cubbyhole.)

Dylan did not go back to bed though, and the only way for peace to have dominion in the Thomas household was for David to get up and take Dylan, Nancy and the dog for a walk along the beach.

He told Florence, his wife, to stay in bed and make them all a big breakfast in a few hours' time as they would go exploring the caves on the beach down by Mumbles Pier.

Mr Thomas told Dylan to put on his warm coat and wellington boots and young Dylan took the toy rifle his mother had given him for his birthday from his toy box. Nancy not to be left out and said, "My boots were made for walking too," and put them on, then they all trundled down to the beach leaving their mam in bed to have an unexpected lie in.

It was Dylan firing his toy rifle, which was a cap gun that first attracted Jerzy's attention.

Jerzy ran down the beach towards them barking loudly trying to frighten them away, but he wasn't convincing enough and Thomas's dog ran up to Jerzy to play with him. Dylan and Nancy ran towards him with Dylan shooting his rifle as if engaging the enemy.

This is no good, thought Jerzy and was about to lead them away when Ivan joined him growling menacingly at the Thomas children and their dog. He had been alerted by the commotion and had left Bruce and Irena to take care of the baby giraffe.

Nancy screamed and Dylan began to cry and their dog barked once in defiance, then scarpered down the beach back to Mr Thomas with his tail between its legs and the children running behind.

"My my, what's all this palaver about?" said Mr Thomas. "Has the big dog frightened you?"

"That wasn't a dog," said Dylan. "It's a wolf with big sharp teeth," he added.

"Don't be silly, Dylan; there are no wolves in Swansea," said his father, "Come and see," and he started to walk down to where Ivan and Jerzy had been but Dylan and Nancy tugged at his trouser legs pleading with him to take them home. Grudgingly, he turned around and took them home.

"You're home early," said Florence, who was still in her nightgown and smoking her first morning cigarette, a habit young Dylan followed. "And look at the state of you, your clothes are stinking filthy, I'll have to wash them so that they will be fit for you to go to school and they'll never be dry in time."

Florence had to wash them by hand as they had not invented washing machines in those days and how she wished they had and a machine to dry the clothes. In fact, Florence wished she had a machine for everything that would make her life easier. Unfortunately for her, it would be many years later when another Florence had such a machine.

"Sorry Flo," said Mr Thomas. "Dylan saw a wolf on Mumbles Beach and got scared so we had to rush home through every muddy puddle from Mumbles to home," he said winking at his wife.

"It was a wolf," whispered Nancy and she and Dylan walked to their bedroom taking off their muddy sandy clothes for their mam to wash.

Dylan could have written his first story that day entitled, *The Day I Saw a Wolf at Mumbles Bay, It was the Day I Went to School Soaking Wet.*

He may have written it, but to my knowledge it has never been published.

Dylan grew up to become a very famous poet and playwright; his work is known all around the world.

Who knows what would have happened if he had seen the baby giraffe, Tomas Tomaschevski and his troupe. It wouldn't be me telling you this story now, it could have been him. He may have written, *Under Mumbles Pier* not *Under Milk Wood.*

Then again, he was only three at the time and the episode may have left its mark on him when he wrote his poems and stories such as *Portrait of the Artist as a Young Dog* and *Do not Go Gentle Into That Good Night.*

Meanwhile, Leona was giving birth to a handsome young son, which made his dad, Leon, howl with delight. He was pleased to have a son and let out a loud roar.

Leona also howled and yelped, she had lain under a thorny brier to give birth and the thorns were sticking in her back which made her very uncomfortable and added to the pain of labour and childbirth. Leona also let out a loud roar and rolled away from the bush carefully to avoid crushing her newborn son.

Tinsky slapped Leon on his back to congratulate him but it was so hard that Leon was bowled over and he rolled and rolled down the beach to where Minsky and Dinsky were standing. They too congratulated him by grabbing him by his front paws and dancing him round and round until he was very, very dizzy.

Bruce returned carrying the baby giraffe, whose legs were dangling and dragging in the sand. Giraffe calves, remember, are around six feet tall when they are born, and it was taller than Bruce who was struggling with the load.

He placed the baby giraffe down by Leona and her new cub and said, "Here's another new baby but this one is an orphan. Do you think you can take care of it as its mother appears to have abandoned it?" he asked her.

"How could any mother just abandon its offspring," as she looked at the gangly giraffe calf.

"Don't worry," said Leona still in the euphoria of child birth, I can raise the baby giraffe, he can be a brother to my son, Brion."

Leon who was still dizzy said, "You've named our son already, why Brion?"

Leona replied, "Because I've given birth here on the sand next to this thorny brier and the thorns were sticking in my back all the time I was giving birth."

"Umm Brion, I like it," said Leo. "And as for raising a giraffe as well, we can always eat it if it gets too troublesome."

Leona scolded him saying, "Leon, you old grouch, you know you won't; you're as soft as a brush when it comes to children, we won't let any harm come to this little giraffe, will we?"

"No, of course not," said Leon.

Tomas chipped in speaking to them all so that Anastasia could understand as well, "Right, so the lion cub is named Brion, but what shall we name the giraffe?"

They all thought for a while when Ivor, who had been watching the events unfold said, "Taff. Why don't you name him Taff? He was born in Wales and is a Welsh giraffe and Taff the giraffe rhymes."

They all nodded in agreement and the legend of Taff the giraffe and Brion the lion was born.

So three baby animals were born at Mumbles Bay that night, Elly the elephant calf, Taff the giraffe calf and Brion the lion cub.

Well that was how Tomas Tomaschevski ended up coming to Wales and how three baby animals came to be born in Wales. How they came to end up in Abercwzoo is just as interesting but as this has been so much to take in, we'll take a rest.

In Part Two, I will tell you how Tomas Tomachevsky and Anastasia become Thomas and Anne Thomas and come to live in Oakdale in the Sirhowy Valley in South Wales and form their Animal Dance Circus. How Bruce fights for a World Title and their escape from the Russians and the KKK to a secret hideaway, Abercwmzoo.

I hope you have enjoyed the story so far and have learnt a little history in the process.

If you have, please buy Part Two when it is published, it's sure to be another damn good read.